Other Books by Christina Edgar Olds

Giving Up Grace

Everything Will Be Okay

C E O
publishing

THE FIRST SUMMER

A Novel

CHRISTINA EDGAR OLDS

Copyright © 2023 Christina Edgar Olds

Published by CEO Publishing

All rights reserved.

ISBN: 9798993365817

christinaedgarolds.com

Book Jacket Design: Emily Rollins

Printed in the United States of America

For my husband, Doug—

*Thanks for making every season
of our lives feel like the first summer.*

Chapter One

October

Jason always left for work before 7:00 a.m., but he hung around on the day I moved out as if giving me five more minutes of his time would change my mind. He was keeping our Muskegon, Michigan home for himself, along with our friends and livelihood. He didn't want the divorce but wasn't interested in having the kind of relationship I needed either, and I was done trying to make things work.

Moving day was dark and gloomy and matched how I felt about leaving the custom-built home we'd shared for ten years. I put my heart and soul into that house, spending hours agonizing over every detail. I'd gone back and forth about paint colors, deciding on Roman Column instead of Dover White, a difference so subtle it could barely be seen by the naked eye.

That was back when there was still an *us*, and our future seemed secure and predictable. Maybe I could sense trouble

1

brewing, and my efforts to create the deep roots of the perfect home were an attempt to keep our happiness from slipping away. I'd envisioned living out a charmed existence at that address; my naivete allowing complacency in a marriage destined for failure.

"Are you really leaving me over something that never happened?" Jason always tried to make me second-guess myself. Most of the time, I'd allowed him to succeed in doing so.

"I don't trust you anymore," I said. "It's obvious we want different things, and working together all day and spending the evening trying to avoid you is more than I can take. It was ridiculous to think living together until everything was finalized would work."

Years earlier, we'd graduated from college, married, and moved back to Jason's hometown in Michigan—all in the span of a month. We ran his parents' print shop, which had been in the family for more than three decades, buying them out as soon as we could afford the payments. Neither of us had been aware of how destructive the pressure of working together would be or the personal price we'd pay to achieve *his* lifelong dream.

We'd invested all our time and passion into the struggling enterprise, at first working alongside each other in every way.

With my marketing knowledge and Jason's entrepreneurial spirit, we'd turned Parson's Printing into a profitable endeavor within a few years. We tried new things and spent money on advertising and promotions the elder Parsons hadn't even considered. And it worked, allowing us more success than we could have dreamed of.

Thirteen years later, we were accustomed to passing in the hall like coworkers who hardly knew each other. I couldn't pinpoint when things began to change, but there was no going back.

It had been late summer when I walked into his office after having lunch with a friend, delivering the other half of a Margherita pizza as a peace offering for an argument we'd had the night before. I'd been wrong about insisting we hire another person for the marketing team, and I wanted to make it up to him.

I pulled out his desk chair and sat, grabbing a pen and sticky pad to write a cute note about my willingness to share my food. Jason's laptop was open, and as I began to write the message, I glanced at the screen and saw one of my favorite pictures of him staring back at me.

Online now!
* Fit 35-year-old male, tall, dark, handsome
* Seeking: Women 21-30 for dating and fun

"What are you doing?" Jason's sharp voice from the doorway startled me.

"What are *you* doing?" I answered back, louder than what felt appropriate. I couldn't breathe as a million thoughts raced through my mind. He moved forward and slammed the computer screen shut, the quick slap of the lid making me jump.

"How dare you spy on me. What are you doing in my office?" he demanded.

I couldn't believe he acted like I didn't have a right to be anywhere I wanted to be in a building we owned together. I picked up the small pizza box and deposited it into the trash can.

"I was going to share my lunch, but now I'm leaving you instead," I'd said.

The surprising discovery of Jason's dating profile had been more shocking than it should have been. He'd always been a flirt, and I'd grown accustomed to being ignored while he made every other woman in the room feel special. Knowing he could give others the attention I craved made his lack of affection toward me more devastating.

4

Jason swore he never acted on the dating ad he'd made for himself, but it didn't make it any less hurtful. I couldn't see moving forward with a man who was thinking about romancing someone else, even if that person didn't exist yet. His secret desires, acted upon or not, were proof his feelings for me had waned.

I'd clung to the illusion of our love for too long. Seeing in black and white that the mirage had vanished gave me the resolve to do what needed to be done, and I felt as much relief as sadness about my decision.

The doorbell rang just as I heard the garage door close as Jason left for the office.

"Are you Meg Parsons?"

"Yes, come in," I said, opening the front door to the moving crew. I'd taken the day off, but in twenty-four hours, I'd be back at my desk running a business with a man who was becoming a stranger to me.

"You don't look ready to move—you were supposed to have this stuff boxed for us. I hope this isn't going to take longer than what we agreed to. We have another assignment at noon and were told this was a small job."

"Not everything is going. I've organized and marked what I'm taking. The rest is staying here, so if you follow me, I'll show you what needs to be loaded."

5

This wasn't a favor the guy was doing for me, and I was in no mood to take his crap. I'd had my fill of a soon-to-be ex-husband, aggressive attorneys, and my well-intentioned parents trying to tell me what to do, and I wasn't going to be pushed around.

As we walked through the house, I could almost hear my belongings calling out, begging me not to go. It was difficult to pick the things that would join me in my new life, abandoning the rest like children not chosen for a team on the playground.

Three hours later, I pulled my car behind the moving van and followed in a caravan to a month-to-month rental across town. As the fall colors of the tree-lined streets in our upscale neighborhood disappeared in my rear-view mirror, I tried to let go of a life that no longer belonged to me.

February

I took the last drink from a cappuccino and tried to look at ease in an environment that had become insufferable to me. Four months had passed quickly in my dingy, one-bedroom apartment, but living separately hadn't changed the undercurrent of tension between Jason and me. Everyone was on edge at our monthly staff meeting, and employees I'd cared about for years no longer made eye contact or engaged in small talk with me when we gathered as a team. I was on my way out, and everyone knew it.

As the meeting ended, Jason made a parting comment about his plan to buy a larger commercial printer with the hope of taking on more work for Muskegon Community College.

"I want this completed by the end of the year. I'd like to have an employee committee in place to help us reach out to the college about what they might need from us," he said as employees collected their notes before returning to their desks.

I hung back to talk with Jason while we were still in a public space. A discussion in our private offices usually led to a fight.

"Starting a major project when we're in the middle of a divorce isn't a good idea," I stated firmly.

"I don't think you have anything to say about a business I'll be running by myself very soon. Why would you care?"

"It's not the time to spend money on an expansion. I still own half of this place, and you can't do anything without my approval."

His glare held longer than was comfortable, as if we were playing a game of stare-down, and neither of us wanted to blink first.

"What do you want from me?" His face flushed red, and his jaw clenched.

"I want you to wait to spend any large amounts of money until we agree on a settlement."

"And I want *you* to stop coming into work. I'll pay your salary if you just get out of here and let me run the place."

I hesitated for a moment as I contemplated my response. I was used to considering my words carefully before addressing controversial subjects with Jason. Since I'd filed for divorce, there weren't many topics that didn't fit into that category.

"That's the problem. We *both* own this company, but you've never seen it that way. I'll go because this is no picnic for me either. But make no mistake—you don't pay my salary any more than I pay yours. It's called a partnership. And if you understood what that meant, we might still be together."

That was the last conversation I had with Jason before loading a POD with everything I still owned and headed for my childhood home in Washington, Iowa. My attorney handled the details of my abrupt exit, and I left without saying any goodbyes.

***

I'd heard of the term "boomeranging," when adult children return to live with their parents, but I never thought I'd be a statistic in the growing trend. Even a bad relationship is hard to get over, and during my divorce, I felt like an unlovable failure who needed to be taken care of. Although returning home wasn't my first choice, it did help me realize how much my parents loved me.

In the beginning, Mom made all my favorite foods, and Dad planned fun nights out for the three of us. Howard and Virginia Royce had never been the kind of parents who put their children on a pedestal, and their overabundance of attention was both comforting and off-putting. They'd never risen to an occasion so valiantly. Still, it wasn't long before we realized a double chocolate cake or an order of chicken fettuccine from DiBonito's wouldn't get me back on my feet again or help Dad's rising cholesterol.

I needed something to look forward to, and thinking about frozen drinks garnished with umbrellas and warm sand between my toes were my go-to fantasies whenever things got complicated. What started as a fluke after entering "Daytona Beach VRBO" into my search engine grew into a longing so strong I couldn't stop thinking about it.

After my move back to Iowa, it took three more agonizing months to finalize the divorce. Just when the bickering

9

between our lawyers started to feel like *they* were the ones splitting up, everyone retreated to their corners, and a deal was signed.

My attorney told me it was Jason who ended things, agreeing to give me what I wanted. It was the kindest thing he'd done for me in years.

I'd significantly impacted the success of Parson's Printing, and my divorce settlement provided the immediate cash flow I'd been waiting for. Although I would need to invest the bulk of the money and find a job eventually, it gave me a financial cushion, allowing me the luxury of being able to do whatever I wanted in the short term.

My parents weren't as thrilled about my plans or lack thereof. They were pragmatic baby boomers who didn't believe in employment hiatuses, which might look like a questionable gap on my resume. I followed my gut anyway and rented a beach house for the entire summer, taking time for a life reset they couldn't begin to understand.

May

I'd been driving for two days with an overnight stay in a sketchy motel on the way from my parents' house to the Atlantic coast. Mom had suggested a reservation, but I wanted to travel as far as possible with no plan for stopping. I should have heeded her advice. The bed was lumpy, and my neighbors were anything but quiet. I was on the road again before 6:00 a.m., which wasn't long after the people in the room next to me had stopped arguing.

"Hi, Mom. Just wanted to let you know I'm back in the car," I said, recognizing she'd appreciate a call even if it was early.

"I still can't understand why you're going to Florida for the summer. You know your dad could get you on at the insurance agency. Why do you need to take more time off instead of getting a job right away?"

"Let's not do this again, okay? I'll call you when I get there. I love you and Dad so much, but I'm a grown woman and know what I'm doing."

I spent the time traveling between Iowa and Daytona Beach listening to an eclectic mix of pop and country tunes I'd chosen for my trip. The Spotify playlist included all my top picks, plus a few breakup ballads, which had become my battle hymns. My mood volleyed between mellow reflection and excited enthusiasm as my favorite songs kept me company in my Volkswagen Beetle.

The sporty little car had been a birthday present from Jason, and I'd adored that tiny black Bug from the moment I'd seen it parked in the driveway with a red bow attached to the antenna. I'd felt special that day, knowing the effort he'd put into trying to make me happy. It was an emotion I hadn't felt often in our life together.

The car's impractical sportiness had never been more evident than driving cross country with my belongings stuffed in every nook and cranny. Had I known it would be the car I'd end up with, I'd have begged for a midsize SUV, giving me a more functional vehicle for the long term.

Traveling down the interstate, the wind from each passing semi attempted to blow me off course—like the challenges I'd faced over the previous months. However, the heavy traffic and rain-soaked highway did nothing but inspire me to keep pushing through. As I got closer to my tropical destination, exhilaration began to replace the stiffness in my body caused by sitting for too long.

"Daytona Beach—twelve miles!" I exclaimed, reading a sign posted on I-95. Fist pumping to the beat of the music, I danced in my bucket seat, thinking about arriving at the place I'd been dreaming about for weeks.

***

The small cottage sat close to the road. A driveway led to a double garage tucked underneath, and the textured exterior was pale pink. Paned glass highlighted by white shutters had window boxes not yet filled with flowers.

The home was old, but had been loved and cared for, looking more shabby chic than used and worn out. Many of the older houses along Atlantic Boulevard had been razed to make room for multi-million-dollar mansions. There were a few, like this one, left with the charm of days gone by and personalized with a name as if it were a beloved member of the family. A pastel-colored house would have stuck out as an eyesore in the Midwest. On the sunny coast of Florida, a place called The Pink Shell was the perfect summer escape.

My temporary home materialized before my eyes as the old door creaked open. Vertical blinds covered the back windows, so I dropped my purse and phone on the kitchen counter and moved toward the sliding doors. As the wand moved the slats to one side with a whooshing sound, light poured in from the wall of glass along the back of the house.

It reminded me of when I was a little girl and was chosen for a small role in the Southeast Iowa Ballet's production of *The Nutcracker*. When the heavy velvet curtain opened, and we danced onto the stage, it was a thrill beyond anything I'd ever experienced at my young age. The ocean view from my beach rental made me feel like I was taking a theatrical cue to enter the second act of my life, and excitement swept over me.

The beach house was small, but with the open floor plan, it didn't seem cramped. The woodwork was white-washed, and the furniture was eclectic. The wide baseboards and crown moldings gave the small cottage a calm and pleasant vibe. Patterned chairs in brown and slate blue brought the color palette of the sand and sea inside with subtle touches of beach décor enhancing the home's ambiance.

It didn't seem stuffy, and the air-conditioning had been set so it was already cool. The owners lived on Long Island, and I assumed a management company looked after the place to ensure things were taken care of.

I couldn't wait to make my morning coffee and sit on the screened lanai, which extended from the glass doors toward the water. I unlocked the slider and went onto the porch, where the waves pounded against the shoreline. The air was hot against my face, and the smell of the ocean wafted through the space as the early-evening sky began to cast shadows in every direction.

I'd been nervous the place wouldn't be as nice as it looked online. Beachfront property would be hard to beat no matter what the inside looked like, but it was better than I'd expected.

The first summer of the rest of my life was about to begin, and I felt like something wonderful was going to happen.

Chapter Two
May

"You must be Meg," a woman's voice said behind me as I unpacked the car.

"Hi," I said, wiping my sweaty palms on my shorts before extending my hand in a greeting. "How did you know?"

The Pink Shell was nestled between a large gray contemporary and a smaller green house, which appeared to be where she'd come from.

"I've lived on this beach for more than thirty years. I know most everything going on and everyone who's doing it! The owner of your cottage always lets me know who's renting the place. I keep an eye on things and let them know if something or *someone* needs to be looked into. I was happy to know I had a nice, single woman as a neighbor this summer. Of course— a nice, single *man* would have been better!" She laughed heartily, finding herself to be quite funny. "I turned your air conditioner down this morning. Was the temperature okay?"

"Yes, thank you. I wondered if the place had a caretaker."

"This place isn't usually rented for three months at a time. Most people want a larger place if they stay for an extended period. Is this your first time visiting Daytona Beach?"

"I've been coming here for about thirty years myself," I said. It wasn't a coincidence I'd chosen Daytona Beach as my vacation spot. Since childhood, it was where I'd made every major decision of my life. My grandparents had come to Florida in the winter to dodge the cold Midwestern weather. I looked forward to visiting them each year, and during those times, the beach became my favorite place. It was where I felt the most grounded and relaxed, which were feelings to replicate now that I was starting over.

"There's no better place on Earth. It's why the day starts at this place and spreads to the rest of the nation from here," the lady said.

I'd never thought of it like that, and I loved her spunky personality.

"My sweet Charlie and I used to rise every morning before dawn and watch the navy sky turn from yellow to orange and red . . ." she closed her eyes as if she were lost in another time. She regained her composure quickly and continued.

"Darling, you simply *must* have cocktails with me tomorrow. If we're going to be neighbors, we need to get to know each other. Can I count on you to join me at five?"

"Sure—I'd love to." It wasn't like I had other plans to consider. I was excited to be invited to do something fun and happy to meet my new neighbor.

"I'll see you then," she said as she turned to walk away.

I bent over the trunk to retrieve another suitcase and remembered she'd forgotten to tell me one important thing.

"Hey, I don't even know your name!" I called out as she walked back toward her house.

"Sophia—but everyone calls me Sophie! See you tomorrow, dear."

***

I brought a variety of clothes, knowing tropical evenings could get chilly. Most days would be spent outside, so I'd purchased three swimming suits, which looked good on me after losing a little weight when the breakup made it difficult to eat.

I'd gained and lost the same ten pounds hundreds of times while married to Jason, hoping a thinner version of myself might get his attention. I finally concluded I was invisible to him anyway and didn't need to starve myself for no good reason. I was grieving the loss of many things, but the pounds I'd shed during the divorce had boosted my confidence and made me feel like my younger self. Once I began to take control of my life, the real me began to emerge again, as if I was a butterfly breaking out of a desperately tight cocoon.

I'd cut my dark hair into a sassy, short style to declare my freedom from who I used to be. Then, when I'd gone in for a trim before leaving for Florida, I had my stylist add highlights, which framed my face and accentuated the makeup I was applying every day. I'd even changed my perfume from the cheap drugstore stuff I'd been wearing since college to a more sophisticated scent I felt was more appropriate for a woman my age. A new life meant an updated version of me, and I was enjoying the chance to get to know myself again.

After my last bag had been carried upstairs to the lofted bedroom, I looked down over the rest of the cottage, feeling like the queen of my summer kingdom. It made me happy to have a sense of control, which had been missing from my life for years.

I hung some of my clothes and folded my shorts and T-shirts before putting them away in an old dresser. The

18

bedroom had a queen-sized bed with a soft comforter and plump feather pillows, and they beckoned my sleepy body. The loft included a bathroom with a claw foot tub, and the thought of pouring myself into a steaming hot bath almost kept me from getting the rest of my things unpacked and organized.

With the upstairs in order, I moved to the first floor and began to explore the cupboards. I was happy there was a coffee maker and high-end wine opener, in addition to a variety of other useful items. I found some empty shelves and unloaded the groceries I'd purchased on my way into town.

Two days of travel began to take its toll, and I decided I'd done enough for one day. I opened a bottle of cabernet and filled a wine glass, grabbing a spoon and a pint of chocolate ice cream to go along with it. I breathed in the smell of oak and dark fruit, and the first swallow of rich, red grapes was delicious. The flavor contrasted with the cold sweetness on my tongue, making my dinner choice palatable.

Enjoying the first thing I'd eaten since lunch—I was overcome with a feeling of peace. The serenity I felt was a sign I'd made it through one of the worst times in my life. The exhale of a deep breath came with the release of some of the stress I'd gotten used to carrying.

My cell phone vibrated on the kitchen counter, and I moved to answer it.

"I just got here," I fibbed, remembering I'd promised to call my parents the minute I arrived. It felt like my independence was being squashed again when my mother's voice came through the phone.

"Good, Meg. I've been worried sick since you left. That trip was too long to make alone. You've been through so much, and I couldn't bear it if something happened to you.

Here, your dad wants to say hello."

"Hi, Peanut! How was your trip? Your engine light didn't come on again, did it?"

"The car is fine. Please don't worry about me. You'll have to get used to me being on my own. I appreciate everything you and Mom have done for me, but I'm happy to be here. This is a good thing. In fact, this is the best thing that's happened to me in a long time."

I tried to pacify my parents' fears while balancing the phone on my shoulder as I organized the last of the supplies in the kitchen.

"Can I call you back tomorrow? I've been driving all day and want to get unpacked and relax," I said to my mom after Dad turned the phone back to her.

"Okay, honey. But don't forget. Also, your dad found a little bungalow for sale a block from us. We think it would be ideal for you."

"Mom, I'm not buying a house right now."

"Well, it has a wonderful spot in the back for a garden. Just the right amount of sunlight, and it already has raised beds for tomatoes."

"I don't garden."

"I know, but I do—and I'd be happy to come over every day and water and weed, and we could share the bounty. It would be fun and give us a chance to do something together."

I'd been listening to them try to convince me to move back to Iowa for months. Dad bragged about his ability to make *anyone* into an insurance salesperson, which said more about his capabilities than mine. I appreciated the offer but didn't feel any real passion for actuarial tables, and having my dad for a boss would be worse than answering to Jason every day.

20

"I'm not buying a house a block from the two of you. We've gone over this a hundred times." I put an end to her ranting and finished the call. I imagined her turning to Dad as soon as she hung up saying, *"She's going to think about the bungalow."*

***

I woke up early even though I didn't have to be anywhere for three months. It felt like I'd slept on a fluffy cloud once I drifted off. It had been my first good night's sleep in a long time, the result of deep satisfaction at arriving in Florida.

My body ached from being behind the wheel of a car for hours and unloading everything upon my arrival. It didn't help that I'd moved a few pieces of furniture into an arrangement I liked better than how it had been set up. My muscles objected to the workout they'd been given, but the place felt more like home as a result of my efforts.

I crawled out of bed, wrapped myself in a light bathrobe, and went downstairs. Before falling into bed, I hadn't pulled the blinds shut, and bright sunshine bathed the room with light. I examined the reconfigured room layout and admired the glass pitcher holding flowers I'd purchased at Publix.

I poured a cup of coffee, and the smell of vanilla filled the room as sweet creamer made the dark liquid a perfect tint of beige. I sipped the cup low enough to walk across the floor without spilling and proceeded to the lanai, where I sank into the comfortable cushions of an old wicker chair.

I hadn't seen a red bike leaning against the wall of the screened porch the night before. It looked a little rusty, but a repair kit and tire pump sat nearby. I hadn't gone to the trouble

21

of bringing my bike for the long drive to Florida and was happy I'd have one available. I couldn't wait to ride along the sand and have the wind blow through my hair and the sun kiss the bridge of my nose with color.

Although it was early, the beach was beginning to come alive. People were walking and jogging, and two older men placed fishing poles not far from the sandy walkway leading from my house. Seagulls flew overhead and dipped down, screeching as they skimmed the top of the water, eating their breakfast from a school of fish swimming beneath the surface.

I saw Sophie walk toward the shore in her swimming suit, only stopping to place a towel on the sand. She walked into the surf and swam toward the horizon. At her age, I was surprised to see her swimming alone and with such abandon. She seemed to reach a magical line in the sea and then turned around and swam back.

She emerged with her suit sucked into each crevice and curve of her body. She plopped herself on the towel and sat without moving for at least fifteen minutes. Then, as if an imaginary alarm clock went off, she got up and returned to her house without looking in either direction.

Sophie looked to be in her eighties, although it was hard to tell with her dyed brown hair and sense of style. She carried herself with a tremendous amount of poise, but some things couldn't be hidden in a swimsuit at the beach. I looked forward to getting to know her better, and cocktails seemed like an excellent alternative to spending another evening alone.

***

I made my way down the path from the cottage and unfolded

my beach chair. I walked barefoot in the surf with a few inches of ocean washing over my feet. The tide was foamy and felt cool on my toes. I could hear the faraway laughter of children playing as they ran in and out of the waves. It reminded me of times spent with my cousins as we frolicked in the water outside our grandparent's rented condo, and the memory made me smile.

Every few feet, a fish or crab struggled beyond the reach of the lifesaving water. I tried to figure out how to get the creatures back in the sea so they wouldn't die, but the task was too big to undertake as I looked at the miles of beach on either side of me. They'd have to figure out how to survive on their own or suffer the consequences, and it was a challenge I could relate to.

I heard the voices of two children as they ran from the back of my *other* neighbor's house toward the beach. They didn't look very old, and the little girl had a ponytail bouncing in the wind as she ran.

"Wait up, kids!" yelled a woman in a wide-brimmed hat who followed behind them, putting my worries to rest about their safety.

The little ones pulled a wagon from underneath the steps of their wooden walkway and unloaded their toys. The woman set up her beach chair and watched them begin to build a sandcastle.

A man came from inside the house, and he was carrying two coffee mugs. He handed the woman one of the cups and talked briefly to her. She started to read a book, and he joined the kids. He sipped his beverage as he pointed and gestured, giving them ideas for building their beach creation.

I tilted my head, observing the neighbors through my

sunglasses without them knowing. Imagining their idyllic life together made my heart ache for the family I'd always wanted.

Even though I was excited about my future, the grief I felt for losing a man I *thought* would be the love of my life was overwhelming. I'd been hasty to give such an important title to Jason when he hadn't done enough to earn it. I had a lot of years left to be in love and was determined to find the one who deserved my heart. Maybe someday I'd have a handsome husband and children to love, but until then, I'd have to settle for spying on my neighbors, who seemed to have everything I dreamed of.

I sat in my beach chair and applied a protective layer of sunscreen. The smell of coconut filled the beach air as the smooth tanning oil softened and warmed my skin. I closed my eyes and fell asleep as the sun's heat soothed me.

After a few minutes, I was awakened by the bounce of a runaway beach ball hitting my nose. It surprised me, and I let out a gratuitous scream.

"Oh, I'm sorry—sometimes the kids get carried away." The woman with the hat was standing in front of me as she retrieved the rogue inflatable.

"No problem." I was trying to collect myself following the scream I'd let out at something so minor. "It looks like they're having a wonderful time and are good at building sandcastles."

"Construction is in their blood. Hi, my name's Betsy Barts. It looks like we're neighbors."

"Meg Parsons," I said, reaching out to shake her outstretched hand. I had noticed a truck in the driveway of the gray house with the name Barts Construction on the side, but I wasn't sure if the vehicle belonged to my other summer neighbor or a contractor. It looked like I was sandwiched between two residents, and I was happy there would be no weekly renters to deal with from either side.

Behind Betsy, the little boy began crying as the man tried to figure out the issue. It looked as if the kids were arguing over the sand toys.

"Are you here for the week, or are you staying longer?" She seemed oblivious to the bawling going on behind her. I loved how she let her husband take the lead in dealing with the kids.

"I'm here through Labor Day weekend."

"That's great," she said as she looked over her shoulder toward her family. "Sorry. Duty calls."

I watched as Betsy bargained with the kids and tried to solve whatever seemed insurmountable. Another bucket was found in the wagon, and both kids had what they wanted. It would be nice if every difficulty in life was as easy to figure out.

***

I showered and cracked open an ice-cold Diet Coke. There was one more box I needed to unpack, and that was filled with personal mementos I'd brought to make the cottage feel more like home.

I placed a framed photo on the side table next to the sofa. It was a picture of my family on the day of my graduation from college. The faces of my parents and two siblings were young and carefree as we stood with our arms interlocked. I was wearing my cap and gown with the mortar board cocked on my head, and the expression on my face showed how happy I was.

I'd grown up in a rural community of fewer than ten thousand people. Almost everyone I knew had gone to The University of Iowa, only forty minutes away. I'd decided on Illinois State for my college studies and a three-hour car ride that seemed like it took me across the world.

I'd been full of hope when the picture was taken and thought I was so in love with Jason. I wouldn't allow any doubts to seep in and overtake our plans to marry and move to a place where he belonged, but I was only a visitor. I'd pushed aside that little tug, telling myself I *wasn't* making a mistake. I was too afraid to change my mind. The wedding invitations had already been mailed out, and I didn't want to cause my parents to lose the money they'd put down as a deposit on the venue when I was probably just experiencing pre-wedding jitters.

Looking at the photo, I remembered the closeness I felt with my family before moving to Michigan put seven hours of distance between us. The picture represented the last time my life was in a significant transition and seemed like an appropriate point of reference for the summer ahead.

Chapter Three
May

I arrived at Sophie's, and a large piece of iron by the front door declared, "*It's five o clock somewhere,*" and the mood was set.

"Welcome—you're right on time. Punctuality shows commitment," Sophie said as I entered her overly decorated house.

"Wow, this is . . . *something.*" I tried to search my vocabulary for a word to describe her design style without being rude. I hadn't expected to see so much stuff, and it took me a minute to process the scene.

Sophie insisted on giving me a tour, and I could see the pride she had in her home décor choices. It didn't take long to realize each room had a theme, and none of them went together.

The kitchen was decorated with cats. There was a cat cookie jar, curtains with paw prints, and feline-shaped knobs on the cupboard doors. The master bedroom and bath shared a jungle safari motif, with a plastic palm tree in the corner and a giraffe neck peering over the top of the headboard. The living room had a circus theme—complete with a red and white striped big top painted on the ceiling. There were photos and souvenirs from her travels and color everywhere you looked. The sensory overload made me long for the subdued hues of my quiet refuge next door.

"At 5:00 p.m. sharp, I have cocktails. Often my close friends join me for two martinis, and then we call it a night. Every weekend we try to gather for a barbeque to celebrate the fact we're still alive," Sophie said as she poured me a martini I didn't ask for.

I sipped the drink she offered and realized the need for a two-cocktail limit. I'd never had a real martini unless you counted a fruity cosmopolitan. I felt it would be ill-mannered not to at least sip it, but the taste explained why they were called *dirty*. Sophie's martinis were the kind old men drank in the back of stale bars. It tasted like rubbing alcohol and had two olives stuck in the bottom. Since I lived next door and wasn't driving, I didn't see any harm, but a little grenadine and a lemon peel would have made it go down easier.

"You must *love* cats," I said as I surveyed the kitchen again. "Do you have one?"

"No, not anymore. I've had them all my life, but I decided I couldn't take on another one when I had to put my little Thelma down last year. I couldn't be sure I'd outlive her and wasn't about to leave a furry friend behind."

"I understand. I haven't had a pet in a while either, but I've always loved dogs." Jason didn't like the thought of animals in the house, so we'd never had one.

We sat at Sophie's kitchen table and enjoyed the cheese and crackers she'd prepared, which helped sop up some of the alcohol.

"I can't wait for you to meet the gang. You simply *must* join us for our cookout on Sunday afternoon. But for now—

tell me about you, darling."

"Well, what do you want to know?"

"Everything—where you come from, what brings you here, and where you're going. A pretty young thing like you alone at the beach all summer? There's got to be a story."

I could answer Sophie's first two questions, but the third one was more complicated. I began to tell her about myself, leaving out few details. She made me feel comfortable, and it was easy to open up to her. She sat quietly while I presented a synopsis of my life.

She contemplated her reply for a few moments. "Well, you've come to the right place to seek your future. Everything begins at the sea, and you are certainly at a beginning, my dear."

"Sophie, I don't *want* to start over again."

"Nobody likes change. Have you considered this the greatest opportunity of your life—the possibility of a do-over? You must never speak of your unpleasant circumstances again and simply move forward. To focus on something unsavory only gives it power over you," she said. "If something bad happens to me, I try to wish it away by simply imagining it isn't occurring."

"Huh?"

"Do you play golf?" she asked, changing the subject quickly.

"I've played a few times, but I'm not very good."

"Well, this is like a mulligan in the game of golf. It's a chance to take the shot over again. Were you so happy in your old life you never considered what it might have been like if you'd taken a different path? Think about what you've always longed for and create a new life fulfilling your unrealized dreams."

She made it sound easy. There'd been many things I'd longed for in my life. I wanted a family of my own, a man who genuinely engaged in our marriage, and a life that included some of *my* dreams.

"Sometimes you have to take matters into your own hands," she continued. "Happiness is waiting for you, Meg. But it isn't going to come and get you. You have to search for it, and that's half the fun."

Sophie had a gentle way about her, which was both supportive and encouraging. After talking with her, I knew she must have an interesting life story and was anxious to learn more about my new friend.

She poured herself a third martini, and I wondered how often the drink limit was enforced in this nightly ritual. Before returning to the cottage, I'd agreed to join Sophie and her friends on Sunday and was looking forward to the good time I'd been promised. I'd bring a bottle of wine to the festivities and forget the martinis, which had already begun to give me a headache.

***

Sunday morning, I went flower shopping for the window boxes at a local garden center. I found everything I needed and returned home to do the planting before it got too hot.

I unloaded several flats of bright pink and purple impatiens from the trunk of my car and began filling the containers with flowers. The covered porch on the front of the cottage provided enough shade for them to grow well, and all I'd need to do was water them. I loved flowers and outside potted plants but didn't want to go to the expense of doing more for a temporary home.

As I emptied another bag of potting soil into a planter, the man from the gray house pulled into his driveway and waved.

"Hey—you're making us look bad!" he joked. I waved back and continued my planting. He seemed like a decent guy, and I assumed that Betsy was a lucky woman.

After finishing outside, I hit the shower and got ready for my adventure at Sophie's.

***

The smell of grilled meat made my mouth water, and the sounds of music and laughter came from the back of Sophie's house. A darling couple was dancing to music while the others clapped and encouraged them.

Sophie was dressed in a bright red top and white pants and was serving drinks from a tray. As she walked across the deck to greet me, she swatted the behind of a man who was tending something on the grill. This made me laugh, and I could tell they enjoyed each other's company.

"Everyone, this is my beautiful neighbor, Meg Parsons," Sophie said, presenting me to her friends as if I was a special gift to be unwrapped. Before I could respond, everyone greeted me with hugs and words of welcome.

Once the meat was cooked, we went inside and sat around the dining room table. The food was good, and the drinks were flowing. Everyone added to the conversation, and there was laughter and a feeling of inclusiveness in the group.

Bill and Kate had recently celebrated their fiftieth wedding anniversary. They had kids all over the country and beamed when they talked about their eighteen grandchildren.

Sam was younger than the others and had lost his wife two years earlier. Sophie met him at the grocery store while he was standing in the produce section trying to figure out the difference between a honeydew and a cantaloupe. When she'd asked him if she could help, he'd burst into tears, and they'd both left their shopping carts in the aisle when Sophie offered to buy him coffee at the Panera Bread next door.

Then there was Barbara, a sweet and quiet woman. Her warm smile never dulled, and she reminded me of my grandma. She held back a bit compared to the others, but I could tell she had a crush on Sam and hung on every word he said.

As the evening progressed, it was apparent Sophie was the social director of the group. I realized without her hospitality, these people might spend their evenings alone and wondered if she saw me in the same light. I felt a sense of respect for a woman who looked out for the needs of others, enjoying herself in the process.

The get-together ended early, and I was back home before 8:00 p.m. As I poured myself another glass of wine, a child's cry from the gray house next door drew my attention to the window.

The little boy was wrapped in the man's arms, and Betsy was trying to pull the child free and put him in the car where the little girl was already strapped in. When she got him into his seat, the man opened the back of the mini-van and put in several bags. They waved goodbye as Betsy pulled out of the driveway, and I heard the man say, *"See you next weekend."*

Why would Betsy and the kids leave for the week? Maybe they were going to visit relatives, and the husband couldn't get away to go with them.

I took my wine out on the lanai and watched people passing by. Were they vacationing, or were they locals? How many were walking the beach trying to figure out what to do with the rest of their lives?

It surprised me to feel a little homesick after such a fun evening with Sophie and her friends. I decided a call to my parents might help.

"Hi, Mom. Just thought I'd check in," I said.

I saw the man from the gray house walk onto his deck. He looked sad as he gazed out toward the ocean. He probably missed his wife and kids already. He was lucky to have such a beautiful family.

"Meggie, we've had quite a day. Your dad has been having back pain, and he took a muscle relaxer before we went to church. I *told* him it wasn't a good idea, but he insisted on doing it anyway. Then, during the sermon, I heard this awful sound, and I looked over to see your dad's head hanging and the loudest snore I've ever heard coming from a human being. I gave him a little push, and everyone around us laughed. I was so embarrassed."

Hearing her laugh and imagining the scenario she described made me giggle. Sometimes I could be a little hard on them.

***

My first week at the beach went quickly. I enjoyed sleeping late before hitting the beach for long morning walks. In the afternoons, I wandered through antique shops and read from the pile of books I'd brought with me. Each day I sat on the beach and felt the warm sun as it tanned my pale skin.

I'd invited Sophie over, and the blueberry muffins I'd taken out of the oven were almost cool enough to eat, but the egg casserole had a few more minutes to bake. I wanted a chance to thank her for inviting me over to meet her friends, and breakfast seemed like a nice gesture.

Sophie arrived in a flurry and immediately began sharing her life story. It wouldn't take long for me to get the background on my fascinating neighbor.

"I haven't always been the woman you see today," she said. "I scored the dance audition of a lifetime as a favor to my hometown dance instructor and landed a spot as a Rockette when I was only nineteen."

"Wow, you must have been a very talented dancer," I said.

"I was good, but most of all, I fit the "look" of the show. After getting the job, I moved into a tiny efficiency apartment in New York with one of the other cast members and began to live the life of my dreams."

"Is that where you met your husband?"

"Well, it's where I met my *first* one. The girls would go to a little bar around the corner from Radio City Music Hall each night after the show. We smoked and drank, allowing men to buy our drinks and light our cigarettes. We didn't have much money, and it was the only way we could have a little fun in the city. I didn't care much about any of the guys but continued leading them on as long as they were footing the bill. Everything changed the day I met James Callister."

"Oh, this sounds juicy," I said, wanting more of the story.

"I'd seen him in the bar before and had noticed him looking at me from across the room. One evening, he made his way to me, and we began talking. We were inseparable after that. He courted me, impressing me with gifts and a lifestyle I wasn't accustomed to. James was from a wealthy family, and he didn't mind spending money on me, and I didn't mind accepting it."

"It sounds like an incredible love story," I gushed.

"Well, not exactly. We were married six months later at his parents' estate. I gave up dancing when James told me it wasn't a *respectable* profession. After a honeymoon in the Hamptons, we settled into a mid-town apartment where I thought we'd live the perfect life."

As the story started to go in a different direction, I braced for what was coming next.

"The bliss of marriage, however, wore off the first time he slapped me across the face when I burned our dinner. He apologized and told me it would never happen again. I wanted to believe him, but he lied."

At least I'd never been abused by Jason—unless you counted being ignored.

"Finally, the day came when I filled a suitcase with clothes and took $200.00 from the glass jar on top of the refrigerator. Two black eyes made it impossible for me to keep his secret any longer. I bought a bus ticket to Florida where my sister, Audrey, was working as a waitress. And the rest is history."

"Oh, Sophie. I'm so sorry. Did you ever marry again?" I asked.

"A few years later, I met and married an air force sergeant stationed at Patrick Air Force Base in Cocoa Beach. He was kind and handsome, and I thought my prayers had been answered as I started to build my life as a military wife. But everything ended again when he was killed in a helicopter crash during a training mission two years into our marriage."

There was more to Sophie than I'd imagined. Maybe I

could learn something from a woman who'd been through so much.

"I met the love of my life, Charles Beatty, while working an office job in Orlando. He was my boss and the owner of the company. As we got to know each other and fell in love, he told me he was unwilling to date an employee. So he fired me and proposed marriage in the next breath."

"How long were you together?" I asked.

"Thirty-five wonderful years, splitting our time between a house in Orlando and the one next door. We traveled, entertained guests, and lived the good life until he dropped dead of a heart attack at sixty-six. We never had children because we didn't want to share our time with anyone else. Charlie left me with a load of money in the bank and a lifetime of adventurous memories to get me by, but I make it a point to entertain and have people in my house because I can't stand to live my golden years *alone* at the beach."

"How did you survive it all?"

"Like I said, I don't allow myself to dwell on negativity. I've had some dark moments in my life, but the good times far outweigh the bad—so I focus on the good. I've had three husbands, and two of them were gems. If I'd given up after James's mistreatment, I'd have missed the best years of my life."

I wasn't the only woman who'd gone through a life change. Sophie made it with little more than determination, and I could do the same.

Chapter Four
June

Sunday morning was bright and sunny, and humidity hung in the air like damp laundry. The white, stucco church my grandparents had always attended when staying in Daytona Beach looked the same as I'd remembered. When I was a little girl, I'd complained about going to services when we were visiting, but Grandma was a staunch Christian and had always pointed out that, *"God doesn't take a vacation from us, so we shouldn't take a vacation from God."* Her words of wisdom echoed in my head as I felt the need for spiritual renewal and slipped into a pew near the side entrance.

The organ music swelled with a familiar hymn as the congregation stood, and the minister and choir began to proceed down the center aisle. Overcome with emotion and nostalgia, my eyes filled with tears. I felt alone in a sanctuary packed with people and wished my grandma was standing beside me, holding my hand as she always did. Even though the divorce was what I wanted, I was feeling sorry for myself to be facing the challenges of starting over when Jason and I should have been enjoying the life we'd worked so hard to build.

After the sermon, the congregation began to file toward the

front to receive the wine and bread symbolic of the Last Supper. I watched as people of all ages and ethnicities left their pews, moving forward with the common goal of receiving communion. One older couple drew my attention and helped me to put my situation into perspective.

"Where are we going?" the woman asked. The gentleman helped her get up, and they walked toward the altar as she looked to him for guidance. She took communion following the example of the people in front of her, and the man steered her back to their seats.

"Are we going home now?" she asked without whispering. The man said something to appease her, and she looked straight ahead for the rest of the service.

She obviously had a form of dementia, and a lump formed in my throat again when I thought about their challenges. The plight of the strangers at church reminded me that marriage wasn't always an easy path. Someday I'd have a man in my life who would love me as much as the older man must love his ailing wife. I said a silent prayer for the couple and also one for the man I hoped was making his way toward me to share the life we both deserved.

***

Every day I walked, jogged, or biked on the beach in front of The Pink Shell, and the daily exercise made me feel good and sleep well. I stood at the end of the sandy path and stretched. A jogger made his way down the beach, and the figure approached me.

"Hey, Meg—how are you?" It was the man from next door. He was sweating profusely, and his dark hair dripped with perspiration and formed damp curls around his face.

"Hi," I said, realizing Betsy must have told him my name.

"I was hoping I'd get a chance to meet you before much more of the summer passed. I'm Brian Barts," he said as he tried to catch his breath. "I was thinking when Betsy and the kids are here next weekend, maybe we could get together for a drink or something."

I'd seen Betsy arrive on Friday night with suitcases and groceries, and the Barts Construction truck pulled into the driveway not long after. They'd taken a picnic to the beach, and I'd seen Brian carrying a bottle of wine and two glasses outside and felt a pang of jealousy at the life they seemed to be living. Maybe Betsy had a job somewhere else that took her away from the beach during the week. It was a strange arrangement and not ideal for raising kids.

"If it works out, that would be nice." I didn't want to feel like a third wheel during a family weekend and had no intention of joining them.

"Well, nice to meet you. By the way, your flowers look beautiful out front."

"Thanks," I said as he started to walk away. Maybe it wouldn't be the worst thing to have a drink with my *other* neighbors.

Brian continued to walk up the stairs to his own place, and I couldn't help following him with my eyes. He was medium height, athletic, and good-looking without being too buff. I was sure years of construction work had kept him in shape. He had a confident air about him and seemed like someone who took care of himself but wasn't so dedicated to the gym and the mirror that he couldn't see anyone else around him.

Brian Barts would have been the one you talked about at your class reunion. He'd have been the solid, well-mannered guy who'd become a success in life, contrasting to the star quarterback who was overweight and underemployed once the shine of high school wore off.

Betsy was a lucky woman.

***

The grocery run I'd made on my way into town hadn't sustained me for long, and I stopped at the store to pick up more supplies. I'd been surviving on whatever sounded good, and one day it consisted of an entire bag of potato chips and a Snickers Bar.

I'd shopped on an empty stomach and had to stop myself from buying everything on the shelves. I was starving and decided to start my healthy eating plan another day and treat myself to Chinese takeout. I'd seen a restaurant not far from the beach house advertising the best egg rolls in Daytona, and I wanted to know if they were telling the truth.

The lighting inside the restaurant was dim and small candles burned on each table. It wasn't the dive takeout joint I was expecting. Soft music played in the background, and a beautiful Asian woman dressed in a red silk dress served as a hostess by the front door.

"May I help you?" she asked in a beautiful accent.

"Yes, could I see a menu?"

The woman nodded and handed me a booklet with pictures of delicious-looking food on the inside.

"I'll have an order of the number seven *to go*, please." I decided my poor eating habits should go out with a bang and ordered sweet and sour chicken with fried rice.

"Hey, twice in one day . . ." I recognized the voice behind me, and as I turned, Brian Barts smiled as he made his way past me from the dining room.

"Oh, hello again," I said. He smelled fantastic as he passed by. I was missing male companionship in the worst way, and having a good-looking man brush past me reminded me of what I didn't have.

He walked into the restroom, and I wondered what he was doing at the restaurant. I figured he was like me, eating for one and never thinking about it until the hunger was so intense all you could do was get takeout or eat the first thing you could find in the refrigerator.

I was sitting on a bench waiting for my order when Brian came out and passed by again.

"Have a good night," he said.

I peered past the hostess stand and saw him going toward a table where an attractive blond woman sat. As he approached, he smiled and touched her back as he found his seat again. I felt uneasy at how he smiled at her and listened intently as she talked to him quietly. She was probably a friend or client, but I didn't think he should be touching her in such a familiar way and gazing into her eyes when he had a family to consider.

When I got home, I opened the Chinese food boxes at my kitchen counter and ate from the top of them. The first few bites were delicious, but I lost my appetite when I couldn't get the thought of what I'd seen at the restaurant out of my mind.

What if Mr. Barts wasn't such a good guy? How could I observe him carrying on a charade with his family each weekend and watch him rendezvous with another woman during the week? I didn't want to see anything else to make me suspicious of my handsome neighbor.

I settled into the most comfortable chair in the room and watched TV, hoping something would take my mind off what I'd seen. Before long, headlights appeared in the driveway of the gray house. I turned the light off so he wouldn't see me spying on him and carefully peeked through the closed blinds. The door of his truck opened, and he made his way toward the front door *alone*.

I had to admit I was suspicious of men after what happened with Jason. I hated to think all men were in various stages of cheating—planning, engaging, or making up for an indiscretion that would eventually surface. Maybe I'd been wrong about what I'd seen. I was an Iowan, and my faith in the goodness of people was strong. There was a chance Brian didn't deserve my mistrust, but until I knew for sure, I'd keep my distance from Brian Barts.

***

Sophie and I had brunch together in a quaint café near the beach shops at the Daytona pier, and I filled her in on my *other* neighbors.

"I pride myself on knowing everything about this neighborhood, but the only thing I know about that stunning gray house is that it recently sold. I haven't met the people there, but they seem like a lovely family. We should all get together over martinis and introduce ourselves," Sophie suggested.

"I'm not getting any closer to those people until I know what's going on. If you want to invite them over, you'll have to do it without me," I said.

"Well, that Brian is quite a hottie. I'd love to spend the

evening with such a fine specimen of a man. In fact, I could do a little flirting with Mr. Barts myself and see if he takes the bait."

"Oh, Sophie," I giggled, wishing I had her self-confidence.

"Perhaps you should forget about the Barts family and move on with your own life. You need to have fun and get out and enjoy yourself. Maybe meet some people your age or find a young man to take you out on the town."

"Where am I going to meet someone in Daytona? I'm only here for the summer, and I'm not the type to hang out in a bar to pick up guys."

"Well, it's quite a coincidence, but I happen to have a wonderful nephew who would love to take you out on a date," Sophie said as her eyes danced.

My first inclination was to decline her offer without hearing more.

"Meg, he's a delightful young man who simply hasn't found the right girl."

Sophie continued to tell me about Audrey's son, Carl, who lived nearby in New Smyrna Beach. He was a CPA with a successful business, a good personality, and a big heart. She shared that she'd already mentioned me to him, and he was interested in meeting for dinner.

"I don't know, Sophie." I didn't want to hurt her feelings but wasn't sure if I was ready for a fixup.

"It would be such a favor to me, the poor boy works too hard, and I'd love for him to meet someone like you . . . He's going to call you tomorrow."

Sophie was beginning to remind me of my mother, and I knew there was no use trying to refuse her offer to meet up with Carl.

43

***

It was mid-evening when I heard a car door. I went to the window to see if Betsy and the kids had returned early for the weekend. Instead, I saw the blond woman from the Chinese restaurant head toward the front door with a bottle of wine, and my heart sank. Brian hugged her before she entered the house.

How could he do such a thing to Betsy and the kids? I tried to put it out of my mind, but nothing would distract me from what was happening next door.

Brian and the blonde went out on the expansive back deck and sat on the same side of the dining table, looking toward the ocean. They were drinking wine, and he put his arm around her. They talked and laughed, and it was apparent by the end of the evening she was *not* just a friend. I decided to keep my distance from the Barts family. I had enough to deal with and didn't need to get involved.

***

Sunlight peeked into the loft, waking me from a night of restless sleep. I splashed cold water on my face and changed into shorts and a T-shirt, preparing to take a quick run before my morning coffee. I planned to spend part of the day working on my laptop, researching possibilities for a career change. A run would feel good and clear my head before looking at job prospects.

I started to stretch and was bent over in an unflattering position when I heard his voice.

"Beautiful day, isn't it?"

44

Why wasn't Brian at work at 9:00 a.m.? Was he planning to spend the day with *her*?

"I suppose," I answered flatly. I was so *over* men who thought they could get away with anything.

I continued to prepare for my run, not wanting to give him my full attention.

"Betsy and the kids will be here tomorrow afternoon. Let's plan to get together for that drink after they get settled," he offered.

Maybe he thought I was on to him and wanted to get me on his good side so I wouldn't blow his cover.

"I'm pretty busy this weekend." I could see by the look on his face that my coldness did not go unnoticed.

"Oh . . ." he started to walk away but turned back to me before he reached the steps to his deck. "Hey—is everything okay?" he asked.

"Yeah, just trying to get out for my run." I didn't make eye contact with him.

Brian turned and continued to walk toward his house, and I took off running down the beach feeling smug.

Chapter Five
June

I'm unsure why I agreed to go on a blind date with Sophie's nephew. It was more of a favor to her than a prospect for love. Her description of the lifelong bachelor didn't sound that bad, but I wondered how a guy could fly under the radar of marriage for so long. I figured it was either commitment issues on his part or the rest of womankind making a subtle but definite statement on his romantic qualities.

Carl called me the night after Sophie brought his availability to my attention, and we decided to meet later in the week. I wanted to hurry up and get it over with, which demonstrated my lack of hope for a future between us. We decided to meet at a local sports bar called The Last Inning. The name of the place made me feel like a loser before I even got there. I hated to think my only chance at love was with the nephew of someone I'd just met—who needed his aunt to fix him up.

We planned to meet at 7:00 p.m. I arrived five minutes early and chose a booth near the front door. Our server, Scott, was a handsome and muscular twenty-something. For some reason, I felt the need to impress him with my ability to date anyone who walked in the door dressed in a red shirt. That was what Carl said he would wear and how I would know it was him.

At least ten men, aged six to ninety, came through the door wearing a shade of crimson. I never knew it was such a popular color. I kept trying to make eye contact or see searching in the face of those who entered. Each patron seemed to know where they were going and who they were joining.

When I started to think I was being stood up, Carl came into the restaurant asking for directions to our table. He was already ten minutes later than he should have been, but I gave a little wave, and he came over to our booth.

"Hi, you must be Carl. I'm Meg Parsons," I said, stating the obvious.

"Good to meet you. Aunt Sophie has told me a lot about you," Carl replied as he slid into the seat across from me.

We exchanged some pleasantries and talked about the humid Florida weather while we looked over the menu. I could tell right away he wasn't my type. I wanted to order something to go and call it a night but felt I needed to give him a chance out of respect for Sophie.

Carl was about my height and a little pudgy through the middle. He was balding like many men his age, but he'd decided to try and hide it with a hideous comb-over. I imagined his hairstyle would be ever-changing in a swimming pool or on a windy day.

Even though he lived in Florida, he was pale, like he didn't get outside much. I learned in my first few minutes with Carl that he suffered from severe allergies. He'd brought his own box of tissues, and they held a prominent place in the middle of our dining table.

For the entire evening, I tried to be interested in Carl. I asked about his life and shared a little about mine. I wanted to make him feel comfortable, which was not an easy task for someone who seemed so unsure of himself. The ticket finally came, and I was glad our evening was ending.

"Would you like me to pay my part of the bill?" I asked, not sure about the current trends for paying on a blind date.

"Sure, let me figure out what your portion would be," Carl said, whipping out his phone to start working figures on his calculator.

"You had a glass of wine and the iced tea. That would be $8.00 plus $2.95, and I will give you half of the appetizer, bringing it to $15.45. Then your salad was $10.95. So, your total would be $26.40 plus tax and tip."

I could tell Carl was an accountant by trade, and since I didn't want to do the calculations to figure out the extra amount due, I just rounded up and put $35.00 on the table. Carl snagged the money, combining it with cash of his own. He continued to figure out how much should be left in total.

"Hey," Carl said, "do you have some extra ones? I'm running short of cash for the tip, and I hate to have to put the entire thing on my credit card."

"Sure," I said, fishing in my wallet for more money. Scott, the handsome waiter, looked on with a grin plastered across his chiseled face, willing us to hand over the money and get out of his section.

Unfortunately, I was fresh out of ones. I threw another five down and grabbed my purse to leave. We walked outside the restaurant, and Carl began to tell me what an enjoyable time he'd had. I looked longingly toward my car.

"I had a lot of fun, Meg. Maybe we could go out again

sometime. Could I call you?"

I never wanted to see Carl again. No amount of giving him the benefit of the doubt would change my feelings. If I left the door open for future contact, it would only delay the inevitable.

"Thanks, Carl, but I don't think so. It was nice to meet you." I had no choice but to rip the band-aid off and be done with him.

"Okay then, take care of yourself, and maybe we'll run into each other at Aunt Sophie's." He walked behind the building toward his car. I had a feeling most dates ended for Carl in much the same way.

***

I saw Sophie through the window as she sauntered to the ocean for her morning ritual. I took my coffee and chair to the beach and waited for her to come over and discuss my date with Carl. She was smiling in anticipation as she set her towel beside me and pulled up a piece of beach for the conversation.

"Well, darling—how did it go?"

"It was fine. Carl is a nice man," I said.

"Carl is a splendid boy, but did you feel a spark with him? We're looking for a spark for you."

"I'm sorry, Sophie. There was no spark. But I appreciate your effort in setting us up." I didn't want her to feel bad about her choice for me or to be offended about my lack of feelings toward her nephew.

"Sweetheart, I didn't think you would hit it off with Carl. He's single for a reason. I just wanted to help you out by giving you an *opportunity*. The more you go out with men, the sooner you will decide what's right for you. Knowing what you *don't* want is as important as knowing what you *do* want. There was a slight chance the two of you would hit it off, but I knew it would probably be the other way around. I did it for both of you—knowing it would get you further on your journey toward happiness. Even if you aren't going to take the rest of the trip together."

I was glad to hear Sophie's declaration of purpose in arranging the date with Carl. I knew she understood the situation, and I wouldn't have to make up something about not seeing him again.

"Thank you, Sophie. I'm grateful to you for understanding it didn't work out."

"Not another word, dear. Don't speak of unpleasantness, or you'll bring more upon yourself. You will find your special someone. He may be closer than you think, but you must keep looking. The day I met my Charlie, I woke up in the morning in a terrible mood. I was feeling sorry for myself. I'd been through a divorce from one husband and the death of another. At thirty years old, I felt defeated. But that day ended up being very important. If I'd stayed in bed as I'd wanted, depressed and unhappy, I would have missed meeting the love of my life."

Sophie had a great outlook on life.

***

I heard Betsy and the children arrive on Friday night. The squeals from the kids rang out as they ran up the front steps and into their daddy's arms. Their happy voices alternated with the slamming door as they made several trips to and from the car with their supplies for the weekend.

I wondered how Brian Barts felt knowing he had another woman with him just a few nights earlier. Was it an ongoing relationship or someone he'd just met? Did Betsy think her husband loved her unconditionally, never knowing he had a secret life that didn't include her? I planned to make myself scarce over the weekend to avoid an unwelcome invitation to have a drink with Betsy and the cheater.

***

Saturday consisted of errands and shopping. I even spent the afternoon at the movies trying to stay away from the beach house. I returned to the cottage around dinner time and planned a quiet night alone. Unfortunately, my evening was interrupted when I heard a knock on the front door.

"Hi!" Betsy said when I opened the door.

"Hi, Betsy—how are you?" I asked, thinking about the betrayal at hand.

"I'm good. It's great to be out here on the weekends. The kids love it, even though they miss their dad during the week. They are wound up when we get here on Fridays, and I'm ready for a break!"

"It must be tough being a single parent all week."

"Well, it isn't that bad, and I have my parents to help out. We all pitch in to make it work. Hey, would you like to come over for lunch tomorrow? I thought it would be nice if we had a chance to get to know each other since we're going to be neighbors all summer. I'd love for Brian to have someone out here for company. I worry he gets lonely here all week by himself."

Brian's loneliness was the last thing Betsy needed to worry about.

"Oh, that isn't necessary. You don't get much time with Brian. I'm sure you don't want to waste any of it with outsiders."

"What do you mean?" she asked with a puzzled look.

"Well, it must be hard to be away from your husband and only have weekends together as a family. I don't want to intrude."

"You think we're married?" she asked as her eyes widened.

"Well, I thought . . ."

"Brian's my *brother*," she said, laughing. "I figured the two of you had talked. He said he'd seen you a few times, and I assumed he'd told you about our situation. "

I could feel my cheeks turning red.

"He's your brother?" My mind raced as I tried to comprehend what she was saying.

"Yes. I hoped you would join us tomorrow. I'm sorry I'm being a little selfish, but Brian has been through so much. I thought if we got together, maybe the two of you would hit it off. He could use a friend in Daytona."

It was apparent Betsy didn't know anything about the blond woman, and I suddenly felt compelled to protect Brian's privacy.

"My brother's wife died of an aneurysm about a year and a half ago," Betsy continued. "When she died, he was devastated—totally broken. But, he's getting back to his old self again, and our family has been helping him with the kids. He's putting his life back together as much as possible given the circumstances."

"I had no idea," I said quietly, trying to remember everything I'd said to Brian. I thought back to my blatant rudeness, and my heart sank at the way I'd come across.

"This job in Daytona is a huge step for him. Even though it meant being away from the kids, we thought it was a fantastic opportunity for him. The job included using the beach house during the construction project. Otherwise, he would have had to travel back and forth to our home in St. Augustine."

"So, you take care of the kids while he works here during the week?"

"Well, our entire family does. The timing was perfect because I got laid off around the same time. Brian needed my help, and I needed the cash. So, here we are!"

"Here you are . . ."

"How about lunch tomorrow? Brian is great with the grill."

"Sure," I said, trying to process the information I'd been given.

As Betsy walked back to the gray house, I was relieved that my suspicions about Brian Barts were unfounded. It never dawned on me that Brian and Betsy were siblings. I'd never seen him show affection toward her or heard the kids call her Mom, but it seemed like it all fit together.

I felt terrible about the way I'd treated him on the beach when he was just being friendly. How could I explain my rudeness without looking like a complete idiot?

***

I carried a fruit salad and balanced a plate of homemade cookies on one arm as I knocked at Brian's front door. I imagined there had been a conversation about my assumptions concerning their family relationships, and I felt like the butt of a joke with only myself to blame.

"Hi, welcome to the neighborhood," Brian said as he opened the door.

"Hey," I said sheepishly. His cheerfulness only made me feel worse. "I brought a couple of things for lunch. I hope the kids like chocolate chip cookies."

"Their favorite, thanks! Hey, kids—*cookies!*"

The two of them came running from somewhere in the big house. They were grinning from ear to ear and excited to have a visitor.

"I'm Jenna, and I'm eight, and this is Jack, and he's four. I can swim the entire length of the pool, but Jack can only go part way. I've had lessons."

"Okay, Jen—let Meg get in the door, and we can tell her about your swimming lessons a little later."

The children ran off in the direction of the back of the house, and it was quiet again. They were cute and overly friendly, and my heart was heavy at the thought of the two of them left without a mother.

The interior of the modern house was stunning. It was different from my homey cottage next door, and I couldn't imagine having kids around such expensive-looking design pieces. We walked into the large kitchen covered in what seemed like miles of white and gray marble.

"Hi, Meg! Can we get you a glass of wine?" Betsy asked as she cut vegetables at the counter.

"That would be great." I was happy to have plans outside the four walls of my little beach house and with people my own age.

"Would you like red or white?" Brian asked.

"White would be fine."

54

Brian took a bottle out of the wine fridge and poured three glasses. It was fruity and delicious, and the mood was relaxed. Van Morrison played in the background, and when the horns took over on "Into the Mystic," Betsy swayed to the music and pretended to play the trumpet.

"Sorry, we're a little crazy around here. Thanks for the fruit and cookies. You didn't have to do that," Betsy said.

"I'm happy to have something fun to do, and I *love* the music. A little crazy sounds like fun today," I joked.

"To new friends," Brian said, raising his glass.

"Here, here," added Betsy.

We toasted by clinking our glasses and sat at the breakfast bar getting to know each other. They had an easy rapport, and both parented the children with natural skills. It was easy to see how I'd misconstrued the relationships.

I told them a little about myself, sharing I'd grown up in Iowa and had attended college at Illinois State and then moved to Michigan with Jason to take over his family's business. I kept the sordid details to a minimum but told them I was spending the summer at the beach house on the way to life *without* Jason Parsons.

It was a sunny day, but the ocean breeze made it cool enough for us to eat outside. A large stone fireplace was the focal point of the deck. I couldn't imagine a time when it would be useful in the Florida heat, but it was beautiful and added something unique to the covered porch. The outdoor dining table anchored the space and gave us a spot to relax.

A storm was brewing in the Atlantic, and even though it was hundreds of miles away, the waves were bigger than usual. The site was breathtaking, with the navy-blue water crashing along the shore. I could see why Brian had brought his blond friend to the spot with the best view in the house.

We ate barbecued chicken, grilled vegetables, pasta salad, and the fruit I brought. The kids told stories, and we all talked and laughed as we enjoyed the food and wine. Before long, Betsy and the kids were talking about heading home.

"I'm sorry. I've overstayed my welcome. Thank you for lunch, but I should let you all get back to your day."

"No, don't worry about it. We never leave until later in the evening," Betsy replied.

"Let's get together again soon," Brian said as I gathered my things.

Knowing the *real* story behind the family next door made another invitation to join them very appealing.

Chapter Six
June

With a storm on the way, the air was cooler on my morning walk. I planned to do some shopping and spend the day cleaning the cottage. As I breathed in the sea air, I could see Brian running toward me. His pace slowed as he got closer, and a warm smile spread across his face.

"Beautiful this morning, isn't it?" he asked as he stopped to talk with me.

"Yeah, most mornings are. That's why I love it here."

"Do you run every morning?"

"I walk or run, but usually a little later. When I have the entire day to myself, there's no reason to get out here too early," I answered.

"Agreed, but there's nothing like the sunrise," he said.

"You go out that early?"

"Sometimes. Well, have a good day," Brian said, continuing toward his house.

I decided to seize the moment.

"Hey, I wanted to apologize for how I acted the other morning. It was rude, and I'm sorry."

Brian turned back to me. "No problem. Had I done something to offend you?"

"Listen, Brian—I'm sure Betsy told you I thought the two of you were married. I saw you at the Chinese Restaurant with a woman, the same woman who visited the other night, and I thought you were having an affair. I had no right to judge you, and I'm afraid I may have been overly critical toward you considering my recent divorce."

Brian started to laugh. "Betsy said you had our family dynamic all wrong, but it's understandable. I didn't realize you'd seen me with Anne at the restaurant that night we ran into each other. I can see how it would have raised an eyebrow."

"Yes, but it was none of my business. And I didn't mention it to Betsy, so don't worry about that."

"I thought you were just unfriendly," he laughed. "When Betsy insisted we invite you for lunch, I made a thousand excuses why I didn't think it was a good idea. Then you came over, and we had such a good time. I couldn't believe you were the same person who'd practically accosted me at the beach," he said, exaggerating his negative feelings toward me to get his point across.

"I'm sorry. Can we forget the entire thing and start over?"

"That's exactly what we should do. Hi, I'm Brian Barts," he said, extending his hand to me.

"Meg Parsons, *friendly* next-door neighbor," I said, looking into his beautiful blue eyes, which were offering forgiveness.

He placed his other hand on top of mine and said formally, "Good to meet you, Meg. Now it's time for me to get to work."

***

I opened my computer to search for the day's job postings. Researching marketing positions had become part of my morning routine, and I was used to being discouraged at what was available to someone with my experience. Maybe I'd have to expand from marketing roles to consulting or abandon my skill set for a different career path altogether.

I started to wonder if a future at my dad's insurance company would be my only option. I pictured myself bringing a completed report to my new boss, who would reply cheerfully using my childhood nickname, *"Thanks, Peanut!"*

I'd slink past the other insurance agents' desks, returning to my cubicle, where the name Peanut Parsons would be emblazoned on the nameplate hanging outside the entrance. Nepotism was a surefire way to get a job, but it wasn't a sound approach for building relationships in the workplace.

A television news story filled the beach house's quiet space as Al Roker did a remote from Key West. He talked about the tropical storm forming near the Leeward Islands and moving toward Puerto Rico. The weather models showed it hitting the Florida coast without turning into an actual hurricane, but the potential for bad weather was making me nervous.

I knew it would be windy and wet for a few days, and Al specifically gave a shout-out to those living along the Florida coast and said we should make plans for the inclement weather. My mind went to sleeping on a cot in a high school gym, eating ham sandwiches on white bread, and washing them down with cold coffee. I hoped to stay put in the comfort of The Pink Shell but needed to be prepared regardless.

My phone rang, and I settled in for a conversation with my mom.

"Megan, are you aware there's a hurricane headed right for

your house? I'm watching the *Today Show*, and Al Roker has me in a panic." Even though I knew my mother was being dramatic, a call from her caused me to feel more stressed about what could happen.

"I'm watching it too, but I don't think it will be that bad. I've talked with my neighbors, and they don't seem too worked up about it." I didn't want to add to her concern, so I downplayed my own fears.

"I guess you forgot to tell me you have meteorologists living next to you," she said sarcastically. "The national news reports an emergency situation, and your father and I are beside ourselves. You should book a flight home today."

"That's going a little far, even for you, Mom. The storm is still a couple of days out, and there's a chance it will change direction by then. They aren't asking people to evacuate, and the warning is for Puerto Rico with the expectation it will diminish the longer it lasts. What if I promise to keep in touch and check in with my friends here if I have any problems?"

"I guess it will have to suffice. You seem hell-bent on making your own decisions and ignoring anything your father and I have to say, so we'll sit by the television and watch, hoping Mother Nature doesn't prove our point."

"Mom, everything will be okay. I love both of you, even if you drive me nuts."

***

It was mid-afternoon by the time I started cleaning the cottage. Of course, I wouldn't have had to clean except that I'd waived the weekly housekeeping package offered on the condo to keep the cost down. I'd procrastinated most of the day away but knew I could still accomplish my goal before evening with a bit of hard work.

I started upstairs, and by the time I made it to the first floor, the house was beginning to smell like Pine Sol and bleach. I continued to clean everything in sight, not slowing down until late afternoon.

I was ready for a relaxing evening and an early bedtime when there was a knock at the front of the house. I opened the door to Brian holding two brown paper sacks.

"Hi," I said, wishing I'd put makeup on after my shower and was wearing something other than yoga pants and a ratty T-shirt.

"I understand you like Chinese food. Since we're reintroducing ourselves, I thought I would treat you to dinner. Unless you've already eaten . . ."

"No—I haven't eaten. In fact, I've been cleaning and am famished. Come on in."

"Wow," Brian said as he came through the door. "This place is awesome."

I surveyed my work, scanning the cleaned and organized great room. It was beautiful, even if it wasn't as grand as Brian's place next door.

"I hadn't had a chance to clean yet, so I decided to take the day and get it done. I don't think it even needed it, but it gave me something to do."

"It looks like I came on a perfect night. You need a little dinner after your hard work, and I want some company."

I was surprised Brian would appear on my doorstep with dinner but was happy for the opportunity to show him I was not a rude and nosy neighbor.

"There's white wine in the refrigerator or red in the wine

rack. Glasses are on the top shelf next to the sink. You get the food ready while I run upstairs and change into something more presentable."

"You don't need to change on my account," he said, "I think you look great." The comment made me blush as I hurried upstairs.

I pulled on a pair of jeans and a lightweight hoodie. I put a little powder and blush on my face and touched a tiny dab of gloss on my lips. I used the blow dryer on my damp hair and added styling gel to give my hair a little body. I saw a better version of myself in the mirror before returning downstairs to join my unexpected guest for dinner.

Brian had opened a bottle of red wine and had poured two glasses. He'd put plates and silverware out for each of us and had six different entrees on the table, along with crab Rangoon and egg rolls. For two people, it seemed like an incredible amount of food. He was standing by the table, looking proud of the dinner he'd laid out for us, and I couldn't help but be attracted to him.

"I don't know if I'm *that* hungry," I said, looking at the spread of food.

"Well, I wasn't sure what you'd like, so I got a little bit of everything. We can each take some of the leftovers to sustain us for the rest of the week."

"Good idea—thank you. This is such a nice surprise."

We finished dinner and took our wine out to my lanai. It was a beautiful evening, and I was thankful for the breeze, which kept the room cool enough for us to enjoy the sights and sounds of the beach.

I was careful about the subjects I brought up. I wasn't sure how much Brian would want to share about his life. He'd been through so much, and I didn't want to make him feel uncomfortable. We discussed our experiences at prominent universities and how we'd both married our college sweethearts.

I found out Brian and his dad were in the construction business together and had lived in Charlotte before opening a branch in St. Augustine. Eventually, his entire family settled in Florida, closing the North Carolina location. Between the lines, it was easy to read that Brian was a successful businessman, even if he'd had a lot on his plate in the previous months.

He'd come to Daytona to work as the project manager for the building of a beachfront condo. As Betsy had told me, the gray house belonged to the developer, and staying in the house during the construction was part of the deal for taking the job.

Brian wanted Jenna and Jack to be able to stay in their own home instead of leaving their lives in St. Augustine, so the plan for Betsy to take care of them was ideal. He got to see them every weekend and would sometimes travel the hour and a half back home to stay with them during the week if they needed him.

"What about you?" Brian inquired. "Do you have children?"

It was a strange question because if I had kids, wouldn't they be with me?

"No, my ex-husband and I didn't have any children together."

"What about nieces and nephews?"

He wasn't going to let this go.

"Yes, I have three nieces, so I get my kid fix through them."

The topic of kids always made me feel inadequate.

The conversation got around to the woman he'd been seeing. He expressed his concerns that Anne was younger than him and didn't seem prepared to take on the needs of a family. He went on to say they'd had a few dates, but he knew they didn't have a future together.

"That's why I never mentioned her to Betsy. And I'm grateful you didn't say anything to her because I don't want to involve my family in something that isn't going anywhere in the first place. They're anxious for me to be happy, and they don't always give me the space I need to figure out the new landscape of my life," he said.

"You should meet *my* parents," I added with a laugh.

"If I were someone like you, with nothing to tie me down in starting over again, I might choose all kinds of things. But I'm not," he offered openly. "Jenna and Jack are my main priority. My life has to reflect what's best for them."

"I can understand that. Without children, I do have a lot more options. The problem for me is too many choices. At least you've narrowed your path a bit."

"Anne and I gave it a chance in case there was something there, but I don't think either of us wants to spend any more time on it."

I was not disappointed to hear this news.

After we finished the bottle of wine, Brian decided it was time for him to leave. He seemed ready to call it a night with an early morning ahead and a long day of work after that. We boxed the leftovers, and Brian took a few with him, leaving the rest for me.

I walked him to the front door. "Thanks for dinner. It was so thoughtful of you."

"Thank *you* for indulging me," Brian replied. "I knew I was taking a chance buying all that food, not even knowing if you were home. But I wanted to let you know I didn't harbor any hard feelings about our earlier misunderstanding."

"It was *my* misunderstanding, so I appreciate it. I'm glad you took the risk," I blurted out, surprising myself with such a bold statement.

There was an awkward silence as we tried to figure out how to end the night. It wasn't a date—but it felt a little intimate for a meeting between neighbors. I was happy when Brian broke the silence.

"Hey, give me your cell phone number in case I need to check on you if the weather gets bad."

I gave him my number, and he put it into his cell phone.

"Should I do anything to prepare for it? Aren't you supposed to board up windows or something?"

"It wouldn't hurt to shut your hurricane shutters. They make a lot of hype out of these storms, and they don't usually turn out to be anything. Unless they turn out to be something," he said, laughing. "I'll take care of you if you need me to!"

It felt like he was flirting with me, but it had been such a long time since I'd had that kind of attention, I wasn't sure if my instincts were still reliable. Nevertheless, riding out a storm with a handsome man might be fun, especially now that Anne was out of the picture.

"Let's do this again, okay?"

"I'd like that," I answered.

"And thanks for looking out for my family—even if you did have it all wrong."

I closed the door and leaned against it as Brian made the twenty-second journey back to his house. I'd spent a wonderful evening with an attractive guy, and it had gone well. I was proud of the way I'd handled myself.

My phone beeped, and I saw a text from Brian.

You didn't ask for my number. What if you have to look after ME? Add me to your contacts. Thanks for a fun evening.

B

Chapter Seven
June

"Hi, you're up early this morning," I chirped to Sophie at my front door. She was carrying a basket, and I hoped it was filled with something sweet.

"Hello, yourself. Do you have an extra cup of coffee for an old lady?"

"Sure, come on in. Whatever you have in there smells fantastic!"

"I figured I should bring breakfast if I was going to beg some java off you!" Sophie said. "I'm driving to Atlanta later this afternoon. I've decided to spend a few days with Audrey and avoid any weather problems."

"Do you think it's going to be a bad one?" I asked. "They said on the news it's only going to be a tropical storm. Should I be worried?"

"Stop—don't say another word. You know how I feel about discussing unpleasant things. If you speak of it, you give it power. You'll be fine unless you go around talking about all the terrible things that might happen, and then fate will swoop in and make a big mess for you."

I felt nervous knowing Sophie was leaving. I wanted to

believe what Brian said, especially the part about him taking care of me—but I thought I needed to take care of myself too. And now Sophie's superstitions made it impossible for me to discuss it with her.

"I'd rather be sitting in my sister's living room listening to her brag about her grandkids than worrying about things I have no control over. I'm going to close my hurricane shutters while the sun is shining bright and vamoose."

I knew Sophie well enough to know I didn't need to waste my breath on a conversation she didn't want to have. We sat together eating warm cinnamon rolls while we *didn't* discuss the storm. I loved time with my unusual neighbor, even if I had to watch what I said.

"I had dinner with Brian last night, and he said he'd be around to help if I needed him for any reason."

"Brian, the cheater?" Sophie asked with a surprised look on her face.

"Well, I hadn't had a chance to tell you what I found out about the Barts family over the weekend," I said, sharing with Sophie the latest information about our neighbors, including the fact that Brian and Anne weren't together anymore.

"I told you sometimes things are not what they seem," Sophie replied. "Of course, sometimes they are exactly what they seem. This brings me to my next point. You like him, don't you?"

"I *do* like him. He's an amazing man caring for two adorable children and trying to make the best of it. But I hardly know him."

"That, my dear, is what a tropical storm is for," Sophie said with a twinkle in her eye.

"I'm not planning on taking advantage of the weather to get

a man's attention," I said, envisioning myself breaking out my own window and having to call Brian to come over and board it up.

"Darling, when life hands you lemons, you make lemonade, add a little vodka, and invite your cute neighbor over to ride the storm out. That's making something positive out of a negative for sure!"

"Sophie—you're something!"

"I have a lot of years on you, and this is what I know for sure. Most couples get together because one of them makes sure they are in the right place at the right time. Many an impromptu party happens because someone is getting set up on a date by a meddling friend and doesn't even know it. People say those things are due to fate, but it's usually *manipulation*. And I mean manipulation in a good way. What those two people do after that is up to them."

When Sophie was done handing out romantic advice, it was time for her to go. As we said goodbye, I promised to call her if anything looked out of place at her house during the storm. She rejected my offer with a flurry of hand motions made to dismiss my negative energy, and she left.

***

The grocery store was crowded with people preparing for the storm. I picked up bottled water, a few groceries, and the ingredients to make peanut butter cookies. We'd always baked when we had a snow day from school, and I figured a tropical storm would be more fun with the same tradition.

When I returned to the cottage, the clouds were beginning to roll in. The storm wasn't supposed to hit until after midnight, so there was still plenty of time to prepare. I took a quick walk and noticed the waves were getting more prominent as the ocean churned in response to the beating it was taking miles away in the Atlantic.

People were closing their hurricane shutters and bringing in deck furniture. I knew many people were cursing at the weather for ruining their vacation, and I was glad to have the rest of the summer to enjoy the beach.

Some tall condos had workers securing the buildings and closing up for residents who weren't there. I thought about what a big job it would be to ensure everyone's belongings were taken care of. Brian and his crew would have a busy day at the construction site.

By evening, I'd put the bike and my beach chair in the house and checked to make sure there wasn't anything else that might take flight in the storm. Finally, I unhooked the flower boxes from the front of the house and set them inside the front door for protection.

As I began to close the shutters, Brian pulled into his driveway. I waved at him and returned to my work as he went inside. After a few minutes and a change of clothes, he came over to assist me.

"Looks like you could use some help getting those closed," he said as he walked toward me.

"If you help me—I'll help you," I answered.

"Sounds like a plan," he said, grabbing a ladder leaning against the side of the house. He went up ten steps to unhook the highest window shutter, which I'd left for last.

"Thank you. That was a little high for me," I said.

"This is easy compared to what I've been doing all day to secure the construction site."

"I'll bet. I can't even imagine how much work it must have been."

"We moved everything at risk to the underground parking garage and walked away. The wind shouldn't be strong enough to damage the site, but we had to tie everything down so the materials wouldn't blow away."

After we secured the cottage, we went next door, and I helped Brian take care of his deck. We moved everything into the back of his house through the sliding glass doors, but we didn't have to unhook the shutters because the modern design included automatic coverings, which closed with the touch of a button.

"Well, that looks like it will about do it," Brian commented as we finished bringing in the last items. "How 'bout a beer?"

"Sure," I said as we walked toward Brian's kitchen. "I appreciate your help. I feel more confident knowing I had an experienced Floridian getting the cottage ready for what might be coming."

"You helped me too. It sure is easier to have two people when you're preparing for a storm," Brian added, opening the stainless-steel refrigerator door. He handed me a beer as he popped the top on one for himself.

There was something attractive about a handsome man drinking a beer. Brian was tanned and toned from the construction work he did, and his shirt showed circles of dampness from the hard work we'd just completed.

I opened the can and took a sip, hoping those same sweat patches weren't visible on my T-shirt. Although it was windy, the Florida humidity had taken over while we worked outside, making us hot and sweaty. The ice-cold beer slid down my throat. The flavor of the malt beverage filled my senses with a taste I'd never enjoyed much.

Brian looked at me with a grin, and I wondered what he was thinking. "You're not a beer drinker, are you?"

"It's not my favorite. I never really acquired a taste for it." I just wanted to spend more time with him and didn't care what we were drinking.

"What else can I get you? I'm sure you're thirsty after all that work," he said, taking the can from my hands and opening the refrigerator again. "I have bottled water, Diet Coke, and an entire cupboard of other kinds of liquor. What's your pleasure?"

"A Diet Coke would be fine."

Brian laughed and looked at me with a gaze that made me nervous but happy. He made me feel special, and the attention was more intoxicating than any drink he could serve me.

The moment was interrupted by the ring of his phone. He excused himself to take the call, and I could hear him talking to the kids and reassuring them everything would be okay. He was sweet with them, and there was love in his voice as he spoke in a calming way.

I felt sad for all of them, knowing how difficult their lives must have been over the past months. I imagined the things Brian must have had to say to Jenna and Jack as their young hearts processed the information that their mommy wouldn't be coming home. Tears came to my eyes thinking of a young father setting his own grief aside to make sure his children felt safe and secure.

"Hey, I'm sorry about that. The kids wanted me to come home before the storm, and it may be a better idea. But I don't want to be so far away from the building site if it ends up being worse than what they think."

"You're so good with your kids, and I can understand why they'd want you home with them."

"Thank you," Brian said. "I consider that the greatest compliment you could ever give me. It's hard being away from them. But hopefully, this job will be done by the end of the year, and I can get back home so we can resume our lives—I guess resume our *new* lives is a better choice of words."

The expression on Brian's face softened.

"I'm sorry about your wife and all you've been through. I know it must be tough."

"Thank you," he said quietly. Then, he changed the subject quickly, making me feel like I shouldn't have said anything. "Are you feeling okay about the storm?"

"I'm a little anxious not knowing what to expect. But if you say it's no big deal, I'm going to choose to believe you," I said.

"Remember, call me if you need anything—I'm right next door."

That was something I was sure I wouldn't forget.

***

I made the peanut butter cookies and sat down to dinner in front of the TV. It was almost 8:00 p.m., and the wind was blowing hard outside. The noise changed pitches as it howled through cracks in the house, making me feel like it was Halloween instead of the middle of summer.

The shutters were pulled tight over the windows, giving the room an eerie feeling. I was thankful for the company of the television and flipped through the channels several times until I settled on something to watch. The storm was supposed to hit around midnight, so I wanted to stay awake to see what happened.

By 1:30 a.m., when nothing had changed outside, I was too tired to care anymore. I climbed the stairs to the loft and crawled under the covers, drifting off to sleep while the storm took shape outside.

At 3:20 a.m., I was awakened by something hitting the house. It startled me, and I bolted upright in bed. I knew it was probably just a branch, but it scared me anyway.

I wondered what it looked like outside, but with everything closed up, I couldn't get a glimpse of the conditions. The front door had a small window allowing me to see out, but I didn't want to leave the warmth of my bed to take a look. I flipped on the bedroom TV and tuned in to the local forecast. A reporter was doing a remote broadcast standing somewhere along the Daytona Beach coastline.

"The Florida coast is getting hit with the rain and wind promised in the past few days," the meteorologist said from an empty beach parking lot. He was being filmed while rain beat on his black raincoat and palm trees swayed behind him. It was still dark, and he warned it would be a soggy day.

Hearing everything was all right, I turned the television off and tried to get back to sleep. There was no reason to get up early. There would be no walks on the beach or bike rides for a day or so.

I tossed and turned for another hour, listening to the rain beat against the metal roof. I tried all my tricks for a sleepless night. I counted sheep, daydreamed about buying a house, and prayed. Praying always did the trick as I worked through my list of things to be thankful for and things for which to be forgiven, but sleep wouldn't come.

It was 4:30 a.m. when I gave up, threw on my robe, and

went downstairs to make coffee. I stopped at the front door to peek outside and saw the rain coming in sheets as it blew across the road. The raindrops were illuminated by the fluorescent glow of the streetlight, and the slant of the pouring rain made it look like snowflakes falling from the sky.

There wasn't any traffic, and everything looked deserted. It made me feel lonely and afraid. I missed the security of my old life and wondered how Jason was doing. Had the divorce been as hard on him as it had been on me? I wondered where we'd gone wrong and if I'd been too hasty to leave him.

When we'd started dating in college, it seemed like Jason ticked off every box I had for a good boyfriend. In my early twenties, I had no idea how many boxes I should have on my list. He was sweet, funny, and intelligent. But, looking back, I could see there were other things to be considered. We'd settled into an uncomplicated relationship of two people with great fondness for one another. It was hardly the reason to marry someone, but I didn't know any better. And it might have worked out; many marriages lasted the test of time with less going for them.

Life with Jason hadn't always been strained and broken. There'd been many years early on when we'd lived as best friends and lovers. We worked side by side at the print shop and spent fun weekends doing things either as a couple or with friends. We enjoyed spending quiet evenings at home watching movies and just being together. Our initial attraction to each other had turned into a comfortable existence that worked for a while.

Ever since I started the long journey of divorce, I watched people to see how they interacted. Were they close and loving or cold and aloof? Did they seem to have the *secret* great couples share? Were they able to be in a room full of people and only see each other?

I formed opinions about everyone I knew. After this unscientific research, I concluded that few people were lucky enough to have found the deep love and intimacy I longed for in a marriage. If I allowed myself to fall in love again, it would be for the once-in-a-lifetime partner I dreamed of. Accepting anything less simply wasn't worth the hassle.

Tears burned my eyes. I was scared, but I didn't fear the raging storm outside. What was I going to do with the rest of my life? I shouldn't have expected that coming to the beach for the summer would give me all the necessary answers. A haunting vision of my life flashed before my eyes, and I felt lost and alone. I sat on the sofa and began crying like I hadn't done in months.

As the coffee finished brewing, I tried to pull myself together. I went into the downstairs bathroom and splashed my face with cold water. The simple act of freshening up made me feel better, and I ambled into the kitchen to pour a cup of steaming hot coffee.

I settled into the overstuffed chair I'd moved in front of the TV and covered myself with a light blanket. I turned the television on and hoped I could wait out the darkness of the early morning with my friends from WESH 2 News out of Orlando.

Chapter Eight
June

I'd allowed myself to doze before the lights flickered several times, and I woke up. After the fourth time, it went dark, and the air conditioner's hum was silent. I sat still for a minute in total darkness and listened to the wind blow. The rain was pounding, and I could hear the water splashing as it surged out of the gutters and ran along the house toward the ocean.

Sitting in the dark, I thought of Sophie telling me how this time in my life was a chance at a "do over," and my little pity party was over. I smiled thinking about our conversation and remembered my life mulligan. I *could* redirect my life, and the opportunity was a gift and shouldn't be wasted.

I felt my way to the kitchen and lit several candles. I put one in the bathroom and the other three throughout the great room. I sat back down and sipped my vanilla-flavored coffee. I was lucky to have a whole pot brewed and hoped it wouldn't get cold before I could pour a second cup.

I heard the text notification on my cell phone and checked for a message.

How are things over there? You okay?

It thrilled me that Brian was making good on his promise to check on me. I forgot about feeling sorry for myself, and the dark morning took on a new and exciting light. I texted him back.

Things are dark over here. I'm okay. Thanks.

I stared at the phone, willing it to alert me of a return text.

Will be light soon. Wish I'd made coffee!

I had coffee, and there was no way I could drink it all before it went to waste. I thought of Sophie's advice and knew what I needed to do.

I have coffee. I'll share.

I held my breath.

Really?

My mind raced as I thought about Brian coming over—me in my bathrobe and him in who knows what? Both of us unshowered and fresh out of bed. It seemed very intimate, especially considering the way I'd been thinking of Brian since we had dinner together.

Yes. And cookies.

I didn't hear anything back. I should have texted, *"Thanks,*

I'm fine," and left it at that. I could have felt my way back upstairs and slept until the electricity came on. My regret was cut short by a knock at the door, and I froze.

I saw my black and white polka-dotted pajamas underneath my robe. They were cute with lace around the legs and arms— but still not what I might have chosen had I known I'd have an early morning visitor.

"Wow! It's terrible out here," Brian exclaimed as he came through the door. "I considered running over without the umbrella but knew I'd be drenched, even if it only took me a few seconds to get here!"

As he shed a sopping wet coat and lowered his umbrella, I could see he had on thin sweatpants and a long-sleeved T-shirt. He pushed his tennis shoes off and entered the cottage in white tube socks. I saw his hair was tousled and showed a hint of bedhead as I took a good look at him.

"You were expecting a tux?" he asked with a sideways smile, aware that I was staring at him.

We both laughed, and I made a lame comment about my own outfit as he followed me toward the kitchen. I set my mug on the counter, and Brian sat at the table.

"Coffee?" I asked.

"Well, that *is* why I'm bothering you before 5:00 a.m. You were smart to make it before the power went off."

"It's going to be cold soon, so I'm happy to share." I hoped coffee wasn't the *only* reason he was bothering me so early in the morning. I poured a large mug for Brian and refilled my cup, placing them both on the table before putting cookies on a plate.

"I guess you never acquired a taste for coffee either," he said as he looked at the light beige liquid in my mug.

"Nope—I like it the way I like it. Would you like cream or sugar?"

"No, I drink it black. I'm happy to have this, so I won't give you a hard time on your coffee drinking habits." Brian's easygoing manner drew me in, and I started to feel less self-conscious about hosting him in my nightclothes in the dark.

I told him about snow days back in Iowa and the tradition of baking cookies, which he seemed to be enjoying. We spent the rest of the cup of coffee and part of another talking and getting to know each other better.

We moved to the living room when the coffee got too cold to enjoy. Brian sat on the couch, and I reclaimed my spot in the chair as the room began to warm from the lack of air conditioning. He picked up my commencement photo next to where he was sitting.

"Is this your family with you?" he asked. "Looks like you graduated with honors considering all the cords around your neck."

I knew the confident young woman in the photograph was still inside me. I just had to figure out how to find her again.

I told him about my sister and brother and their families, all living near my parents. I left out the part about putting everything I had into my life with Jason to the detriment of my other relationships. I always had something more important going on when a family gathering called me home, letting the closeness I'd once shared with my siblings fade when I got too busy to keep in touch.

I'd done well in school, graduating summa cum laude with a double major in marketing and business administration—but Mom was just as proud of the MRS degree I was about to get a few weeks after graduation day. She'd always pointed out that choices for a suitable partner decreased significantly once you were out of college, so I should take dating seriously during those years. Even as I'd accepted Jason's marriage proposal, that fear echoed in my head and clouded my judgment.

Marriage had been the next thing for Jason and me after graduation, and I couldn't see past the bridesmaids' dresses and honeymoon to Mexico for other options I might have considered. I was sure we'd grow old together, and I'd love him the way I was supposed to. Maybe he felt the same way, but we never discussed it and plunged into a lifelong commitment neither of us would be able to honor.

"Can I ask you a question?" Brian asked.

"Sure. I can't promise I'll answer it—but you can ask," I replied, wondering where the conversation might lead.

"Had you been crying before I came over?"

I knew my face must have been red and splotchy. It was a trait I'd had since childhood that couldn't be hidden.

"Yes," I admitted.

"Why? Were you scared about the storm?"

"No, not really."

"What then?" he asked.

"I was a little homesick. The dark and the rain made me think about being far away from my family and friends. I've left everything I've known in my adult life, and I'm starting on a new path. I'm just longing for something to feel like home again . . ."

"It's hard to start over. Having your life turned upside down is scary."

"I try not to feel sorry for myself, but sometimes I think of Jason continuing to live the life he and I created, and I'm filled with jealousy. Why do I get left out in the cold? He gets the house, business, and the comfortable lifestyle we built, while I get a chance at a *do-over*."

"I bet things aren't as easy for your ex-husband as you think. He stayed in the town where you lived, and everyone he encounters knows his story. He has to rebuild his life without you, and I'm sure that isn't an easy task."

"I know you're right, but I can't stop replaying everything over in my head, trying to figure out where it all went wrong."

"It's natural. I did the same thing for a long time. I would dwell on everything said and done the day Jayne had her aneurysm. I couldn't remember if I'd told her I loved her or if we'd kissed goodbye before she left the house. You never know when your last moment with a loved one will be, and it bothered me."

I felt like a whiny, selfish child as Brian began to talk about the loss of his wife.

"I didn't want to live in a place where Jayne didn't exist anymore. It kills me that the kids won't know their mom how I wanted them to know her. Answering their questions about death and making sure I don't hurt them further with my answers is difficult," he said.

"Brian, I'm sorry. I know you've had it so much worse. A divorce is nothing like losing your spouse to death."

"It isn't a competition. We have a lot in common. Different circumstances have led us to a point in our lives where we have to continue on in an alternate direction, but the actual act of moving on will come from the same place inside us."

"Are you as scared as I am?" I asked.

"How scared are you?"

"Scared enough that I'm sitting in the dark in my pajamas,

thousands of miles away from the only life I've ever known, sharing my secrets with a stranger."

Brian cocked his head and rubbed his chin with his thumb and forefinger, "Yeah, I'd say I'm about that scared. But I hope you don't consider me a stranger anymore."

If I hadn't been sweating profusely, I would have wished the electricity would never come back on, and we could spend the rest of the summer holed up in the cozy candlelight of The Pink Shell.

***

I woke up as soon as the TV came back on. Our conversation made me feel supported by Brian's friendship, and we'd drifted off to sleep across the room from each other.

The room smelled like apples and cinnamon, thanks to the aroma of the burning candles. They would no longer be needed with the return of electricity to the cottage. I wanted to offer to make Brian breakfast and convince him to stay with me for the rest of the day so we could watch movies and eat buttery popcorn until it stopped raining.

I knew the most appropriate thing was for us to end our time together. Brian must have agreed because he was moving toward the door.

"Well, I can't remember when I've enjoyed a power outage more," he said, putting his shoes on. "Hearing you talk about how hard it is to move on makes me realize I'm not the only one. I've been so busy making sure everyone else is all right that I've thought very little about what I need. As I listened to you talk, I wanted you to know it was okay to be unsure and realized I need to give myself the same advice."

My only real relationship with the opposite sex, besides those in my immediate family, had been with Jason. I'd never found him to be interested in feelings, and even getting him to say, "*I love you,*" was a struggle. I liked that Brian was in tune with his emotional side, and it made me want to spend more time with him.

"Well, I'd better get going. I should run over to the construction site and check it out in a little while. We won't work today—but I need to get those guys back out there tomorrow if I can," he said.

"It does seem to be letting up. Now that it's light out, things look a lot better."

"This should all be out of here by evening. No worries," Brian reassured me.

"Well, thanks for riding the storm out with me and listening to me wallow a little." I was sincere in my appreciation of the time I'd spent with him.

"Thanks for the coffee. A little caffeine makes everything better," he said.

We stood there, not knowing how to say goodbye again, until Brian offered an invitation of his own.

"Hey—Betsy, the kids, and my parents are all coming out this weekend for a big Fourth of July celebration. Why don't you join us? Unless you have other plans . . ."

"No, I hadn't even thought about it. I guess this weekend *is* the Fourth." My weeks were running into each other, and I hadn't remembered that a holiday weekend was coming up. "It sounds great!" I said, not hesitating to accept the offer.

"We'll have a lot to celebrate because it's Jack's birthday too."

As he left, I was excited to think I had weekend plans to

look forward to and made a mental note to buy a birthday gift for Jack before Saturday.

Brian was right. The rain stopped in the afternoon, and the sun came out. Everything was wet and dirty from the storm, so I spent time drying everything on the screened porch with several large bath towels. I'd put the cushions inside, but everything else was sopping wet, including the rug on the floor, which splashed on my bare feet when I stepped on it. The air was warming quickly, and the cold water on my foot startled me. I rolled up the rug and hauled it outside, hanging it on the wooden railing of the walkway leading to the beach.

Since my feet were already wet, I went to the water's edge. The sand was damp and clumped between my toes like cold, sticky oatmeal. A few people walked along the edge of the water, investigating what had washed ashore during the storm. Unlike the Gulf of Mexico on the other side of Florida, the Daytona Beach coastline didn't usually give up many shells. However, the storm had disturbed many creatures hidden in the ocean, and they were vulnerable in the hours following the bad weather.

It was evident by the water line on the beach that the tide had been extremely high. I knew the debris from overnight would be recovered quickly by the sea, as if the ocean knew it had a responsibility to take care of the mess it made the night before.

***

Sophie returned around noon on Friday. She'd had a good trip to see Audrey and was happy the storm had not materialized into anything other than a lot of wind and rain. She quickly credited this to the good karma of the people of Florida. I helped her unhook the hurricane shutters from her windows and dry out her porch furniture like I'd done at The Pink Shell. She treated me to lunch to repay me for my assistance, and the discussion eventually came around to Brian and me.

"So—did you spend time with the handsome Brian Barts while I was gone?"

"You were only gone for a couple of days, Sophie. But yes, I did see him."

"Do tell, darling!" Sophie said with excitement.

"Well, we helped each other get our houses ready for the storm, and we had a cold drink together."

"Sweetheart, those aren't the juicy details I'm looking for. That sounds more like common courtesy, and I'm looking for romance. Did anything else happen indicating he might be interested in you?"

"I'm getting to that! Anyway—the electricity went off early in the morning during the storm, and Brian texted to make sure I was okay."

"Now we're getting somewhere," Sophie interjected with a grin.

"I'd made a pot of coffee before we lost power, so I invited him over to share it with me."

"And?"

"And he came over and spent a couple of hours in the dark with me. Well, it wasn't dark because we had candles burning."

"Nice touch, Meg. Candles always set the mood."

"Sophie, it wasn't like that. The candles were necessary, so we didn't trip over the furniture. It was pitch black with the hurricane shutters covering the windows. We drank coffee and talked about our lives. It wasn't a big deal." I didn't want to get Sophie all riled up before I knew if there was something to get riled up about.

"We'll see, darling. . ."

Sophie was a hopeless romantic. She was right—there had been more to the time we spent together. But until I knew if Brian felt the same way, I was going to play it cool.

Chapter Nine
July

Summer was half over, and my first weeks at the beach had been better than I could have imagined. I'd already read most of the books I'd brought with me, and I'd spent plenty of time basking in the Florida sunshine. I loved the time I shared with Sophie and was optimistic about my new friendship with Brian. The one thing I'd successfully avoided was deciding what I would do after my time at the beach was over. With the Fourth of July looming, I began to panic.

Like clockwork, Betsy and the kids arrived on Friday night, and Mr. and Mrs. Barts were with them. Bob and Linda were in their early seventies and were fit and stylish. Bob had gray hair that curled around his face, and Linda's hair was dyed strawberry blonde and cut into a cute style. They looked like friendly people, and I was excited to meet them.

I was invited to join the family on Saturday night for a barbeque and birthday party, and I spent Friday evening with Sophie and her friends. I felt like a popular socialite with such a busy schedule on a holiday weekend. All I had to worry about was what food to bring and which red, white, and blue outfit I should wear to the parties.

After dinner and drinks with the gang at Sophie's, I took the rest of my wine and walked out to the beach. I wanted a minute by myself and to breathe in the fresh air as the sun was beginning to set. I stuck my toes in the surf, and the cool water felt good on my feet.

"Hi there," Brian said from behind me.

"What are you doing down here? Too much family time?" I asked, turning around.

"I saw you coming out Sophie's beach walk and thought I'd join you and say hello. How 'bout you? Too many senior citizens?" I giggled at his ability to read my mind and was flattered he'd come out to the beach to see me.

"Maybe," I said. "They're all lovely, and it's so nice of them to include me."

"Why wouldn't they? You bring their average age down by at least two decades."

"You'd be surprised at how much fun they are. And they like to drink. They have a two-martini limit but are usually too drunk to enforce it!" Brian laughed at my joke, and it made me happy to see him smile.

"I love your sense of humor," he said.

We talked for a few more minutes, and Brian excused himself to get back to his house. He confirmed my invitation for the next day, and I told him I was planning to bring a veggie tray and a salad.

I didn't tell him I wanted to kiss him.

I drank the rest of my wine and returned to Sophie's, where the group was beginning an exciting game of charades. I loved their spirit, but I'd had enough for the evening.

I thanked everyone for another great night and promised to have coffee with Sophie soon.

"Darling, what are you doing for the rest of the weekend?" she asked as I began to leave. "You're more than welcome to join us for dinner tomorrow night. We're going to Sam's to make homemade pizza in his new pizza oven."

"I'm going to spend tomorrow evening with Brian and his family," I said.

"Oh, you are? Well, I look forward to seeing you early next week. I can't wait to hear all the sordid details," she said with a sly grin.

I made my way next door and climbed into bed with a smile on my face. I was having a fantastic summer.

***

The morning air was hot as I walked along the beach, and it was already filling up with people getting ready for Fourth of July celebrations. Families were setting up tents, and people were hauling grills out to the beach from their condominiums. There would be the smell of barbeques combined with the sweet scent of tanning oil wafting through the air later in the day.

After breakfast, I made a trip to the store to get a few items to take to the Brian's, including a birthday gift for Jack. The store was crowded with people buying last-minute picnic food and filling coolers with ice and beer. I was glad I had plans for the day and didn't have to spend the holiday alone.

I bought sparklers for the kids and grabbed a cute stuffed dog wearing a little red jacket from the toy section. His fluffy fur made him look snuggly, and I thought Jack would like him. I bought a card and a gift bag with tissue paper to complete the birthday gift. As I was checking out, I spotted red, white, and blue flip-flops and threw them in my grocery cart.

When I returned home, I cut the vegetables and placed them on a glass tray with dill dip I'd thrown together from one of my mom's old recipes. I'd made a broccoli salad and had a good time preparing for the party.

I showered and put on white cargo shorts and a red V-neck. By the time I slipped the flip-flops on and walked next door, I was ready for some fun.

***

I added my food to the tremendous spread already laid out on the marble island before Brian introduced me to his parents.

"Mom and Dad, I'd like you to meet my friend, Meg Parsons," he offered. "Meg, these are my parents—Bob and Linda."

"It's so nice to officially meet you. I've heard a lot about you," I said.

They were friendly and told me how happy they were to have the chance to spend part of the day with me. Their warm greeting made me feel like either Betsy or Brian had filled them in on me, and I wondered what they'd been told.

It was nice to see Betsy again. I liked her, and it was a welcome change to be able to talk to another woman of my age. Jenna and Jack loved the sparklers, and Jack wanted to open the gift I'd brought right away.

"We have to wait until later," Betsy told him. I could tell she was doing an excellent job at being a surrogate mom to both children.

Brian was busy getting drinks for everyone and encouraging us to get a plate of appetizers. It made me smile thinking about the love and support this family shared with each other, and I was glad Brian hadn't had to face the tragedy of his wife's death alone.

Bob and Linda took the kids out on the deck, and Betsy followed behind them. I hung back on purpose, and when everyone was outside, I took my opportunity to thank Brian for including me.

"I love this—thank you," I said.

"What do you love?"

"I love your family. You all have such a good time together."

"I thought you might enjoy it. I'm glad you're here." He looked at me in a way that made me feel like we were at the start of something.

***

It wasn't long before the kids wanted to go swimming, so we all took chairs out to the beach, where families had already claimed most of the sandy space to celebrate the holiday. We continued to visit as we watched the kids run in and out of the waves.

"Do you want to come to the house and help me with a few things before dinner?" Betsy asked.

"Sure, I'd love to," I said, welcoming the chance to get into the air conditioning. The Florida sun felt like a blow torch as it crossed the bright July sky.

Once inside, I put up a few birthday decorations for the party while Betsy prepared vegetable and meat kabobs for dinner. We continued to nibble on the appetizers and sip our wine while getting to know each other better. We visited about various topics, including the kids' activities and the latest movies.

Betsy said, "Can I ask you a serious question?"

"Sure," I answered, putting a scoop of smoked fish dip on a cracker and popping it into my mouth.

"Are you interested in my brother?"

I almost choked on my cracker. I hated to reveal my true feelings without knowing the reason behind Betsy's question.

"Why do you ask?" I tried to buy myself more time.

"Meg, I'm going to give this to you straight. Brian likes you, but he's afraid to ask you out on a real date because he's not sure you want kids . . . there, I said it. I'm sorry to be so blunt, but my brother and I are close. Brian told me you've spent some time together, and he thinks you're great. He's been beating around the bush about kids, and you've never taken the bait. He doesn't want to come out and ask you himself, so I'm left making this middle school move to help him out."

"Why would he think I don't want kids?" My mind was racing as I thought about our conversations and what I had and hadn't said, combined with the thrill that Brian was interested in me.

"Because you don't have any," she said.

I started to answer, but Betsy cut me off.

"I know. I've tried to tell Brian just because you don't have kids doesn't mean you don't want any. There are many reasons why a person doesn't have children, and I've told him going on a date doesn't mean you're going to get married and have a family anyway."

"I wanted kids. I *longed* for children, but it never happened for Jason and me."

Betsy interrupted me again. "You don't have to tell me

93

anything else. I'm sorry to ask such a private question. I want to be able to tell Brian to go for it. I needed to know you were not opposed to the idea of children in your life before I felt like I could do that. I think the two of you, and hopefully the four of you, might be good together. I just want him to be happy again."

Jenna and Jack were adorable kids. When I thought about the possibility of dating Brian, I knew the kids would have to be a part of it. You can't be in your thirties and think about dating someone without picturing a life with them. I was excited about the prospect of going on a date with Brian, but the feeling was followed by anxiety that the summer would be over soon. Was it wise to start something with him when I was leaving in a few short weeks, especially when children were involved?

We finished getting the food ready, and Betsy avoided any more probing questions. I knew she'd gotten the information she wanted, and the rest would be up to Brian.

We enjoyed dinner, followed by a bakery cake decorated with a picture of a starfish on top. We sang to Jack, who was hamming it up as the center of attention. He had plenty of presents to open, and as he neared my gift bag, I felt like maybe I hadn't purchased a big enough gift. I didn't want to seem inappropriate, so I'd gone with something small.

Before getting to mine, he'd unwrapped five other gifts, including an art set and some books about marine life. He squealed with joy when he pulled the stuffed dog out of the bag.

"This is my most favoritest thing I've ever gotten!" Jack exclaimed, hugging the little dog and kissing him on the head. "I'm going to name him Gus!"

"That's a good name," Brian said. "What do you say to Meg?"

"Thanks, Meg. I love him!" he said as he came over to give me a hug.

I wasn't expecting such a great response from a last-minute gift. I knew Jack's reaction was genuine because after he finished opening his other presents, he put them all aside and continued carrying Gus around wherever he went.

The night ended with a beautiful fireworks display ignited from the pier a mile away. Brian's family crowded at the deck railing overlooking the ocean. He and I stood back, leaning against the side rail. All eyes were on the colors in the night sky, and no one saw Brian put his hand on the small of my back and pull me close.

***

Brian's truck was already gone when I came downstairs on Monday morning. The game Betsy had played with me of *"Brian likes you—do you like him?"* was a means to an end, and I couldn't wait to see where it would lead.

I spent the day by reading a book on the screened porch and enjoying the sea breeze coming through the lanai. I took a long bike ride on the beach and stopped to watch several dolphins frolic in the water. By late afternoon, I'd returned to the cottage and poured myself a glass of iced tea. My cheeks were flushed from the sun, and I was hot and sweaty. The coolness inside felt good, and I contemplated what to do with the evening ahead.

I heard a loud knocking toward the front of the house. I made my way across the kitchen and opened the door to find a man holding a bouquet of flowers.

Are you Meg Parsons?" he asked.

"Yes," I said, surprised to have flowers being delivered to me on a random day in the middle of the summer.

"Here you go. Have a good one," he said, handing me the vase covered in plastic.

I took the flowers into the kitchen and cut the covering off. There were a dozen pink roses arranged with baby's breath and greenery. The card read:

Let's take this up a notch. Dinner?

Brian

It had been a long time since I'd received flowers from a man. I assumed the card indicated a date and marked the official start of something more than friendship for Brian and me. I did a happy dance and clapped my hands together in excitement.

I looked to see if Brian's truck was next door, but the driveway was still empty. It was only 4:30 p.m., and there was a little time before he would get home from work. I decided to write him a note and tape it to his front door. I had to thank him for the flowers, and I didn't want to do it in person. Suddenly, I was shy and embarrassed that Brian liked me.

I went upstairs and looked through the boxes I had stored in the bottom of the closet. I knew I had packed some note cards that would be perfect for this occasion. I found them right away and went downstairs to get a pen. I sat at the kitchen table and tried to decide what to say. After several attempts, I came up with something I could live with.

Brian –

Thank you for the beautiful flowers. They made my day. I would love to join you for dinner!

Meg

I licked the envelope shut, grabbed a piece of tape, and went next door to attach it to the door. I didn't want Brian to come home while I was leaving the note, so I hurried back to the cottage, dizzy with anticipation.

Did he mean dinner tonight? Dinner next week? Dinner sometime before the end of the summer? I figured he meant soon, and I was dying to know the details. A real date could change everything, and I was ready to find out what was going to happen next.

Chapter Ten
July

Brian's truck didn't show up in his driveway until 10:00 p.m. Either he'd worked late or had other plans. I thought about texting him earlier in the evening, but since I'd already taped the note to his front door, I was afraid another contact from me might seem too needy. He hadn't been in the house long before he called me.

"Hi."

There was something in his voice I hadn't heard before, and it worried me.

"Hi," I said. "Thank you for the flowers. They're beautiful."

"Beautiful flowers for a beautiful lady."

Whatever I was hearing didn't seem to have anything to do with me.

"Sorry it's late," he continued. "I hoped to get back here earlier and give you a call. But unfortunately, I had to run to St. Augustine to discuss something with Betsy. She said she wanted to talk face-to-face, so I needed to go."

"Is everything okay?" I asked, sensing it wasn't.

"Yeah, it will be. I need to make some big decisions."

"Do you want to come over and talk?" I asked.

"No. It's late, and I've had a long day. I think I'm going to get a shower and go to bed."

Brian was obviously upset, and his demeanor was bursting the bubble I'd surrounded myself in since getting the roses.

"What about tomorrow night?" he asked. "Can we do dinner and spend a little time together? I promise I'll be in a better mood by then."

"That sounds great. I can't wait." I exhaled, relieved to know his dinner offer was still on—despite whatever was going on in his life.

"I'll pick you up at 7:00."

"What should I wear?" The answer to my question would give me an idea of what he had planned.

"Just something casual. I want to take you to one of my favorite places, and it isn't fancy."

I didn't care where we were going if it meant more time with Brian.

***

I began getting ready late in the afternoon, spending the first half-hour soaking in the tub. I shaved my legs and painted my toenails bright red. I applied makeup with more effort than usual and sprayed my favorite perfume on my neck and wrists. I wore jeans and a black top, finishing the ensemble with a pair of silver hoop earrings and cute black wedges. I caught a glimpse of myself in the full-length mirror. I looked like someone ready to move on with her life, and I couldn't imagine a better guy to do it with than Brian.

There was still time before he was due to pick me up, so I answered the phone when I saw Mom was calling.

"Hey, what's up?" I said, hoping she wouldn't want to talk for long.

"Well, your dad and I just returned from the grocery store, and I had to call to let you know I saw Candice. She's having another baby!"

Candice had been my best friend growing up. She'd married her high school sweetheart the summer after we graduated to beat the impending birth of their first child. She proceeded to have three more children before she turned thirty. Another baby was unexpected, but the news did remind me that women do get pregnant later in life. I still had time.

"Mom, can I call you back tomorrow? I have plans tonight, and I'm ready to leave the house."

"Are you having dinner with your neighbors again?"

"Something like that. I'll call you in the morning, and you can tell me all about Candice."

It wasn't long after the call with my mother ended that I opened the door to a freshly scrubbed man. Brian's hair was still damp, and he smelled like expensive cologne. He wore an awesome pair of jeans and a white button-down shirt, which was untucked but nicely ironed. The color showed off his tan from working outside in the Florida sun. He had on a pair of casual sandals and a big smile.

"Hi," he said, thrilling me with his simple sexiness.

"Come in. Would you like to have a drink before we go?"

"If you don't mind—I'd like to take you someplace before dinner. We can have a drink there if you'll indulge me."

"Sounds great. Let me get my purse."

We got in Brian's truck, which I noticed had been cleaned inside and out. Most days, it looked like a mess as it sat in the driveway next door. Keeping a work truck clean was hard work, and I appreciated his effort. We drove a few miles down Atlantic Boulevard until we reached a tall building still under construction.

"I thought you might enjoy seeing the project I'm working on this summer. Now stay right there," he told me.

I waited in the passenger seat until he opened my door and held out his hand for me to get out. It was a massive vehicle, and I was thankful for the help. I couldn't remember the last time a man had opened the car door for me, and I loved it.

"Thank you," I said, hopping out of the truck.

"You're welcome. It's a little high for someone who isn't used to it."

"Can we get in here?" I asked, looking up at the high rise.

"You forget who you're with. I'm in charge of this development and can get in anytime I want," he said proudly.

We entered the covered garages, and Brian used a key to open the door. We took the elevator to the top floor and got out in a large area not yet divided into condos. The glass windows weren't in yet, and a beautiful breeze was coming through the space. I walked to the edge and looked out at the vast ocean below. The view was breathtaking, even if it was scary being up so high. I was glad the openings were small, and the rest of the walls were closed off with thick boards and steel beams.

"Wow, this is something!" I was awestruck by the site in front of me.

"You said you've been coming to this beach for years, but I didn't think you'd ever seen it from this far up," he said. He didn't come close to the window openings, and I wondered if he was afraid of heights.

"It's beautiful," I said, looking out across the familiar landmarks. I could see the beachfront and the houses. I saw the Ponce Inlet Lighthouse not far away, which was a brilliant red color in the evening sun.

Brian walked over to a backpack on the floor. He pulled out a bottle of red wine and two glasses. He proceeded to open the wine, and I realized he'd set everything up earlier for our arrival.

"You did all of this for me?" I asked.

"Well, I guess I'm showing off since I'm in charge of building this thing," he laughed. "But yes, I thought you might like it."

"What a thoughtful thing to do."

"I'm a thoughtful guy," he said as his eyes embraced me.

After finishing our wine, we took the elevator back downstairs to walk the short distance on the beach to a restaurant called The Seaside Grill. We both took our shoes off, and I was glad I'd heeded his advice and dressed comfortably. The sand was warm, and my feet looked tanned with the red polish setting them off.

When we got to the restaurant, I could see a bar along one side and picnic tables with umbrellas throughout. There were tables outside on the beach, and we chose one next to a palm tree lit with white lights. The place was busy with a local crowd, and the atmosphere seemed fun and laid-back.

"I hope you don't mind if we sit outside where it's a little quieter," Brian said.

"It's perfect," I said, sliding onto the bench.

We ordered drinks and a plate of peel-and-eat shrimp. By the time we'd finished our appetizer, I was relaxed. We'd already discussed most of the obvious parts of our lives, so the evening's conversation began to delve a little deeper.

Brian asked me more about Jason and our life together. I told him we'd grown apart over the years, and the discovery of his dating profile was the final straw. However, I didn't share with him that I'd been looking for a reason to leave for a long time, as I didn't want it to seem like I wasn't committed to marriage.

"Your ex might have been smart at business, but he was a foolish man," Brian said. "I would have given anything to spend the rest of my life with my beautiful wife. I hope you know not all men are like Jason."

Tears came to my eyes at Brian's comments. Meeting him had already improved my self-esteem and restored my faith in men. No matter what happened between us, I felt as if I would carry that into the next chapter of my life.

"I'm counting on it," I said quietly.

Brian reached over and took my hand. "I promise."

We enjoyed a bucket of steamed seafood combined with ears of corn, potatoes, and sausage. After dinner, we shared a piece of Key lime pie. The atmosphere at The Seaside Grill was ideal for a first date. The soft light of candles on the outside tables was beautiful. The glow and the constant sound of the waves lapping onto the shore set the backdrop for a romantic evening.

"When I opened the door to the flowers you'd sent, my first inclination was that my parents sent them because they missed me. I couldn't believe it when I read the card. It's been years since anyone sent me flowers, and it meant so much to me," I said.

"You aren't used to being treated well, are you?" he asked.

"Well, I've never been *mistreated*." I didn't want Brian to feel sorry for me.

"You do know that not being mistreated and being treated well are two different things, don't you?"

"Jason wasn't an emotional kind of guy."

"Jason is gone, and you don't have to settle for how he did things anymore," Brian said as he picked up my hand and leaned in to kiss my fingertips. I wanted to climb into his arms and kiss him without regard for decorum. But instead, I smiled and lost myself in his warm blue eyes until the server came with the bill.

I thought of the uncomfortable ending to my date with Carl, with figures and money flying across the table. I was grateful when Brian pulled out his credit card to pay the bill.

We laughed and talked as we walked back down the beach to the construction site to get the truck. When Brian pulled into his driveway and walked me back to the cottage, I was as happy and content as I'd been in years.

"Goodnight, Meg. I had a wonderful evening," he said, kissing me softly on the lips and then pulling me in for a hug.

"Me too," I said. "Thank you, it was so much fun." I went inside as Brian walked away toward his house.

I thought about the two of us, replaying the conversations of the evening in our heads, just feet from each other in our separate houses. I went upstairs to the bedroom and plopped onto the comforter, feeling like a teenage girl again.

***

The next morning, I stretched and yawned as I rolled over in bed, and my thoughts went to the evening I'd spent with Brian. It felt like he genuinely wanted to get to know me. I didn't need to try to impress him, I just needed to be myself. Brian had been through a lot and wasn't interested in playing games, and his sincerity made me feel safe and hopeful.

Brian had told me he wanted to move on with his life, but as the father of two young children, he had to think about three lives in every decision he made. I felt lucky I didn't have my own kids to consider but knew a future with Brian would mean falling in love with all of them and having them fall in love with me too.

I glanced at my cellphone on the nightstand and saw I had a message. It was a text from Brian, which had come in at 11:42 p.m.

Can't sleep . . . thinking about you. Tomorrow night?

The message excited and scared me at the same time. Was Brian smitten with me or desperate to find a woman? I wasn't used to men allowing themselves to be vulnerable. Brian hardly knew me, and a text like that could scare me away. When I'd started dating Jason, our idea of romance was using his fake ID to get a cheap bottle of Moscato and driving out to Lake Bloomington to drink it on the hood of his car.

Being pursued as an adult was a new experience for me, and I loved it. I was falling for Brian, and I knew there was nothing left for me to do but jump in with my heart wide open.

What did you have in mind? I texted back.

I was glad I hadn't seen the message the night before. It wasn't that I wanted to play hard to get with Brian, but I didn't want to seem too eager. I got in the shower, hoping to hear back from him soon.

The smell of jasmine filled the bathroom after I used my favorite body wash and shampoo. The soapy suds slid down my tanned body, cleansing and refreshing me. I felt good about myself and was intrigued about dating a man like Brian. I grabbed my towel and began to dry off. I glanced at my phone on the vanity and saw a text was waiting.

Whatever your heart desires.

What *did* my heart desire? All I wanted to do was get to know Brian better and spend the evening close to him.

Wine, beach, conversation? I replied back.

I dried my hair and continued to get ready for the day until I got another text.

See you around 7.

I was glad I had another exciting evening to look forward to. My biggest dilemma was figuring out how to pass the eleven hours until I got to see Brian again.

Chapter Eleven
July

I thought about the evening ahead and what it might bring. I put on a casual sundress and a pair of flip-flops and went downstairs as soon as I heard a knock at the door.

"You look beautiful," Brian said. I breathed in his aftershave as we hugged, and it made me swoon.

"Thanks. How was your day?" I asked as he entered the cottage.

"I had a great day. We accomplished a lot, plus I had tonight to look forward to."

He always knew the right thing to say without being overconfident or arrogant. He was comfortable in his own skin, which allowed me to be comfortable in mine.

We ended up in the kitchen. After working all day, I thought he might be hungry, so I'd put out a few snacks.

"Help yourself," I said, opening some wine.

"Hey—let me do that," he said, taking the bottle from my hands.

Brian poured two glasses of dark, red merlot. I swirled my glass and breathed in the rich scent before taking a drink.

"Do you know a lot about wine?" Brian asked.

"No, but I've seen this done in the movies. And I enjoy the wine's aroma before I drink it."

Brian copied my actions with his own wine.

"Do *you* know anything about wine?" I asked.

"I know what I like to drink—basically, anything offered to me!"

There wasn't much about Brian that was too complex.

We nibbled on the food and decided to head out to the beach. He ran to his house and got a beach chair, and I joined him on the sand between our houses.

"There sure are a lot of people out here tonight."

"It's probably because of the launch," Brian said nonchalantly.

"Really? I had no idea. I've always wanted to see a space launch. Do you think we'll be able to see it from here?" I knew Kennedy Space Center was an hour south of Daytona Beach.

"I thought that's why you wanted to stay here instead of going to a restaurant."

"I guess I wasn't paying attention to the news, but I'm glad we'll get to see it. Have you seen one before?" I asked.

"Jenna is crazy about space. She wants to be an astronaut, so last year I took the kids to Cocoa Beach, and we rented a condo for a couple of days when a launch was scheduled. I was afraid it would be called off, so I didn't tell the kids what was happening until it was almost time for liftoff. It did go off, and we went out on our balcony and watched it soar into space. I loved seeing their excitement."

"What time is it supposed to happen tonight?" I asked.

"If it launches, it will be at 9:11 p.m. I looked it up before I came over. I've got the app loaded on my phone, so I'll keep an eye on it."

Our conversation returned to other surface subjects, which always began our time together. Brian seemed preoccupied, and I started feeling awkward with him for the first time.

After a long silence, Brian said, "I'm sorry about my mood a couple of days ago. I got some news that changes everything for me, and I needed to be by myself and think about it. I guess it's on my mind tonight too."

"Do you want to tell me what's going on?" I asked. I was worried it was something serious for him to have made a trip to St. Augustine right after his family had been together all weekend. I hoped it wasn't a health issue with either his parents or Betsy.

Brian began to open up as he told me of his dilemma, which I didn't think was all that difficult to solve. It thrilled me that it didn't have anything to do with me.

"The day after Betsy and the kids returned to St. Augustine, she got a call from the investment firm she'd worked for previously, and they want to re-hire her. But they need her to start in August, and that puts her ability to watch the kids in a different light."

"Couldn't the kids go to daycare for the rest of the summer and stay with Betsy at night?" I asked.

"That's what she thinks we should do, but I can't put that on her. It was one thing when she needed the money and was free all day. I want her to concentrate on her career and not what she's making for dinner for the kids. She's already put enough of her life on hold for us, and she needs to get back to it."

"I can understand. Has she ever been married?" Betsy was younger than me, but she'd never mentioned much about her personal life.

"She'd been living with a guy when Jayne died. Betsy took over when I needed her, putting so much time into *my* family that she neglected her own, and they split up. She says he was never the *one*, but sometimes I wonder."

"I think you have to trust her on that. I'm sure she didn't do anything she didn't want to do."

"I need to take care of my own family and let her get back on track," he said. "It's time."

The construction project would take a few more months, so he'd decided to enroll the kids in school in Daytona Beach. He was worried about uprooting them and moving them from their home, but he was even more concerned about being away from them any longer.

I could feel his anxiety at making such a big decision impacting his children. I listened as he fretted over what would happen if they needed him during the day, and he couldn't get to them. I could sense he was feeling their mom's absence and was frightened at the prospect of having the kids to take care of all alone for the first time since her death.

"Brian, this doesn't seem to be too complicated. The kids are young. Moving them for a few months and returning home when your job is completed will be okay. They're resilient, and you're a great dad."

"You're right," he said. "I'll be like many single moms and dads doing this every day of their life."

With that declaration, he changed the subject.

"What have you concluded about your *own* dilemma? Have you decided where your life is going after the summer? In case you haven't been looking at the calendar—the weeks are rushing by," he said.

"I haven't made any solid decisions about what I want to

do. I can always return to Iowa. My dad has made a lucrative living in the insurance industry and thinks I would be good at it. I've even thought about going back to school."

"What if I enroll you *and* the kids in school in Daytona this fall? We can register Jenna and Jack at Ocean Breeze Elementary and get you signed up at Daytona State College. I'm sure they have a degree program in something you'd be interested in!"

"It would be nice to have a plan in place. Would you like for me to do that?" I asked. Were we at that place in our relationship already?

"I think so," he said.

I wasn't sure what Brian wanted me to say. I liked him a lot, but dating at this time in my life was new to me. I wasn't sure how quickly things should move. I knew it didn't make sense to spend time with someone you couldn't see yourself with for the long term, but I wasn't sure where either of us stood on the topic.

"What does that mean, Brian?"

"I was married to a wonderful woman. We had about the best marriage I could have hoped for. I have two children and a career in Florida. I'm looking for a partner to share my life with and someone who wants to be a part of a family that needs her. I realize it can't be just any 'ole woman, but I don't want to waste my time with someone who doesn't want the same things."

"That's why you aren't seeing Anne anymore?"

"Anne is a nice woman, but she travels for her job. She isn't ready to settle down with a family already in place."

"So, you're definitely not seeing her anymore?"

"No–I wouldn't see two women at the same time. I've

111

never cheated on anyone in my life. I'm a one-woman man."

"I didn't know—I'm new to this dating thing," I said. I didn't want a man in my life who had the potential to be a cheater, and I was glad I'd had a chance to ask Brian that important question in the context of another conversation.

"I want to find the person I'm supposed to be with and begin living my life with her. I don't want to scare you off or make you feel pressure, but I don't have the luxury of playing the field. I don't want to put a lot of time into a relationship that isn't going to work. I realize we don't know what the outcome of seeing each other might be at this point. Right now, I need to know that we're interested in the same goals and share the same values. I want to take this further with you, but I have to know we're on the same page before we move forward."

"What are you asking me?"

Brian's face softened. "I think you're funny and beautiful, and I'd like to see where this might lead. I want to spend the evening talking about *your* hopes and dreams, and I want you to hear mine. I want to know if we've got enough in common to see each other for the rest of the summer and figure out where we go from there. I realize I might have too much baggage for you. But I'm laying it all out here to see if you are interested in me enough to take this further."

"What if it's me who has the baggage?"

"I promise to protect you if you'll do the same for me. But if you know you aren't interested in taking on a man with two kids, I'd be grateful if you'd just tell me. My idea of a good time is a steak on the grill and a couple of beers. I understand you have every option open to you, but I don't. I'm not a party guy, and I'm pretty content just being at home. If that doesn't sound like a life you would enjoy, I'll understand, and we can still be friends."

I was touched by Brian's honesty. He was speaking from the heart and wanted to see inside mine. It didn't scare me to hear him talking in such a serious way. Why not get right to it? At least you knew upfront if you wanted to invest more time in another person before your heart was so far in you couldn't get out.

"Where do we start?" I asked.

"Tell me what you would do with the rest of your life if you knew you could have or do anything you wanted."

I thought for a moment. I knew right away if I was candid, it would seem like I was trying to give Brian the answer he was looking for.

"I'd want to find a man I could love and trust who would be my best friend. I'd like to have a chance to have a family of my own and live the happy life I've always dreamed of." I looked down as tears began to pool in my eyes, and I didn't want Brian to see them.

"Why do you say that as if you should be embarrassed about it?" he asked, taking my hand.

"Because I don't want you to think I'm giving you that answer to match what you're looking for. I'm not desperate to find a man. I'm capable of living my life alone and on my own terms. But I want that great relationship I've never had. Maybe I want something that isn't possible."

"It's possible. And once you've had it, there's no way you could accept anything less. That's why it's hard for me. Jayne and I had what you're talking about. Our life wasn't perfect, but we adored each other. We were there for each other and lived our life with as much gratitude as we could muster because we knew what a gift we'd been given."

"And you think you can find it again?" I asked.

"I hope so. I know I'm capable of it. I believe people can have more than one great love in their lives."

"Let me ask you something. This is personal. Maybe I shouldn't ask it." I hesitated to share what was on my mind.

"You can ask me anything," Brian replied.

"How do you expect someone to feel about coming into your life after Jayne? Having gone through a bitter divorce, my standards aren't quite as high as yours might be. How do you think you can accept another woman into your life and not always wish it was Jayne?"

"Jayne is dead. I'm not going to lie to you, If I could have her back, I would be the happiest guy around. But it isn't going to happen, and I've accepted that. I think she'd want me to move on."

"Do you think you're ready?" I asked.

"I'm ready—but it doesn't mean you're ready to move on with me. You've got a past too. Have you dealt with the grief of your failed marriage, and are you ready to open your heart to someone else?"

"I know I *want* to be ready," I offered.

"That's all I need to know."

We finished our wine and ate the sandwiches and chips I'd packed in a cooler. Our conversation made the time pass quickly, and Brian's phone finally indicated the launch window was closing. He turned up the volume as the final ten seconds passed. When the countdown reached zero, the bright red tail of the rocket sailed across the darkening sky. We could hear people cheering and clapping up and down the beach as the roar from the launch broke the sound barrier and reached us with a loud rumble.

"That was amazing!" I said with enthusiasm. When I looked at Brian, he was smiling and looking at me instead of the dramatic event in the sky.

As night fell, we walked back to the cottage hand in hand. I asked Brian to put music on while I took care of the food and drinks from the beach. He linked the Bluetooth on his iPhone to a speaker next to the sofa, and light jazz filled the room.

I stared out the kitchen window, and the reflection of the glass served as a mirror. I looked relaxed and content, and my face seemed softer because of it. I was happier than I'd ever been in my life. I didn't know if it was because of Brian and how he made me feel or the independence I felt at being in charge of my life for the first time in a long time.

"What are you looking at?" Brian asked as he came up behind me and put his hands on my shoulders.

"Me."

I turned to face Brian, who had a puzzled look.

"What do you mean?" he asked.

"I looked outside and saw my reflection in the glass of the window. I realized I look different than I did a few months ago."

"I don't know what you looked like a few months ago, but I think you look gorgeous now."

I blushed as I reached out to take his hand.

"I look relaxed and happy. I haven't seen that face in a long time. I think I've been underestimating the toll the past months have taken on me," I said.

Brian put his arms around me and held me tight. "Stress does terrible things to people. I still look in the mirror and see a guy I vaguely remember as a young husband and dad. That man has been replaced by someone trying to make everything right for everyone around him. Sometimes I wonder how well I'm doing."

"I think you're doing better than you think," I said as he released me.

Brian smiled at my comment. "I hope I've had something to do with making you feel happy and relaxed."

"You have," I said quietly. "I don't know where this is leading, but I know it will impact me for the rest of my life. You've made me feel so special."

"You *are* special. You just need to believe it."

I don't know if it was the bottle of wine or the openness we'd shared throughout the evening giving me courage, but I was ready to move forward.

"I want to thank you for being such a gentleman over the past couple of weeks and treating me with respect and kindness—but what I would like right now is if you would kiss me like you mean it."

Brian looked a little surprised, but he took my face in his hands and pressed his lips to mine, giving me a delicious kiss lasting just the right amount of time.

"I've been waiting for that," Brian said softly.

"It was worth the wait."

"Do you want to try it again?" he asked.

"I think we better, just in case the way it made me feel was a fluke."

Without hesitating, Brian kissed me again. This time the kiss was longer and deeper than the first one. My entire world fell into place, and I felt like I was finally home.

Chapter Twelve
July

I spent my days reading on the beach or shopping for the dinners Brian and I cooked together. I enjoyed looking for unique desserts or the perfect wine pairings, anticipating the evening we'd share. Sometimes we got takeout and ate in front of the TV or ordered pizza if we didn't feel like cooking. Whatever our plans were, I found myself thinking about Brian every second of the day, and there was a constant smile on my face.

Dating in my thirties was like experiencing a relationship in dog years. Each time we were together was like seven dates, and we spent hours engaging in deep and meaningful discussions about what we wanted out of life. We didn't agree on everything, but when we disagreed about something, I liked the way Brian listened to me and respected my opinions. Neither of us needed to be right to be happy, and I started to think about what it might be like to be with Brian for longer than the summer.

The only aspect of our relationship moving slower than I'd expected was the sexual part. Brian never hinted at or made a move indicating he wanted to spend the night with me.

Although we'd been making out like teenagers in the days since the Fourth of July weekend, we'd never slept together.

I wasn't sure if he was waiting for me to give him a sign or if he wasn't ready to move our relationship to that level of seriousness. I realized having a deceased spouse might impact a person's readiness for another partner, and I wanted to be sensitive to those issues.

When I first started dating Jason, everything seemed to progress naturally and in an appropriate time frame. However, I wasn't sure how to conduct myself as an adult divorcee in a new relationship. Brian and I had experienced a deep level of intimacy in our brief time together, even if it wasn't the sexual closeness I craved. Taking our time would benefit us as a couple in the long run, but I didn't know how much longer I could stand it.

***

It was 3:00 a.m. when I woke up and realized we'd fallen asleep watching television. It reminded me of the morning we spent together in the storm, only this time we were snuggled in each other's arms. It was the first night we'd spent together, and even though we were fully clothed and sleeping on the sofa, it felt wonderful having him close to me.

"Hey, we fell asleep," I said softly, nudging him.

"What?" Brian asked sleepily.

"We fell asleep. Do you want to go home and get a couple of hours of rest before you have to go to work, or do you want to stay here?"

"What do you think?" he asked.

Brian pulled me closer to him under the blanket, and we

drifted off again. The warmth of our bodies touching each other made me want him more than ever.

We slept for a couple more hours until I felt Brian kissing me softly. When I opened my eyes, I could see it was still dark.

"Good morning," he said.

"Barely . . ." I snuggled close to him, wanting to go back to sleep.

"You told me you loved to watch the sunrise over the Atlantic, and that's something we haven't done together yet," Brian said.

I could think of quite a few things we hadn't done yet.

Brian never forgot anything I said or stopped trying to make me happy. We pulled on our running shoes and hit the beach.

It was warm already, but there was a slight breeze in the pre-dawn hours. It was dark, but orange and pink hues were beginning to illuminate the horizon. You could see bright stars and a sliver of moon hanging in the clear sky as the sunrise waited to burst into a new day.

Brian took my hand as we walked along the shore. It was quiet except for the sound of the waves and the heavy breathing of an occasional jogger running by. The air smelled fresh, and it felt good to be out in the early morning.

As we passed houses and condos, I saw a few lights were already on. Most people were still sleeping as they enjoyed their vacation or retirement at the beach. I was glad I could count myself as one of the lucky ones experiencing such a beautiful time of day with a man like Brian by my side.

"Isn't this something?" he asked.

"It is. During my first week here, Sophie told me there's a reason the day begins in this place and moves to the rest of the country. She said the sunrise represents a chance at a new beginning and that I'd come to the right place to start my life over again."

"Sophie's right," Brian said as he stopped walking and pulled me into his arms. "Meg . . . I think *you* might be my sunrise."

He held me tightly, and I didn't say anything for fear of disrupting the moment. I held him close, letting him know I understood. His declaration didn't scare me in the least. It made me feel like we were both in the place we needed to be.

"Come on," I said after we let go of each other. "I'll race you!"

***

As we returned to our houses, I decided it was time to have a needed conversation with Brian.

"There's something I want to talk to you about," I said as we got to the end of our route. I'd been thinking about the conversation since we ran past the North Turn Restaurant and headed back toward our houses.

"What's up?" he said, bending down to catch his breath.

"Let's sit for a bit," I said, leading Brian to take a seat on the hard-packed sand.

With all the time we'd spent together, I'd never taken the opportunity to discuss my possible infertility. I knew Betsy had filled him in on the high points, but he deserved more from me—even if it would be difficult. It was time Brian knew why I didn't have kids and that Jenna and Jack only added to my attraction for him. Maybe he couldn't move our relationship forward unless I opened up to him.

"I feel like I owe you a little more on the topic of having children, since we're sharing everything else about our lives," I started.

"I'd like that," Brian said quietly.

"Jason and I wanted a family. It was our goal from the beginning to work the business together for a few years, and when we were blessed with children, I'd stay home with them and be a full-time mom. I wanted to be the PTA president, make sack lunches for class trips, and sew Halloween costumes."

Brian held my hand as I continued.

"We tried for years to have a baby, but it never happened. I can't tell you exactly why we weren't successful at becoming parents, and it's been the biggest heartache of my life. That's why it's taken a while for me to open up to you about it. I wanted the husband and the three kids I'd always dreamed of, and I didn't end up getting either."

"Yet . . ." Brian added.

I smiled at his optimistic attitude.

"We never imagined we wouldn't be able to have children. That's something you take for granted until you know differently. When I look back at the flaws in our marriage, I can't help but think our inability to conceive was where it all started. I think Jason didn't want to investigate it further in case it was him. It was easier to silently blame me—like he did with everything else in our lives. Jason wanted his own child and wouldn't consider alternative options like adoption. I even suggested surrogacy, but he thought that was too risky."

"You don't have to tell me everything if you don't want to. That's all personal stuff between you and your ex-husband. I just needed to know you were open to children because, in case

121

you haven't noticed, I have two of them."

"And I adore them," I said, smiling. "I just wanted you to know it's possible that I can't have my own children."

"What if I shared mine?" Brian asked.

"I'd accept children however they find their way to me," I said.

Brian put his arm around me.

"You're going to be a great mom someday, and your kids will be lucky to have you."

Brian always knew what I needed to hear.

Maybe Jason had made the dating profile looking for a woman who could give him a baby, as if my role in his life was to provide the womb for children who could just as easily come from someone else. If Brian chose to have me in his life, it would be because he wanted *me*—regardless of my reproductive capability.

***

I continued to have coffee with Sophie each week. Her simple take on things helped me to feel as if I was in control of the direction of my life. Her superstitions would often stop a conversation if she thought we were going in a negative direction, bringing us bad luck. On the other hand, she would make an exception to the rule if she thought I was about to reveal something juicy about my love life.

I felt secure building a relationship with Brian, and the only thing bursting my bubble of happiness was the anxiety I felt when I thought about how quickly the summer was slipping away. How could I say goodbye to a man like Brian and return to Iowa? How could I stay when we'd known each other for such a short time?

The closer Brian and I became, the more I thought about a life in Florida. My online perusing of job postings hadn't given me anything worthy of a serious look, and Brian and the kids were only going to be in Daytona for a few more months. It made a job search complicated.

I had enough money to get through the summer, but once my vacation rental was up, it would be necessary to find another living arrangement. Employment would no longer be a choice. It was a dilemma without a clear solution, and when I wasn't thinking about my handsome boyfriend, I was trying to figure out a plan to make it all work.

Betsy and the kids seemed to take to me well, and they were all supportive of Brian and me as a couple. They came every weekend, and we spent time together on the beach, enjoying family activities like making s'mores in the fireplace on cooler evenings and having picnics at Ponce Inlet State Park.

Sometimes we'd lose ourselves in the crowds of visitors as we watched bungee jumpers and those riding the Ferris wheel on the Daytona Beach boardwalk. The bright colors of the carnival rides against the backdrop of the night sky were breathtaking. There was never a lack of things to do to keep us occupied in a place where thousands of people flocked for vacation each year.

***

Brian took an afternoon off, and we visited the elementary school where the kids would go once they joined him at the beach. The staff assumed we were married, and Brian didn't tell them differently. I tried to help him with the decisions he needed to make for his family, and it made me feel good that he listened to my advice about what he should do.

I fell for Brian even more when I heard him talk about what was best for his children. I saw how he anguished over the decision to move them to Daytona or leave them in St. Augustine with his family. I could feel him leaning toward relocating them to be with us, and I knew it meant he was ready to take back the responsibilities he'd allowed his parents and sister to share with him after Jayne's death.

We talked about daycare options. He was worried about what would happen if the kids needed him during the day, and he couldn't get to them because of work.

"Brian, I'll help you with the kids however I can. I know at this point in our relationship you might feel like you can't depend on me for the future . . ."

"Why wouldn't I be able to depend on you?" Brian interrupted. He looked hurt by my comment.

"Looking very far ahead might not be possible for us. We've fallen into this fantastic relationship, but I have to make a plan for what happens after Labor Day weekend. The lease on the cottage will be up, and I have to start looking for a job. That's a month after the kids get here."

"Meg, I don't want you to leave. I want us to figure out a way for you to stay."

It was a topic that hadn't been discussed, and I wasn't sure how to bring it up.

"Let's try to figure something out," he continued. "Don't consider leaving without giving serious consideration to staying. There are other places to live and all kinds of jobs in Florida. I don't want time restraints put on us. Don't let the fact you were only planning to spend the summer here keep us from having the life we were meant to have."

His words touched my heart. We were falling for each other, and I had to figure out a way to stay in Florida until we knew where we were headed.

Chapter Thirteen
July

I heard my phone ring and glanced at the caller ID, hoping it was Brian. I was surprised when my ex-husband's name and number showed on the screen. My first inclination was to let it go to voicemail. However, when he didn't hang up after a couple of rings, my curiosity was piqued, and I knew it hadn't been a butt dial.

"Hello?" I tried to answer with a lack of recognition as if I'd deleted Jason from my life—even though his contact information was still in my phone.

"Hi, it's Jason."

"Hi," I said. My mind was running through all the reasons he could be calling me.

"I'm sorry to bother you, but I thought you would want to know—Dad had a heart attack last night and died a couple of hours ago."

I was gripped by overwhelming sadness and shock as tears began to well in my eyes. It was the last thing I could have imagined him telling me.

"Oh, my God . . . I'm sorry. How are you doing? How's your mom?" I found myself plummeting back in time to my old life with a sense of closeness to Jason I didn't know still existed.

"We're okay, considering. I know how much you cared about Dad, and I didn't want you to hear it from someone else."

I loved Russ and Doris Parsons. They brought me into their family as one of their own, and my connection to them was important to me.

"What can I do? Do you need anything?" It was a stupid question. The days of me giving Jason what he needed were over.

"I just can't believe it." He started to cry, making me feel helpless on the other end of the line. "I know this might seem strange, but I just needed to talk to you for a minute. Being alone at a time like this reminds me of how much you mean to me."

Apparently, his online dating matches hadn't worked out the way he'd hoped.

"Do you think you could come to the funeral?" Jason continued. "I know we're not together anymore—but I don't want to go alone."

It wasn't necessary to bring a "plus one" to a family funeral, but he sounded so devastated that I felt myself considering it.

"Oh, Jason . . ." I wasn't ready to return to Michigan, but I couldn't imagine missing Russ's funeral either. "When is the service?"

"It's on Thursday. I know it's a lot to ask, but I was hoping we could put our differences aside for one afternoon. It's what Dad would want."

"I'm not sure if I can make it work," I said. "I'm sorry." As Jason played to my emotions, I could feel guilt seeping into my heart.

"If you do this one thing for me, I'll never bother you again." He always had a way of making me feel obligated to him, even if it wasn't in my best interest. "Please just think about it," he added.

After we ended the call, I sat for a few minutes staring out the window at the ocean view. I couldn't believe Russ Parsons was dead.

I first met Jason's parents when he asked me to join him for Thanksgiving during our second year at Illinois State. I was hesitant to miss a holiday with my own family, but I didn't want to turn down such an important invitation. I'd fallen in love with Jason during our Freshman year and didn't want to spend the long weekend without him.

The five-hour car ride between Normal and Muskegon was spent talking, holding hands, and listening to our favorite music. Jason had made a CD for the trip and had written "First Road Trip with Meg" in black sharpie on the front of the disc cover. It made me feel like I was special to him, and at twenty years old, I was looking for reasons to make him the center of my world.

We had a wonderful time that weekend, and when we left, I knew I'd won his family over. We were engaged the following year, and getting Russ and Doris as my in-laws was a bonus for which I'd always been grateful.

Since our breakup, I'd only spoken to Jason's parents a few times. They came into the shop periodically and were always cordial, but neither had checked on me. Their single comment about the divorce was to say they *weren't taking sides*, and I understood that meant I was out of their lives forever.

It seemed unlikely Jason would have said to them, *"Mom*

and Dad—I was looking for a girlfriend online, and Meg found out and is divorcing me," so I had no idea what they'd been told about our split. But, knowing how their family handled things, it was probably swept under the rug as something unfortunate but not insurmountable.

My thoughts were interrupted by the phone. I hadn't noticed Brian's truck had pulled into the driveway, and he was checking in like he did every night when he got home.

"Hey, gorgeous. Ready to get our evening started?" he asked in his usual charming way.

"Sure, I'll be right over," I said quietly.

"Is something wrong?" Brian could already read me.

"My father-in-law—I guess I should say, *former* father-in-law, died today."

"Oh. Are you okay?"

"I will be once I see you."

"Well, get over here."

I was at Brian's door within a couple of minutes and, upon seeing him, dissolved into tears again. Brian was the closest thing I had to home in this unfamiliar place, and I needed to be in his arms and cry my heart out.

"Tell me what happened," he said.

"Jason called and told me his dad had a heart attack and died. He was so young, and he was active and healthy. . ." I began crying again. "Russ was always good to me, and I feel so sad about it."

"What is it, Meg? It seems like there's something else bothering you. Tell me what you're feeling," he insisted.

"I'm devastated but feel stupid for feeling this way, because he's been out of my life for months. He and Doris stayed on the sidelines during our divorce, making me feel like

I wasn't important to them all those years. And the other thing is that Jason wants me to come back for the funeral."

"It's natural to feel sad when someone you've loved dies. Just because Russ hasn't been in your life on a day-to-day basis lately doesn't mean you didn't share a bond with him. Things happen. But it doesn't take away all the wonderful years you had together. And the fact that Jason wants you to come to the funeral doesn't matter. What matters is if *you* want to go. Do you?"

"I do. Is that crazy? That part of my life is over, but I want to go to the funeral and pay my respects."

"Well, then you should go. Let's get online and buy you a ticket, and we'll get you up there and back to Florida as soon as possible."

It wasn't long before I felt more in control of myself. I'd left Michigan so abruptly in the spring when things turned ugly, and it had never felt right to me. My trip back to Muskegon would be my last visit to a place where I no longer belonged. I'd pay my final respects to Russ and say a proper goodbye to my old life at the same time.

***

I joined Sophie for coffee the next morning and told her I'd be gone for a couple of days. Our time together was always enjoyable, and she'd begun to be a mentor to me with her witty conversation and sage advice.

I told her of Brian's support and how he'd made all my travel arrangements. We'd spent a lot of time talking about Brian, and she knew I was falling for him. Sophie, a self-proclaimed romantic and matchmaker, was our biggest cheer-

130

leader.

"What's eating at you about Brian, Meg? I can feel you holding back, and there must be a reason," she said.

"The end of the summer is not far off. I don't want to give up on a relationship that seems so great, but maybe we should leave this alone and go on with our lives in a few weeks. There are kids involved. And it's all happening so fast. I just wish we had more time. I can't stay here forever without a plan for someplace to live and a job to pay my expenses. We haven't even slept together. Maybe he's not that into me." I blurted this out, knowing it wasn't the case. I needed Sophie to reassure me.

"You haven't slept with him yet?"

"No, I've been waiting for him to make a move, but I get the feeling he's holding off out of respect for Jayne or *something.*"

"Meg, darling, it hasn't been that long since you started seeing him romantically. Your relationship has been on the fast track because you've been able to see each other every day and become close in a short time. I know society makes it seem like everyone is jumping in and out of bed at the drop of a hat. The truth is, often it happens much more gradually. People have their own anxieties and fears about sex. This man may be taking it slow because he doesn't want to get hurt. Or he might be worried that you are apprehensive and afraid of being vulnerable, so he's giving *you* time and space to be sure."

"I don't think he will hurt me, and I'm *sure* I want to sleep with him!" I said as we both laughed.

"Will Brian even be here after September?" Sophie asked.

"He'll be here until at least the end of the year and will move his kids out here soon and enroll them in school. Without

131

a place to live and a job, my only option is to go back to Iowa. Maybe we could survive a long-distance relationship."

"There are always options, Meg. You *must* follow your heart. If you want to be with this man, we'll find a way."

"I do want to be here. I think I'm falling in love with him. But with kids involved, we have to worry about hurting them if things don't work out. I don't want their hearts broken again."

"Believe in yourself and in Brian. You can never be sure of anything unless you try. I think you let your ex-husband steal your confidence. Jason has made you feel like a failure as a woman, and you're afraid if you allow yourself to fall for Brian, he'll leave you too. You need to realize you are loveable, or you'll never be able to accept love from any man."

Sophie was a wise woman, and I wanted to heed her advice.

***

Brian took the morning off and drove me to the airport in Sanford. He held my hand and told me how amazing I was. I knew he was trying to boost my self-esteem so I could face the people from my past feeling good about myself. I was touched he would be so sensitive to my needs after knowing me for such a short time.

"I'm going to be counting every minute until you get back," he said.

"Me too."

"Are you scared the trip will make you want to return to Michigan?" The trepidation in his voice made me realize he had his own fears about my unexpected time away.

"No. I'm never going back. This trip is about goodbyes," I

said flatly.

Brian parked in short-term parking and insisted on walking me into the terminal. He could have dropped me at the door but said he wasn't dumping me off at the curb. I'd never met a man who treated me so well.

The line was short, and I was checked in and ready to go to the gate within a few minutes. When we reached the escalator, it was time to say goodbye. I set my carry-on bag beside me and turned to face him. Brian took my hands and held them tightly.

"I'm going to miss you," he said. "I'll be right here waiting for you when you get back, and I'm going to plan a surprise. When you feel apprehensive or insecure over these next few days, you can think about the fun we'll have when you get back. I want you to know, no matter how the people from your past make you feel, you have someone waiting here who wants to be part of your future."

"Thank you," I said in his ear as I hugged him.

He held me as we said goodbye. "I love you, Meg."

It took me a moment to realize what he'd said. When it sunk in, I wasn't sure how to respond. I didn't want to say it right back and have it seem insincere.

"I wanted you to know that before you left," he said, leaning in to kiss me one last time.

As I walked toward the security line, Brian called out to me.

"Check your Spotify playlists. I downloaded a few songs while you were in the shower this morning. I didn't want you to forget me."

I gave him a grateful smile and blew him a kiss. There was no way I'd ever forget Brian Barts.

***

I found my seat between a businessman and a teenage boy and settled in for my flight to Grand Rapids. I checked the playlist Brian was referring to and saw he'd entitled it *"Love Songs for Meg,"* and I planned to listen to the set as soon as we got in the air.

As I started to switch my phone to airplane mode, I saw there was a text from Brian.

I miss you already . . .

A warm feeling came over me, and I smiled at the thought of Brian getting to his car and sending me the sweet message before he drove back to Daytona.

The direct flight would take two and a half hours, and as the nose of the plane lifted off the ground, I began listening to the most beautiful collection of music I'd ever heard. Each subsequent song whispered melodies to me as the story of finding love unfolded in the lyrics. Although Brian and I had taken different paths to get to each other, we were both healing from broken hearts and heading toward new lives, and the music he'd chosen for me reflected those experiences.

I had no idea where things were going to end up with Brian, but I knew I'd never be the same.

Chapter Fourteen
July

I rented a car at the airport, and by late afternoon was checked into one of the only hotels in Muskegon with a last-minute vacancy. Summers along Lake Michigan could get busy, and I was lucky I'd found a room. It wasn't the nicest place I'd ever stayed, but it would suffice.

I had just enough time to shower and freshen up before Russ's visitation. I was happy the wake was the night before, which would give me an emotional trial run for the funeral.

It was a hot and humid evening for a Michigan summer, and I chose to wear a sleeveless dress, which clung to me in all the right places. Although I wanted to be respectful of the passing of my former father-in-law, I needed to look my best to get through the evening. A visitation wasn't the place to make a statement, but I planned on making one anyway.

Tate Funeral Home sat on a hill overlooking the city. The Victorian-style house could be seen from blocks away and had once belonged to one of the area's founders. Its beauty and stateliness always calmed me when I'd attended funerals over the years. I parked my car and took a deep breath before entering the building.

I saw two black limos, a hearse, and several Cadillac Escalades parked in a row at the front of the expansive parking lot. It was as if they knew their place in the day's drama and waited patiently to transport people to their final resting places. It was ironic that a person traveled in such luxury when they were too dead to enjoy it.

I spotted Jason, and he came toward me, leaving the man he was talking to mid-sentence.

"You came . . ." he said, scooping me into his arms.

After a moment, I began to pull away from him, but he continued to hug me.

When he finally let go, I saw several groups of people standing around, and it seemed like every set of eyes was on us. I was sure it was a spectacle watching the uncomfortable reunion of two people who were no longer a couple. I saw Doris making her way toward us, and as she got closer to me, it was my turn to fall into her arms and cry.

"Doris, I'm sorry about Russ. I loved him so much. He was always kind to me, and I can't believe this has happened."

"Meg, I'm glad you're here. Thank you for making the trip. The flowers you sent were lovely. Please be sure to sign the guest book with your address so we can send you a thank-you card."

Jason's mother was always very proper, and thinking of etiquette at her husband's visitation wasn't unlike her. "Will you be staying for a few days?" she asked.

"No, I'm only here until Friday," I answered as one of Doris' friends took her attention away. I was left standing alone with Jason again.

"Meg, you look great. Thank you for coming."

"I wouldn't be anywhere else," I said, thinking about

getting back to Florida and into Brian's arms again.

It seemed like everyone came to tell Russ goodbye. The Midwest knew how to throw a funeral, and being seen at one was as important as showing up at a Friday night football game.

Many people told me how happy they were to see me and how much it must mean to the family to have me there. Others averted their eyes as soon as they realized I was in attendance and avoided me when they didn't know what to say.

Out of the corner of my eye, I saw Liz and Craig Thompson standing by Russ's casket. I'd seen her do a double take when they came in, but when I glanced toward them, she was unusually interested in reading one of the cards on a funeral spray. Craig offered a half-hearted wave, and I returned a tentative nod.

Liz had been my best friend and the person I leaned on at the start of the divorce. When I'd been stuck in my crappy apartment for weeks, she'd insisted I join them at a fundraiser for one of the local charities. She even offered to pick me up, but I only agreed to attend if I could drive myself and leave when I wanted to.

I hated to think of a group of couples crowding in an extra chair at their table for eight, making space for a person no one else wanted. Back then, being single was new, and every experience brought me a fresh set of insecurities. I got dressed up anyway and drove myself to the party from hell.

I wore a knee-length red dress and had my hair and nails done at the salon. I had no idea the efforts to improve my self-esteem would be seen as anything but positive.

Craig bought my first drink, and when he delivered it to me, he gave me a kiss on the cheek and said how nice it was that I could join them. I felt supported and loved by my circle of friends and had no idea that anyone would be threatened by my new single status. It had been six months since that night, but the thought of what happened still brought me to tears.

I decided I'd stayed at the visitation long enough. There was a limit to what I needed to do for Jason and his mom, and I'd reached it.

"Meg—wait up!" I could hear Craig behind me as I walked toward my car.

"Hi," I said, turning toward him. I hoped he wasn't going to get into it.

"I'm so sorry about Russ. Gosh, I didn't know you'd be here. I've been thinking about you and hoping everything is going well for you."

It seemed a little late for his concern.

"I loved Russ, and Jason asked me to come." I didn't know how much Craig knew about what had happened between Liz and me that night, but I had a feeling I was going to find out.

"Jason seems to be doing okay, but my heart goes out to him and his mom," Craig said.

"They're strong people, and I'm sure they'll be fine. Have a good night," I said, turning toward the parking lot again.

"Meg, can I ask you something?" He wasn't going to let me get away so easily.

"Sure." What else was I supposed to say?

"What happened between you and Liz?" he asked.

"The night of the fundraiser?" I knew exactly what he was referring to, but I wasn't sure how I would answer.

"Yeah. You ran off without saying anything, and Liz told me you weren't feeling well. Then you left town the next week, and we never saw or heard from you again."

"I don't think you want me to answer that question," I replied.

Liz and Craig had their own marital issues, and despite how she'd hurt my feelings, I didn't want to make waves between them.

"I just need to be sure I didn't say or do anything to offend you." Craig was such a good guy, and I hated that he thought he might have done something to upset me.

"If you really want to know, I'll tell you. The night of the party, I'd gone to the bar to buy one last drink before leaving. I was having fun and was grateful to have been included with all of you. I'd managed a night on the town by myself and was glad I'd decided to come out. When the bartender said he needed to get another bottle of wine from the basement, I'd excused myself to use the restroom. I slipped into the first empty stall and could hear two women talking while they used the bathroom. I recognized Liz's voice and was about to say something clever—until I realized they were talking about me."

"Go on. I need to hear this," he said.

"Liz said, *'She does look great, but Craig can keep his kisses to himself. The last thing we need to worry about is a friend who's looking for a husband in a pool of men who are already taken.'*"

"Oh, Meg. I'm so sorry. That had to be terrible for you to hear."

"I waited until the two of them washed their hands and left before making my escape out the side door to my car. Liz saw me leaving and asked where I was going. I told her I needed to start hanging out with a group of friends whose husbands weren't already taken."

139

Liz's texts and voicemails of apology ended after about a month. Her last message said, *"I'm sorry. There's nothing else I can say. Please call me. I don't want our friendship to end because you won't call me back."*

I didn't want our friendship to end because she was trashing me to someone in a toilet stall—yet that's what happened. For the first time in my life, I was thankful I didn't have any children to keep me forever tied to a life I needed to leave behind.

"She didn't tell me any of that. God, she can be such a bitch sometimes."

"It's okay. I've moved on, and I won't be coming back. I'm glad I got to see you and shed light on what happened, because you've always been a good friend to me. I'm going to miss you," I said, giving him a hug goodbye before returning to my hotel.

***

Thursday's funeral was somber, with bouquets of flowers and music fitting for a veteran and an elder in the Presbyterian Church. Standing at the gravesite, the American flag was folded into triangles and handed to Doris as four men from the local VFW fired rifles and played taps in honor of a man I'd loved for years. Each shot startled me, as if I didn't know it was coming. I had to hold my emotions in tightly, so I didn't cry out in grief for everything and everyone I'd lost.

After my conversation with Craig the day before, I wondered if Liz would seek me out and try to apologize again at the funeral. And when she didn't, it hurt me all over again.

The luncheon was to be held in the church basement, but I

didn't have it in me to go. I found Doris and Jason standing near Russ's casket. They were thanking people for coming, and I went to the front of the makeshift receiving line to say goodbye.

"I'm not going to be able to make it to the reception," I said. "I wanted to tell you again how sorry I am about Russ."

Doris leaned in for a hug and said softly in my ear, "I'll always love you, sweetheart. Please take care of yourself." It felt like Doris knew it was a final goodbye for us too.

"Meg—don't go. Please join us for lunch," Jason pleaded, reaching for my hand. His eyes were still red and watery from crying.

"No, it's best if I get back to the Baymont. I'm going home tomorrow, and I have a few people to visit before leaving town." It wasn't the truth, but it seemed like a plausible excuse for skipping out on the final funeral event.

"Well, do you need a ride to the airport?" he asked.

"No. But thank you."

Jason looked tired and distraught. Something in his eyes told me he was sad about more than his father's burial. Even though he wasn't in my life anymore, I knew him better than anyone. He embraced me, and as I pulled away, I kissed him on the cheek.

"Goodbye. I wish you nothing but the best," I said. Jason nodded but didn't reply as he returned to his mother's side. I knew his silence wasn't because he didn't have anything to say.

Once in the rental car, I checked my phone and had a text from Brian. He wanted to let me know he was thinking of me. I wished my flight wasn't twenty hours away. I wanted to see Brian and let him care for me in the way only he could.

***

I settled into my room for the night with a white Styrofoam container full of takeout food. I opened a Diet Coke and relaxed in the typical motel ambiance of the Muskegon Baymont Inn. The day had been exhausting, and I was happy to have it behind me.

The evening was spent talking to Brian on the phone and sending flirty texts back and forth. The attention I lacked from Jason was being given back to me quickly, and I was having fun being courted by a good-looking man. I was about ready to go to bed when there was a knock at the door.

I looked through the peephole and saw Jason standing with his hands in his jeans pockets and his head bowed. I opened the door slightly, trying to hide my gray pajama pants and favorite Illinois State T-shirt.

"Hey," I said. "What's up?"

Jason looked at me through glassy eyes, and I realized he'd been drinking.

"I need to talk to you. Can I come in?" he said as he lost his balance and took his hands out of his pockets to steady himself. I'd never known Jason to be much of a drinker, but he had apparently decided to tie one on.

"Did you drive yourself over here?" I asked, worried he'd been behind the wheel of a car in his condition.

"No, I took an Uber."

"Jason, I don't think this is a good idea. I've got a flight in the morning, and you've been through a lot today." I said. "How did you know where I was staying?"

"You mentioned it when we said goodbye. And I gave the kid at the front desk twenty bucks to give me your room number."

Thank God Jason wasn't a serial killer.

"Please, Meg. I'm begging you." He was fighting back tears as he slurred his words.

I hesitated, but considering he'd just buried his father, I didn't have the heart to turn him away or risk sharing the conversation with the rest of the hotel guests. He came in and sat at the small table near the window. I sat on one of the two double beds closest to where he was seated and hoped our chat wouldn't take long.

"I don't know if you realize how devastated I was when you filed for divorce," he started, getting right to the point. "I *did* make that online dating profile, but once you were out of my life, I realized it wasn't *someone* else I wanted. It was *something* else for both of us. And then I didn't know how to get you back. You're my soulmate, but I know we lost our way. I just want us to get back to where we used to be before things got so bad, and I couldn't wait another day to tell you. Dad's death has helped me to put everything into perspective."

He was clear on what he was trying to tell me despite being inebriated. He wanted me back. Jason may have come to realize we were meant to be together, but it wasn't a realization I shared.

Hearing Sophie's voice in my head, I said, "So, you're asking for a marriage mulligan?"

He hesitated as he thought about my golf reference in his cloudy state. "I guess so. That's funny, Meg. God, I miss you. I want you back."

When we first met, my sense of humor was one of the things Jason said he loved most about me. It had been years since he'd paid attention to me long enough to get my jokes, and it was too late to make up for everything that had gone wrong.

"Jason, what's done is done. I'm leaving tomorrow, and I'm not ever coming back. This is goodbye for us."

He looked lost and sad, and I was sure my face had shown similar emotions months before when I discovered Jason was making plans for a life that didn't include me. But no matter what had happened between us, I'd moved on far enough that I had no reason to cause him any more pain.

"I'm going to change and drive you home. Who knows how long it would take for an Uber to get back here, and it's bedtime for both of us," I said.

Jason nodded as he rubbed his temples. He would have a massive hangover to deal with in a few hours.

I grabbed my jeans and went into the sterile-looking bathroom to change. I'd been naked in front of Jason hundreds of times, but now our circumstances called for privacy, even to change clothes. I brushed my hair and put on a baseball cap before coming out of the bathroom.

"Okay, let's go," I said, heading for the door. There was no answer.

Jason was asleep on the bed where I'd been sitting.

"Jason? Come on, I need to get you home."

I moved toward the bed and shook his foot. He was out. I'd only seen him that drunk a few times in college, and I knew he wouldn't wake up until morning. Spending the night with my ex-husband was the last thing I'd thought would happen on my final trip to Muskegon, but I couldn't think of anything else to do.

I took his shoes off, placed them at the end of the bed, and covered him with an extra blanket from the closet. I'd always looked after him, despite his treatment of me. He didn't move a muscle, and I knew it would be a long night. I changed back into my pajama bottoms and crawled into bed. I checked my phone one last time and saw a text from Brian.

I miss you. Can't wait to hear about your trip.

I could hardly message back, *"Spending night with Jason. See you tomorrow."* I texted goodnight, closed my eyes, and waited for morning to arrive. I let my mind go to the surprise Brian had waiting for me and fell asleep dreaming about our future.

Chapter Fifteen
July

It was 5:30 a.m., and the only sound in the room was Jason's rhythmic snoring. I'd packed my bags and organized everything for a quick departure before going to bed and hoped I'd be able to slip out of the room without waking him. I dressed and brushed my teeth, only stopping to gather my toiletries before escaping out the door.

Alcohol played a role in what was said the night before, but it was apparent Jason had regrets about how things had ended between us. He'd always had the final say in our relationship, and my early morning exit sent the message I wanted to convey to him about where things stood.

It was just getting light on a beautiful morning, and I grabbed a coffee from the hotel lobby to drink in the car. I didn't mind spending a few extra hours at the airport rather than face another conversation with my ex-husband. I could have breakfast and freshen up before my flight was open for check-in, and then I'd find a spot to park myself and scroll through social media until it was time to board the plane.

I thought about my time in Muskegon and felt emotional about the goodbyes that had been said. The space between old and new love felt bittersweet, but the promise of what was to come outweighed any sadness I felt.

***

My flight got in on time, and as soon as I landed, there was a text from Brian.

Can't wait to see you. I love you!

I'd only been gone for forty-eight hours but couldn't wait to be with Brian again. Every person seemed to take an excessive amount of time getting off the plane. There was luggage stuck in overhead bins and children throwing tantrums on the floor. More than one family was fighting about who would carry what through the airport.

As soon as I turned the corner in the main terminal, I spotted Brian. He was standing near the entrance and was looking in another direction. I had a few seconds to look at him before he turned his head and our eyes met. The time away and the experiences I'd had with Jason cemented my feelings for Brian. Although we'd only been together for a few weeks, it didn't change the fact that I loved him. I hoisted my bag higher over my shoulder and hurried to him, pulling my carry on behind me.

"Hi there," he said as he gave me a kiss. I'd been thinking about his smile since leaving Florida, but seeing it again was better than I'd remembered.

"I missed you so much," I said.

He took my suitcase and put his arm around me as we walked out of the airport terminal.

"Are you hungry? Do you need anything before we hit the road?"

"All I need is you," I said, walking toward the car.

On the ride back to Daytona, I told Brian about the funeral, leaving out the part about Jason spending the night in my room. The visit had given me the closure I wanted, but not all of the details needed to be shared with my new boyfriend.

"Did you remember I promised you a surprise?" Brian asked.

"How could I forget something like that? Are you going to tell me what it is?"

Brian spent the next few minutes teasing me and making me guess what the surprise might be.

"Well, first, I'm going to help you to the cottage with your bags. Then I thought we could go for a run on the beach together."

"That's the surprise—a run on the beach?" I said, pretending to be disappointed.

"No, the surprise comes later."

"How much later?"

"Quit interrupting me, and let me finish telling you our plans," he scolded. "After our run, I'm giving you one hour to shower and put something comfortable on before you need to get back to my house."

"Are Betsy and the kids coming tonight?" It was Friday, and I assumed they would be arriving soon.

"No. They aren't part of the surprise, at least not tonight."

"Tell me what it is. What are we doing?" I asked, poking at him and giggling at the idea of something fun for the two of us.

"No, I'm not telling you. That's going to be part of the fun.

You have to wait a little longer."

I felt like the luckiest woman in the world and couldn't wait to find out what he had in store for the rest of the evening.

***

Brian's house smelled delicious, and he'd obviously been preparing for my arrival all day.

"What are we celebrating?" I asked.

"Us."

There was a loud thud as Brian opened a bottle of champagne, filling two flutes on the breakfast bar.

"I'm so glad you're back," he said. "Here's to the rest of the night." We toasted each other, and I began to interrogate him again.

"*Please* tell me what we're doing? I shouldn't have to wait any longer," I begged.

"Well, tonight we are dining at Café Barts. The menu will feature grilled pork chops and my famous twice-baked potatoes. This will be paired with a bottle of fine wine and followed by a chocolate mousse I made earlier today. What do you think?"

"I think I'm going to be full!" I exclaimed.

"That isn't all. The surprise isn't just tonight. There's something tomorrow too."

"What is it?" I asked with anticipation.

"I want to take you to St. Augustine."

I knew this was a serious point in our relationship. Going to St. Augustine meant seeing what Brian's life was like when he wasn't in Daytona Beach.

"Is that why Betsy and the kids aren't here tonight?"

"Yes. I want to take you home and show you what my life is like there—what *our* life would be like if this all works out."

"I can't wait." I understood the unspoken importance of what he was offering me.

"I've also decided to move the kids to the beach with me very soon."

"You have?"

I felt like the move was the best thing for his family. It was time for him to have his kids with him full-time again.

We ate our dinner on the deck, where a nice breeze made it a perfect evening. Brian lit candles inside glass jars to keep them from going out in the wind, and it was beautiful with the light flickering and the sound of the ocean in the background.

After we went inside, we worked together to clean the kitchen—talking and laughing as we shared the evening. Brian lit more candles inside, and we found our place on the sofa, where we kissed and cuddled and listened to soft music on the XM radio station. Brian must have tuned to "Romantic Interlude," as each song seemed to be talking about us.

"Brian, thank you for this wonderful night." I was happy to be back at the beach with the man I adored.

"You're welcome. I'm excited about tomorrow."

"Me too. But I also wanted to talk with you about something else."

"Anything," he replied.

"I was so touched when you told me you loved me before I left. I can't tell you what it meant to me. I kept playing it over and over again in my mind when it was difficult for me at the funeral."

"I'm glad. I wanted to be there with you somehow and

figured telling you how I felt before you left was the best way to do it."

"I wanted to tell you that . . . I love you too."

Brian smiled.

"I didn't want to tell you at the same time you told me," I continued. "I was afraid it wouldn't seem sincere. But I *do* love you. It's crazy to think we could fall in love in such a short time, but I've never felt this way before. Being away and thrown back into my old life only confirmed my feelings for you."

"You love me?"

"I *love* you," I declared. "But I'm apprehensive because we don't have much time. The end of the summer is a few weeks away. I'm afraid to start something we can't finish."

"Why can't we finish it? Why does time here at the beach have anything to do with it?" he asked.

"If I go back to Iowa, we'll be so far from each other. And I don't have anywhere else to go. Long distance relationships never work . . ."

"Can't we just concentrate on loving each other? If we want to be together, nothing will keep us apart. Let's worry about it in a few weeks—when it happens."

Brian made me feel like everything would be okay, and I believed him that we would figure it out when necessary. We had more than a month before my lease was up, and a lot could happen in a month.

"I love you, and you love me—right?" Brian asked me again.

"Yes."

"Then I think you might like the rest of my plan for the evening."

"What did you have in mind?" I asked.

"Stay with me tonight. And when we return on Sunday from St. Augustine, move in with me until the kids get out here next week. I'm going to do what has to be done for work commitments, but I want us to spend as much time as we can together—before our relationship goes from a couple to a family."

"Finally!" I teased.

"I want to love you and want us to grow in our relationship. But I want you to know why it has taken me this long to get here with you."

"I'd like to know," I said quietly, hoping it wasn't because he was unsure about us.

"I made a mistake with Anne. I slept with her on our second date and regretted it the minute it happened."

"Oh." I didn't know what to say about that.

"I was nervous about being with anyone after Jayne. To be honest, it had been *so* long, and I felt it was what I was supposed to do to move on."

"I can see how you would feel that way," I said.

"After Anne, I decided I didn't want to have a casual relationship with anyone. I'm not some college kid looking to get laid. I have children to consider, and they don't need a dad who jumps in and out of bed with random women. I know people think most single men are only after one thing, but getting it from someone I didn't really care about made me feel even emptier."

"I haven't been with anyone since Jason. In fact, I haven't been with anyone *but* Jason."

He looked at me with love in his eyes.

"I was saving myself for you," I said.

152

"Then I'm a lucky man."

Brian took me by the hand as we walked through the house, blowing out the candles. After each one went dark, he stopped to kiss me. The kisses were different each time. Some were light and playful, while others were deep and passionate. When we reached his bedroom, neither of us was thinking about our past.

Chapter Sixteen
July

I opened my eyes and saw Brian on his side, looking at me. He smiled as he took me in his arms.

"Did you sleep well?" he asked.

"Yes, this place is like a five-star hotel. My plan was to come to the beach and spend time processing everything that has happened to me. And now, I'm waking up in my neighbor's bed."

"My plan had been to come to the beach and put my mind back on work. But—this is way more fun," he said as he kissed my shoulder.

"If I'm being honest, the pace of how fast things are moving is still making me a little nervous." I hated to break the mood, but I had things on my mind. "I've always heard time heals, and I want to be sure I'm giving myself enough of it before I move on to another relationship. We're falling quickly for each other, and I'm scared we aren't being smart about this because we both want it so bad."

"Meg . . . you know another thing that heals?" he asked.

"I hope you're going to say coffee—because I *need* coffee."

"I'll get you some coffee, but that's not what I'm talking about. Happiness heals. If you find happiness with someone, no matter how long it takes to find it, you need to hold on and be grateful for it. But if you're having second thoughts about St. Augustine, I will understand. I don't want to pressure you into something you aren't ready for."

"I guess after my divorce, I don't trust myself or my feelings. I don't know the rules of love anymore."

"That's the best part. There are no rules. You're an adult now and can decide what you want for your future and who you want to spend it with. Trust me, and know I want what's best for both of us. But I need to show you who I really am before we go any further. I'm not the bachelor who lives in a beach mansion, and you need to see that."

"Then it's an important day, isn't it?" I said, feeling better.

"Today, you'll get a glimpse of my life at home. I want you to see where I live, what the kids are like when they aren't having fun at the beach and get the feel of the community. And . . . I also want you to see the house I built with my own hands," he added proudly.

"It sounds like a job interview." We both laughed, but in reality, it *was* an interview. I just didn't know which of us was trying to get the job.

Before I left to get ready for the day, Brian made love to me again, and my doubts melted away with the warmth of his touch.

***

I needed to shower and grab breakfast before we hit the road for St. Augustine. As I unlocked the cottage door, I saw a note

155

folded over and taped to the glass window.

Meg,

My sister has taken ill, and I've gone to Atlanta to be with her. I will return next week to get a few more things, but I will need to spend the next few months with her. You could stay at my place when your lease is up. I won't charge you any rent as it would be a huge favor to me.

I would be forever grateful to you if you could help me out. Think about it, and we can talk next week. It would solve both of our problems and allow us to be with the ones we love when we need to be with them.

Sophie

Tears came to my eyes, and my heart gave me the answer I'd been searching for. It wasn't the fear of staying that was troubling me—it was the anxiety of leaving. If I didn't have to pay rent, I would have enough money to stay until the end of the year without getting a job. The few months spent at Sophie's house would give Brian and me time to figure out if we had a future together.

As water from the shower soaked my hair and ran down the curves of my body, a body forever changed after being next to Brian in such an intimate way, I felt beautiful and loved. It had been a long time since I'd felt that way.

I was closer to Brian in a few weeks than I'd been with Jason in years of marriage. Now that we could have the time we needed, I had a sense of peace and could go to St. Augustine with an open mind.

I would wait and tell Brian about Sophie's offer until we were on our way back from our weekend getaway. Before telling him the exciting news, I wanted to make sure life in St. Augustine was something I could envision for myself. I'd learned the hard way that following someone else's dreams could backfire on a relationship, and I wasn't going to make the same mistake again.

***

I wasn't sure who would be part of our day in St. Augustine. I assumed Betsy and the kids would be there, but I wasn't sure about Brian's parents. We traveled the hour and a half together, holding hands and talking. Seeing Brian so excited about bringing me to his family home made me feel special.

As we drove into Brian's neighborhood, the stately brick homes nestled between tall pine trees felt familiar to me. It was remarkably northern, except for the gray Spanish moss hanging from the foliage and the palm trees swaying in the breeze. I hadn't spent much time thinking about Brian's economic status, but it looked like he did well for himself.

We drove into the driveway, and Betsy and the kids met us at the door. We hugged, and she winked at me as she said, "Welcome to St. Augustine!" Betsy wasn't stupid. She knew this trip meant we were taking our relationship to another level. She seemed okay with it, as did the kids, who jumped into Brian's arms the minute they saw him.

Jack was still carrying Gus around and hugging him tight like the all-time favorite gift he'd claimed it was. "Gus is excited to see you, Meg!" Jack said.

"I'm so happy you like him. He must love being your little doggy."

"Daddy says we get to choose where to take you for dinner tonight, and we want to go to The Pizza Pit. That's our favorite restaurant," Jenna said.

"I was thinking of something a little nicer than that," Brian said apologetically.

"I'd love to go to the Pizza Pit," I said to the squeals of both children.

It wasn't long before Betsy left, and it was clear the weekend would be only the four of us.

We brought our bags in from the car, and Brian showed me to a beautiful guest room on the main floor. I wouldn't be sharing the master bedroom with him, which might require explanations he wasn't ready to provide to his children.

The bedroom had its own bath, and the navy and white striped wallpaper matched the comforter on the bed. There were fluffy towels and a nautical theme throughout the suite. The throw pillows had anchors and sailboats on them and looked like they had been purchased in an expensive boutique. I thought about Jayne choosing the décor for her guests, never imagining a time when one of them would be her husband's new girlfriend.

After I got settled, I found Brian in the kitchen preparing cheese and crackers. He handed me a Diet Coke and showed me a bottle of wine he promised we would share later in the evening. The kids sat at the kitchen island, telling us about their week. You could see the love in Brian's eyes as he took in every word. He was the kind of man who gave his entire self to those he loved, and when I talked to him, he looked at me the same way.

We spent the rest of the afternoon sitting on the covered patio beside the pool. The kids played, and Brian and I enjoyed a relaxing time together as an outdoor ceiling fan helped to keep us comfortable in the July heat.

When it was time for dinner, we loaded everyone into the mini-van Betsy drove when she brought the kids to the beach and headed for The Pizza Pit. Even Gus went along for the evening of fun.

The restaurant was packed, but we were able to get a large booth close to a row of games set up for the kids to enjoy. Our server came over, and we ordered from the menu and purchased game tokens for Jenna and Jack. The kids found their place in front of a video game, and we were alone again. The place was loud, colorful, and fun. I was glad we could make the kids happy by eating at their favorite spot.

Brian reached across the table and took my hands in his.

"This isn't exactly The Seaside Grill, is it?"

"No, but I love it. I'm with you, and that's all that matters," I said.

Brian grinned and glanced over to check on the kids. They were talking with three other children standing near them at another game. "Oh, the Larsons are here," Brian said as he waved at the oldest girl in the group, and a well-dressed couple made their way to our table.

"Brian, how are you?" the woman asked.

Brian stood, shook the man's hand, and gave the woman a friendly hug.

"I'm good. How are the two of you?" he answered. "Meg, this is Trevor and Mary Larson. They're good friends of mine."

"Hi, I'm Meg Parsons." I took turns extending my hand to each of them. Trevor was friendly toward me, but Mary offered a terse hello and looked me up and down without trying to hide the fact she was sizing me up.

Brian and the Larsons talked for a few minutes discussing the weather and Brian's work in Daytona. He tried to include me in the conversation, but it was obvious Mary wasn't interested in anything I had to say. They asked when he would be returning and offered an invitation to have dinner at their house. It didn't feel like the invitation included me.

Once the Larsons retreated to their own table, Brian's attention was again on us. I wasn't hiding my feelings well because I could see the concern in Brian's eyes.

"Are you okay?" he asked.

"Sure." I didn't want to kill the mood, but I felt anxious and out of place. The encounter reminded me that Brian's life included more people than his immediate family. To be a part of his life in St. Augustine, I would have to fit in where Jayne had once been a loved and respected figure.

"Don't worry about Mary. She's never been one of my favorite people." I felt better knowing he had noticed her coldness too.

I wished my vulnerabilities weren't so close to the surface where Brian could see them. The look I'd been given by Mary was judgmental and negative. I wanted to shrug it off and move on with the evening, but I felt I couldn't do that unless I addressed it with Brian.

"It made me feel terrible," I said quietly.

160

"Honey, please don't do this to yourself. Mary and Jayne were best friends. I'm sure she had no idea I was dating. It took her off guard, and she wasn't as kind as she should have been. It isn't always going to be like that. Change is hard for everyone, and they've never seen me with anyone else."

We were interrupted by the kids as they ran back to the table for more game tokens. Brian waved at the server when he saw she had our order, and she came over with our pizza. She set the cheesy pie on the red and white checkered tablecloth and sold Brian additional game tokens.

"I want to play more games," Jack cried.

"No, we're going to eat our pizza first," Brian said sternly.

"No!" Jack yelled as he left the booth and returned to the game he'd been playing earlier. I saw him set Gus beside the machine and act like he was playing even though no tokens had been inserted.

"Excuse me," Brian said as he walked over to Jack.

Jenna slid in beside me and started serving herself a slice of pizza. "Jack's always naughty. He never listens to Aunt Betsy, and sometimes she has to yell at him."

I watched as Brian knelt beside Jack and spoke firmly to him, convincing him to return to the table. After that, the rest of the dinner went off without a hitch, and after a few more games, we all went back to the house with a promise of ice cream before bed.

***

Dinner took longer than anticipated with the Saturday night crowd and getting a later start than expected. When we returned to the house, both kids were sleeping in the back seat, and dessert plans were abandoned.

Brian woke Jenna, and she walked herself in through the door leading from the garage to the house as he carried Jack to his bedroom. I stayed in the kitchen while the three of them went upstairs, giving me time to look around the house a little more.

It was homey but a little too messy for my taste. I wondered how they'd kept things going after Jayne's death. Did they have a house cleaning service or meal deliveries? I didn't know much about that time in their lives but was curious to know how they'd managed.

Cookbooks were stacked haphazardly on shelves in the kitchen, and they made me think about what the family's favorite recipes might be. Framed photos were in every room of the house, most with a smiling family of four looking back at me. If I ended up with Brian, there were challenges ahead. I'd expected there would be pictures of Jayne, but I had underestimated how they would make me feel. Even though she was dead, her presence was palpable in every corner of the house, making me feel like an outsider.

I heard footsteps behind me and expected to see Brian. Instead, I turned to see Jenna in pink pajamas standing in front of me.

"Goodnight, Meg. I'm glad you came for the weekend."

I realized she wanted me to hug her as she came toward me. I extended my arms and gave her the affection she was looking for before she went back upstairs to bed.

Jenna was old enough to realize why I was there. She spoke like a little adult with obvious wisdom beyond her years.

Could she have the maturity at her age to still be grieving her mother but be concerned about her dad's happiness as well?

I heard Jack crying from upstairs. The sound grew louder and became more of a wailing as it got closer. Brian came into the kitchen with Jack in his arms, along with several stuffed animals. Jack was sobbing uncontrollably, and Brian looked helpless as he tried to figure out what to do.

"Jack left Gus at the restaurant," Brian said flatly. "I told him I'd go back tomorrow and get him. I found these other stuffed animals, which are just as good . . ."

"They *aren't* as good. I want Gus! Meg, please go get Gus for me!" Jack pleaded.

"Honey, I don't know how to get back to The Pizza Pit. I've never been here before and wasn't paying attention to the roads," I said, hoping to talk some sense into the distraught little boy. The thought of making my way through an unfamiliar town wasn't something I wanted to do, even if I could GPS the location.

"Daddy can get him. I can't sleep without Gus. Please— get Gus right now!"

It was only 9:30 p.m., so there *was* time to get back to the restaurant before it closed. I hated to make an offer Brian might not want me to make, but I did it anyway.

"What if I stayed with the kids and you ran back to get Gus? Jack and I can sit here on the sofa and wait for you. Then everyone will be able to sleep tonight with no problems."

"I don't want him to think he can throw a fit and make me do whatever he wants me to do. Jack, you have to listen to what Daddy says, and I'm not happy with the tantrum you're throwing."

163

"I promise if you get Gus, I'll go to bed and won't cry anymore. I love him so much and don't want someone else to take him. Gus would be scared if he didn't have me. I don't want him to think I'm dead like Mommy."

Brian's eyes filled with tears as he placed his son in my arms. As Jack laid his head on my shoulder, I saw a sadness in my new love that I'd never seen before.

"It's okay," I said.

Brian mouthed *thank you* to me as he left to rescue Gus from an unknown fate at The Pizza Pit.

"Do you want me to read to you?" I asked Jack. There were children's books on a side table, and I pulled one from the stack to pass the time while we waited for Brian to return. Jack settled in beside me and nodded off in the middle of the story.

I sat with him as he breathed heavily and drifted further into sleep. His closed eyes were accentuated by long, full eyelashes. He was a beautiful child, and I wondered if I'd have the chance to love him as my own.

I looked at a photo of the Barts family next to the chair we were sitting in. Feeling Jayne's stare penetrating my heart, I tried to imagine myself as a part of her family. If there was any justice in the world, she would be alive, and I would be spending the evening alone at The Pink Shell.

Brian didn't know about the offer from Sophie yet, and I wondered if I had it in me to go any further. If I chose to continue, the road would be bumpy and full of detours. There were easier paths to follow, but none of them included the man I'd fallen in love with. I wasn't sure I could turn back even if I wanted to.

Chapter Seventeen
July

I heard the garage door open and realized I'd drifted off to sleep. It had been a long day for all of us, and I was tired. I wanted Brian to join me in the guest room and tell me everything would be okay, but I'd be left to my own uncertainties until we were back at the beach house and Brian could properly comfort me.

Brian smiled when he saw Jack and I nestled together in the oversized chair. He picked up the sleeping boy and tucked a rescued Gus under his arm as he carried both of them upstairs.

"I'll be right back," he said, giving me a sexy wink.

With both kids asleep, we changed clothes and found ourselves exhausted on the sofa. Brian opened the bottle of wine and turned on some music, allowing me the opportunity to relax for the first time since we'd left for dinner.

"Was Gus still next to the game the kids were playing?" I asked.

"No, he was safe in the lost and found. The manager said a boy wanted to take him home, but his mother had insisted he leave him there in case the owner came back."

"Thank God."

"Thank *you*. I don't know what I'd have done if you weren't here. I shouldn't have let Jack get his way. Jayne was the one who always disciplined the kids. I'm lost when it comes to raising these two on my own."

"I think you're selling yourself short. You're great with them. No one knows exactly what to do all the time. You'll make mistakes, but it'll be okay. You love them, and that's the most important thing."

"I *do* love those two," he said with a wearied sigh.

"Tonight, as I'm here and see how amazing these kids are, I have to tell you I'm really scared. I see Jayne in every direction I look. Like we were discussing this morning—I don't know if I can simply decide this is what I want, and it will magically work out. What if I fall short of what you need?"

"What if we aren't the family you envision?" he asked.

"And I have something else to tell you," I said, interrupting him. "Sophie wants me to stay at her place until at least the end of the year. I want to take her up on her offer—but you're right. The time we've been spending at the beach has nothing to do with your life here. And it's a life you're returning to."

"The time we're spending at the beach has everything to do with my life here. But wait—Sophie wants you to stay at her place?"

"I found a note on my door when I got home this morning. Sophie's sister is sick, and she's going to Atlanta to help her for a few months and has asked me to stay at her place until she gets back. She wants me to house sit for her, and she'd allow me to do it for free. Sophie's a hopeless romantic, and she's using her sister's poor health to give us more time

166

together. I don't even know what's wrong with Audrey, but Sophie will be back this week to get more of her belongings, and I'm going to try and find out what's going on then."

"I'm sorry for Sophie's sister, but I'm happy for us!" he said.

"I can only assume Audrey's illness is serious if Sophie knows she'll be gone for several months. I suppose she'll be going through cancer treatments or something, but Sophie didn't offer any details in the note she left," I said.

"Meg, I love you. I'm not asking you to do anything you don't want to do. But let's keep moving forward, and we'll make whatever decisions are necessary when the time comes. Let's enjoy the rest of our evening together, and we'll have a fun day tomorrow. We have one more week together in Daytona—just the two of us. When Betsy brings Jenna and Jack out next weekend, we'll see how it goes for the *four* of us. Will you take Sophie up on her offer and stay?"

I could see by the look in his eyes how much he wanted it to work. My own insecurity led me to think I couldn't take on a family who needed me as much as I needed them. Why was I scared to have the life I'd always dreamed of?

"And," he continued with a smile, "do you have any better offers?"

"There's nothing I'd love more than to spend time with you and the kids," I said. Brian made it sound easy, and I wanted to trust him. He was right—I didn't have anything else pulling me toward a future with more possibilities.

"Perfect."

"*You're* perfect," I said.

Brian tucked me into the guest room and retreated to his own bedroom. I wanted him next to me, but I knew we could be together at the beach house the following night. I was drifting off to sleep when I heard my phone ding and saw a text message waiting for me.

I can smell your perfume on my shirt, and it makes me want you.

The thrill of having Brian love me was more exciting than anything I'd ever experienced.

Tomorrow . . . I texted back.

A few minutes passed, and my phone rang.

"How can I get any sleep if you keep texting and calling me?" I teased after answering.

"Meg, I had one more thing to say—I love you. I love you for *who* you are and *what* you are, not what you can offer the kids and me. It probably seems like I need you more than you need me. But, if you stay with me and be my partner in every way, I'll make you the happiest woman in the world."

I didn't doubt his offer.

***

I took a quick shower and dressed for the day in shorts and a T-shirt. When I joined the family in the kitchen, I could smell the coffee and hear bacon sizzling.

"Hey, the sleepy head is finally awake," Brian kidded as I entered the room.

Both kids said hello, and Jenna asked if I'd slept well. Jack insisted I say good morning to Gus, who seemed happy to be home where he belonged.

"Would you like coffee?" Brian asked as he handed me a mug already mixed the way I liked it.

"You made my coffee?"

"One sweetener and just enough vanilla creamer to tint it beige—right?" he asked.

"Yes, I can't believe you took note and remembered," I said, unable to hide my surprise.

"I notice everything you do. I'm sorry, would you have rather made it yourself?"

"No, it was very sweet of you." Jason had never made my coffee, not even on my birthday. I'd found someone who wanted to make me happy by the simple gesture of preparing a beverage for me. A man who would do something so thoughtful to please me would certainly have my well-being in mind when we faced the bigger issues of life.

"I'm a sweet guy, aren't I, kids?" He gave Jenna a fist bump and Jack a high five.

I wanted to wrap my arms around him and let him know how much his kindness meant to me, but with the kids looking on, I just took the cup and drank from it. It tasted better than when I made it myself because of the way it made me feel to be taken care of by him.

We all sat together, sharing a delicious breakfast as if we'd done it a hundred times before. Pancakes, eggs, and bacon had never tasted so delicious.

"Daddy, I got all my spelling words correct this week," Jenna said proudly.

"You did? Wow, Aunt Betsy must be doing a good job with your homework," Brian said.

"And I get to be the teacher's helper next week at school," Jack added, not wanting to be outdone by his sister.

"I was the spelling bee champion for my school one year," I shared. "I won a trophy and got to go to the regional competition."

"Really?" Jenna asked. "Will you help me study for my tests when I get to the beach?"

"Of course," I said.

The kids bantered back and forth with their father. The conversation was easy, and it didn't seem strange for me to be a part of the inner workings of the Barts family.

"Are you two excited about moving to Daytona?" Brian asked the kids.

I held my breath for their answers.

"I can't wait!" Jack exclaimed. "I want you to tuck me in every night, not *just* on the weekends."

"I'm looking forward to going to the beach every day, but I'm going to miss my friends," Jenna said. "Aunt Betsy says it will be like a long vacation. Then I'll be back for the second part of third grade, and everyone will have missed me so much they'll all invite me over for a playdate to catch up."

"I'm sure they will," Brian said. "It will be a change, but I think it's important the three of us are together again. We'll have so much fun in that big beach house, and before you know it, we'll be back home for good."

We finished our breakfast, and Brian helped the kids get ready for the day while I cleaned up the kitchen. I dried a frying pan and placed it in a cabinet along the back wall where it had come from. When I was closing the cupboard door, I saw a magnet stuck to the side of the refrigerator. I read the Desmond Tutu quote a couple of times over, contemplating its meaning.

"You don't choose your family. They are God's gift to you, as you are to them."

***

"Want to grill steaks tonight?" Brian asked as we drove south on Interstate 95 toward Daytona Beach. I hadn't had a good steak since I'd arrived in Florida. Iowa corn-fed beef was hard to beat, but I'd risk it if Brian was cooking.

"Sounds great," I said. We'd spent the morning with the kids, and when Betsy had returned after lunch we'd headed back to the beach.

"How long do you think it will take to pack up your stuff for the week and get over to my place?" he asked.

"Considering anything I forget is right next door—not long."

"Good. While you're getting moved over, I'm going to go to the grocery store to get supplies. After that, I want us to settle in and enjoy the next few days without worrying about anything. If things go smoothly, I'll have my foreman take the lead this week. That will allow me to come in late and leave early when possible."

"I like that plan," I said. It would be so much fun to have more time together.

"You seem more relaxed today. Are you feeling better about things?" Brian asked.

"There are such big shoes to fill in your life, and I'm working through my own issues about how that makes me feel."

171

"Do you think you have to measure up to Jayne somehow?"

"I imagine *anyone* would feel that way," I said.

"When someone dies, it's easy to put them on a pedestal. I adored Jayne, but we were a regular married couple. We always treated each other with love and respect, and we would have been married for many years had she lived. But she wasn't perfect. I'm not perfect—and I don't expect you to be either."

"It's funny, but something happened this morning that made me think. I don't want to freak you out, but I felt like Jayne was sending me a message."

"What was that?" Brian asked. I could tell he was wondering what I was going to say next.

"I was putting the frying pan away, and a magnet on the side of the refrigerator caught my eye. It said, '*You don't choose your family. They are God's gift to you, as you are to them.*'"

"Yes, I bought it for Jayne years ago. It was one of her favorite sayings."

"I know this is an unusual situation, but if I were Jayne, I would want to know my family was happy. Maybe she would be okay with us being together—like I could finish what she'd started. Reading the magnet made me feel that way."

Brian was quiet for a few minutes. Had I hit a nerve?

"Say something," I said. "I'm sorry if I upset you."

"It isn't that. I'm just collecting my thoughts. I want to tell you something, but I don't want to freak *you* out. If you felt Jayne was trying to send you a message—I believe you."

"Will you tell me about it?" I asked.

"You may have noticed I've never talked about Jayne's family."

172

I'd never thought about it, but he was right. No other grandparents had ever been mentioned.

"When I first met Jayne, she had a tough time accepting my family and feeling like she would be able to fit in."

"Wow, Jayne and I had a lot in common!"

"She was an only child. She was close to her parents, who doted on her. Jayne had everything she wanted growing up and attended the best private schools. When she turned sixteen, her parents even bought her an expensive sports car. She was spoiled but deeply loved, which kept her grounded. The following year, they were on vacation and got into a terrible car accident. Her parents were killed instantly, and Jayne was hospitalized for weeks. The only family she had left was an aunt and uncle, but they'd never been close. The aunt came to be with her while she recovered, but Jayne was on her own after she was released."

"How sad," I said, feeling the pain in the words he was sharing.

"Once we met and fell in love, she didn't feel so alone anymore, but she had trouble being dropped into a family and feeling accepted. My parents and Betsy did everything they could to make her feel loved, but Jayne always felt like an outsider until we had our own kids. Jenna and Jack finally made her feel connected to the rest of us."

"I can see how she might feel that way," I said.

"I gave her that magnet in her Christmas stocking the year Jenna was born, and it was very special to her."

"The words made me feel as if I didn't need to be so afraid—that maybe I was right where I needed to be."

"I promise you are," Brian said.

Chapter Eighteen
July

After our conversation about the magnet, Brian began to open up. I had many questions about what had happened to Jayne, but I'd never asked them. I knew when the time was right, Brian would share what he wanted me to know, and the car ride back to Daytona provided the opportunity for him to do it.

"Jayne had been running errands all morning getting ready for the holidays, and when she came home, she wasn't feeling well and said she needed to rest," Brian started. "I took the kids outside, and after a while, I went in to check on her. She said she had a pounding headache, and it wasn't going away. The look on her face told me it was more than a migraine."

It was difficult for Brian to talk about something so traumatic, and I stayed silent while he continued. We needed this conversation, and I braced myself for the devastating details.

"It was getting worse by the minute, so I called an ambulance. I didn't want to scare the kids, but it was serious, and I knew time was of the essence. Something inside me went into overdrive, and I was able to keep an eye on Jayne, the kids, and on the driveway so I could wave the paramedics in."

I reached for Brian's hand as he kept talking, letting him know I was there for him.

"The kids and I followed the ambulance in our car, and I called Betsy and my parents on the way to the hospital. It didn't take long after Jayne was admitted for her to be diagnosed with a brain aneurysm. They did surgery immediately, but she never regained consciousness despite their efforts. She survived for almost a week and died with me lying in bed beside her. It was just the two of us, and I pleaded with God to let her parents be there to greet her so she wouldn't be alone."

"Oh, Brian . . . that must have been terrible. I can't imagine explaining something like that to children the ages of Jenna and Jack."

"The day before her death, I took the kids to see her. A young man and his toddler got on the elevator with us. The guy was beaming, and the little boy wore a "Big Brother" T-shirt. The young dad was talking to his son about his new baby sister, and the child looked at Jenna and said, "My mommy is in the hospital." Jenna told him her mom was there too. It really broke my heart, and I lost it. I stood there sobbing with the four of them staring at me. The poor guy had no idea what to do and just said, "Hey, man—good luck," as they got off on the maternity floor."

I searched my purse for tissues. We were both crying, and I didn't know how much more I could take. I needed insight into the experiences Brian and his family had endured, but it made me sad to think about the three of them during such an awful time.

"Later that day, I took the kids for a walk and made a point of taking them to the fifth floor to see the babies in the nursery. Of course, they were too young to understand why we were going there, but it made me feel better to see the happy families and the newborns wrapped in pink and blue blankets. As lives were ending, others were beginning, and I wanted to make sure they saw that. So, that's the condensed version of how I became a widowed, single parent at thirty-six years old. Okay, that's the end of the sad stories for today," he declared.

"Thank you for sharing all of that with me. I'm sorry you've had to go through so much."

"How about you help me bring happiness back to all of us?" he asked.

"It would be my honor," I said.

I'd never wanted anything more in my life.

***

We had five days until Betsy was scheduled to bring the kids to the beach to stay. I wanted to savor every moment we had together, knowing our time as a couple would be hard to come by once the children arrived.

I threw a few things in a duffle bag and returned to Brian's. I didn't need much as I'd spend my days at the cottage when he had to work. I liked my surroundings at The Pink Shell and could only enjoy them for a few more weeks.

Sophie returned from Atlanta on Monday, and we got together the following day. I entered her sensory-overloaded house, and the smell of hazelnut coffee made me feel at home.

"If you're sure, and it would be a help to you, I'd love to accept your offer to watch over your house while you take care of Audrey," I said as we settled ourselves at the kitchen table. "How's she doing?"

"Darling, I don't want to dwell on this. You know I never speak of unpleasantness—it only tempts fate. Everything will work out in the end, but I need to go and be with her for now. That's all I can say at this point. There's a situation that needs to be addressed, and I've told Audrey I would come and stay with her until the problem is solved."

"When are you leaving?" I wondered what Sophie would do without the beach at the tip of her toes for a few months.

"Tomorrow morning. I wanted to make sure you were willing to do this for me before going to the trouble of packing everything."

"What do you mean?" I asked. "If I hadn't agreed to stay on, you wouldn't have gone to Atlanta to be with your sister?"

"Um . . ." Sophie hesitated with her answer. "I would have figured something out. Audrey will be fine eventually, but I need to be with her now. Let's not talk about this any longer. I'd rather hear about you and your young man. How are things going?"

Sophie's superstitious nature was difficult to understand at times.

I obliged her request to hear about Brian and me. I told her about our trip to St. Augustine and the moving plans for the kids. I did leave out some steamier parts from the previous few days, but Sophie's expression told me she knew exactly what was happening.

"This is the best possible news you could have given me. I love a good romance, and until I meet a gentleman as appealing as my sweet Charlie, I'll have to live vicariously through you," she said.

Sophie gave me the information needed to care for her

house and made sure I felt at ease about unpacking and making myself at home. I assured her I'd keep in touch and contact her if there were any problems. We planned to talk each week so that Sophie could keep up to date on the progress of my relationship with Brian. When I asked her to keep me in the loop about Audrey, she scoffed and dismissed the idea with a flutter of her hand.

∗∗∗

"That's your last bag from inside," I said, helping Sophie lift a heavy suitcase into the trunk. It was early, and I hadn't had my coffee yet, but I didn't want to miss telling Sophie goodbye.

"Be careful. That's the one with all my prized possessions," she said.

Sophie had packed three large suitcases and several smaller bags to take with her to Atlanta. One was stuffed with treasures she planned to use to decorate the room she would be staying in. She wanted to feel at home, which meant lots of trinkets surrounding her. She'd also packed puzzles, board games, and everything they'd need for martinis.

"Do you think Audrey will feel up to games and drinks?" I asked. Maybe she intended to show Audrey a good time and *force* her to get well.

"I want to be ready for anything!" Sophie replied.

I hugged her and waved as she backed out of the driveway. I was going to miss our talks and her vibrant personality.

She lowered the passenger side window and yelled back at me from the road, "Don't waste this opportunity!"

With that final piece of advice, she was gone.

***

Brian and I let the outside world disappear for a few beautiful days. He made me feel like it was my birthday, Christmas, and Valentine's Day all wrapped into one. I'd never felt such deep love before.

We spent every night together, becoming closer with each conversation and touch. We stayed up until the early morning hours, not wanting to waste any time we had alone on sleep. I was lucky because I could nap during the day, but Brian was going on sheer adrenaline after a day or two. I felt like we were the only people in the world, and I was basking in his love and affection.

I wondered how long I'd feel the intensity of new love and pondered what life would be like with Brian once those feelings began to fade. With the kids moving in, I feared I'd have the answer sooner rather than later.

Our last night alone was spent running errands to prepare for the kids' arrival. We shopped for their favorite foods and bought a few decorative items to make their temporary bedrooms look more like children's rooms. When we got back to the beach house, Brian put things away while I worked on a welcome sign to hang on the front door. I wasn't sure how the kids *really* felt about moving to the beach, but I knew we'd done our part to make it feel like home.

We were exhausted when we fell into bed together after midnight. Brian reached for me and pulled me close.

"I know it feels like the end of something tonight, but I hope you're as excited as I am to bring the kids into our life. I trust you can see this as a beginning for all of us."

"It's going to be great," I said, hoping my response didn't

sound as uncertain as I felt. I *was* apprehensive about how the children would impact our relationship. There was a possibility we'd become a family, or I could be returning to Washington, Iowa, by the end of the year with a shattered heart and still no direction for my life.

Brian sensed my insecurities and made sure I knew how much he loved me before we fell asleep. I was happy he would be by my side as we headed in a new direction together.

Chapter Nineteen
August

Brian took part of the afternoon off, and we spent time at the beach before we had to make final preparations for Jenna and Jack's arrival. Neither of us said much as we let the quiet embrace us for the last time.

After our return to the house, Brian got burgers ready for the grill while I cut up a watermelon. Betsy would stay the night and help get everything set before she took off to reclaim her life. I imagined she had mixed feelings about leaving the kids with us, but I was sure getting back to the normalcy of her old life was something she was looking forward to.

As we finished the dinner preparations, we heard the dull thud of the van door, followed by the cries of excited children bursting through the front door and into our lives.

"Daddy—we're here!" Jack yelled into the big house.

We met them at the door, and after hugs and kisses and a discussion about how much Jenna had grown in five days, everyone landed in the kitchen.

"They're so happy to be here," Betsy said, smiling.

"How does Aunt Betsy feel about it?" Brian asked.

"She feels ready—but happy to have been able to serve!"

She put her arm around Brian's shoulders and hugged him.

"I'll be forever grateful to you," he said, kissing her cheek.

"Oh, you're going to owe me for a long time," she joked. "Seriously, Brian. I loved doing it. I'm going to miss them so much."

I could see the love between brother and sister as they shared the moment. Brian was ready to move on with his life too, and his appreciation was for more than caring for Jenna and Jack.

The children came back from checking out their bedrooms and seemed happy to see the changes Brian and I had made. They had also found their swimsuits and were ready to hit the beach.

"Gus wants to see the ocean again," Jack declared, placing his little friend on the counter.

"I thought we'd get the rest of your bags out of the car and try to get you unpacked before we had dinner. We'll go out to the ocean tomorrow."

"Can't Meg take us to the beach while you and Aunt Betsy unload? Please, Dad? We've been waiting all week," Jenna pleaded.

I looked at Brian and could see he was considering her request. It would be easier to empty the van if the kids weren't underfoot.

"I'm happy to take them if it's okay with the two of you," I offered.

"Okay—but when we say it's time to come back to the house and eat dinner, I don't want any whining," Brian warned the kids.

Jenna and Jack agreed and accompanied me next door to get my swimming suit and towel, and the three of us went out to the beach. I helped them get their sand toys from under the walkway and put my chair in a good place to watch them. The sea breeze made me happy that I'd drawn lifeguard duty and didn't have to unload the van.

A half-hour later, Brian came out to the beach carrying a bottle of wine and an insulated beach bag with plastic wine glasses, ice, and lemonade pouches.

"I had to come out and see how my three favorite people were doing," he said. "Plus, I thought you might enjoy a glass of wine while we do all the hard work!"

"Thank you," I said, taking a wine glass from him. He poured the crisp, clear wine for me and put the remainder of the bottle back in the cooler.

"When we're done, we'll come and share the rest of the bottle with you. This shouldn't take long." I watched Brian go back toward the house. I'd never been with anyone as caring as he was.

With the van unpacked and the rest of the bottle of Chardonnay consumed, we all sat down to dinner. The conversation was lively as always, and the food was delicious.

After everything was cleaned up, I excused myself for the evening. No one wanted me to leave, but it was the right thing to do. I hugged everyone goodbye, and Brian walked me back to the cottage.

"Thanks for everything," he said. "The kids like you so much. I'm happy to have them back in my life every day. Now that I have you and them here, I feel like I can relax and enjoy things again. You've given me a reason to dream about the future, and I'm so grateful."

As we stood inside my front door, he pulled me to him and kissed me.

"Want to run upstairs for a quickie?" he asked, giving me a sly wink.

"I think you'd have two disappointed kiddos who'd be upset if their daddy didn't come right back," I replied.

"I know," he said, feigning defeat. "Let's do something fun tomorrow. Betsy will leave after breakfast, so it will just be the four of us."

I was already anticipating the day we'd have together.

***

We packed a picnic and drove to Blue Spring State Park. A winter haven for West Indian manatees, it was a popular swimming and picnicking site in the summer. The ocean was always beautiful to look at, but in the August heat, swimming in the warm water wasn't always refreshing. The state park offered fresh spring water at a constant seventy-three degrees. Although it felt cold when we first got in, it was enjoyable to spend the afternoon in the cool, clear water.

We found a picnic table under the shade of a tree and unloaded ham sandwiches, chips, cookies, and fruit. After swimming, we were all hungry and ate everything Brian had jammed into the red and white Igloo cooler.

"Who wants to go canoeing?" Brian asked. Everyone's hand went into the air enthusiastically, including my own.

"Can Gus go too, Daddy?" Jack asked.

"Buddy, I don't think taking Gus is a good idea. Do you remember when we lost him at The Pizza Pit? Let's not take that chance again," Brian said.

"Plus, they don't have a life jacket small enough to fit him," I added.

"Meg, dogs know how to swim, so they don't need life jackets," Jack countered back, unmoved by my knowledge of canine safety requirements.

"The answer is no, Jack," Brian said, standing firm in his decision.

"I want Gus to go with us on the canoe!" Jack cried loudly as he stomped his foot, and others began to glance over at us. I didn't see the problem with including the small passenger but could tell Brian was choosing to make a point, and I planned to support him.

"Jack, don't make me get angry with you," Brian said.

It was early afternoon, and the park was crowded with people. I looked over at the line for canoes and saw at least fifteen people waiting.

"Jack needs his nap. Whenever we go out in the afternoon, Aunt Betsy always makes sure we're home by this time so he can sleep for a couple of hours. But he's not going to stop crying. He never does," Jenna said knowingly. She was only eight years old, but she knew things about her brother that Brian may have missed while he was dealing with their lives.

"It's time to go home," Brian said firmly.

I was proud of the stance Brian took, even though I knew he felt terrible about having to take it. We packed our things as Jack continued to cry. Gus sat at the table; unaware he was at the center of a controversy that would end our day early. Once we were back in the van and on the road, Jack fell asleep, and we had a quiet ride back to Daytona Beach.

"You did the right thing," I whispered.

Brian smiled, took a deep breath, and let it out slowly. I selfishly thought of how convenient it was for me to have The Pink Shell to escape to when I needed it. Brian didn't have that luxury as a full-time dad.

Once we were back at the beach and well-rested, we ordered pizza and spent the evening running in and out of the big waves resulting from a late afternoon storm. Finally, everyone was happy again, and we were all exhausted and ready for bed.

"Tomorrow, we need to take it easy and get the kids ready to start daycare. Why don't you come over after you get up, and I'll make breakfast," Brian offered.

Brian had enrolled both children in an extended-care program at the same school where they would go later in August. Getting them started early would allow them to get to know some of their classmates before the beginning of the school year.

Jenna and Jack both seemed excited about the prospect of heading off to daycare. The program had lots of weekly activities and a huge playground, which Jack was thrilled about. I wondered if I should have offered to watch the kids each day at my house and save Brian some money, but it was important he had a plan in place without my help, and we both knew it would be best if they had structure right away.

"What if I made breakfast for all of *you* at my place?"

The look on Brian's face told me he would welcome the opportunity to be taken care of. It had been less than forty-eight hours since the kids had arrived, but our last moments alone seemed like a lifetime ago.

***

"Who wants sausage?" I asked, serving up scrambled eggs to my visitors.

"I do!" Jenna said as she held her plate for me.

It was so enjoyable to be making a meal for Brian and the kids. I thought about other things we could do at the cottage, which would give us another place to spend time and get to know each other.

"Do you think we could make cupcakes to take to daycare tomorrow?" Jenna asked. "It would be a good way to introduce ourselves."

"What if we *bought* treats to take," Brian suggested.

"I don't mind," I said. "We could make them this afternoon if you don't have any other plans." Of course, I didn't want to assume their little family would always include me in their daily activities, but I didn't think they had anything else going on that I didn't know about.

"Are you sure?" Brian asked.

"I want to make blue frosting for them," Jack requested.

We made another trip to the store and spent the afternoon in the relaxed setting of The Pink Shell. We baked chocolate cupcakes and covered them in teal-colored icing, and the kids took turns licking the beaters covered in gooey sweetness. We dropped heaping spoonfuls of batter into muffin tins and sampled our baked goods until we were too full to eat more.

When the day was over, we'd worn the kids out enough that they would go to bed early. Everyone was tired, and I knew getting the two of them off to daycare the following morning would be different from Brian's normal routine. I hoped a good night's sleep would put them in the right mood and make his job more manageable.

I needed to get home and make the phone call I'd been dreading, so I said goodnight and made my way back to the cottage.

***

"Hi, Mom. What are you and Dad doing tonight?" I asked, making small talk before getting to the point of my call.

"Your dad has been doing a puzzle all day and only has part of the border done. Can you believe that?" I heard my dad laugh in the background as he made excuses about the difficulty of his project.

"Can you put me on speaker phone so I can talk to both of you about something?"

"Sure—did you get a job?" Mom asked as she fumbled with the phone. "Howard, get over here. Meggie needs to tell us about her new job."

"Mom, it's not a new job."

"Well, what is it? Are you moving back home? Howard, get over here. Megan's moving back to Iowa!"

"Mom—it isn't any of those things."

"Hi, Peanut," Dad said. "Is your car still running okay?"

Dad always seemed to start a conversation asking about the car.

"It's fine. But listen, I need to talk with you about something important," I said.

"Howard, *shush*. Meg has something to tell us. Go ahead, honey."

"I've met someone in Florida, and I've decided to remain here for a few more months and explore where the relationship might go." I knew my parents didn't have any say in my decision, but I felt like a scared teenager waiting for her parent's approval about doing something questionable.

"What do you mean you've *met* someone?" Mom asked.

"I'm dating my neighbor, and we've fallen in love." I

declared firmly.

"I thought your neighbor's name was Sophie," Dad said.

"She has two neighbors, Howard. She's certainly not dating Sophie . . . *are you?*" she asked.

"Oh, Mom. For God's sake, no. I'm talking about Brian Barts. I've mentioned him to you before. I spent the Fourth of July weekend with him and his family."

"That must have been quite a weekend," Dad chuckled.

"How are you going to afford to live in Florida longer? Megan, this is getting ridiculous. I know the divorce was rough on you, but it's time to get on track now. You need to get home and back to work," Mom demanded.

"No, Mom. I'm going to stay at Sophie's because she will be gone for a few months. I'm going to house sit for her, so it won't cost me anything."

"Honey, this isn't a good idea. This will never work out," Mom said.

"I'm not asking for your input. I'm just letting you know what's going on in my life. I'd love to have your blessing, but regardless of whether you give it, I'm staying in Florida with Brian for the time being."

"I'm not going to listen to any more of this. Howard, you can finish up—I need a scotch."

There were muffled sounds as Mom switched the phone off speaker, and my father took over the call.

"Meg, let your mom cool off a little. She loves you so much, but she worries about you. We both want what's best for you," he said.

"You need to trust me. Brian is the most wonderful man I've ever met—besides you. I need more time to see if he's the one for me. It's all happening quickly, but is there really a time

189

frame for how long it takes to fall in love? Didn't you and Mom meet and marry in less than a year?"

"Let me work on her, okay?"

I could hear Mom come back into the room and say something to my dad. He covered the phone with his hand, and they spoke in hushed tones for a minute.

"Meg?" Dad was back on the phone again. "Your mom and I are coming to see you. We'll be there for Labor Day weekend."

The soft nest of romance Brian and I had built for ourselves had been invaded by the outside world. I crawled into my lonely bed, overwhelmed by the conversation I'd had with my parents. My mind was racing about what was coming our way as I fell into a restless sleep.

Chapter Twenty
August

I was up before 7:00 a.m., watching out the kitchen window to make sure Brian and the kids left on time. I'd dressed early instead of lounging in my robe, so I was ready in case he needed me to come over. I was already beginning to sense responsibility for Brian's family and loved how it made me feel. I knew it was important to recognize my place and planned to stay out of sight unless summoned.

I got one sweet text to let me know Brian was thinking about me, but I didn't get a call from him until after he dropped the kids off.

"How did bedtime go last night?" I asked when his call came through.

"Terrible. Jack missed Betsy, and we had to call her to get him to calm down. Jenna tried to help and started crying when I told her to get back into bed. She saw I was struggling, and I should have been better at trying to accept the help she wanted to give me. I have a lot to learn as a dad."

"And you have plenty of time to learn it. Don't be so hard on yourself. This is a big change for everyone, and it was only the third night."

"I wish you were staying with me so I could hold you in my arms and not feel so alone at night."

"I'm right next door. If you need me, you can call me," I said.

"I'm so happy to have you close. It will be a challenge for me to fall asleep knowing you're only a few feet away from me. We're separated by cement blocks, plywood, and sea air, but it might as well be a hundred miles," he said.

His assessment of our situation was correct and being apart every night would be difficult. But it was the right thing to do for the kids, and my gut told me it would be the best thing for him as a dad. I needed Brian to want me to be with him for the right reasons, and I wasn't sure he could make that decision unless he had a chance to make it on his own first.

"And what about this morning? Did everyone cooperate?"

"Yes, it went fine. They were so excited to get there. The staff was friendly, and the other kids were thrilled there were cupcakes to share at snack time."

"I'm so proud of you. You're going to be terrific at this," I encouraged.

"I sure hope so. I've got to get busy. I can't get home early if I don't get some work done. I'll see you tonight!"

I put the phone down and poured myself another cup of coffee. I was looking forward to a day of doing whatever I wanted.

My phone rang, and I answered Brian's call again.

"I love you. Don't ever forget that!" he said.

"I love you too," I said with no intention of forgetting how he felt about me.

Jenna and Jack were on my mind all day. I wanted them to love their new school so it would make things easier for Brian. I feared if there was even a single sign indicating they were unhappy, he would blame himself and feel like he'd made a mistake.

I enjoyed a warm day at the beach by catching a few rays and reading a book. I took in the beauty of my surroundings and was grateful for how things were turning out.

Brian's family would spend Labor Day weekend at the beach, too, and my mind wandered to what it would be like to have our families together to celebrate the holiday. My mother could be challenging sometimes, and I wanted her to love the Barts family as much as I did.

Brian and the kids would be home around 5:30 p.m., so I had time to run to the grocery store and still beat them home. I'd been paying attention to the children's favorite snacks and wanted to make sure I had a few of those items at my house when they visited.

I studied the aisles of fruit snacks and granola bars. I'd never realized how many different kinds there were. I chose the ones I thought would be best and hoped they would think it was fun to have other things to try when they came over if I'd made a mistake. The afternoon was getting away from me, and I hurried through the store, hoping they wouldn't beat me home.

It seemed like people were stocking up for the apocalypse by the amount of food in their carts. No lines were open for ten or fewer items, and the others were packed with customers.

I had no choice but to wait it out, even if it would put me behind schedule.

**

I glanced at the clock in my car as I left the grocery store parking lot and knew I'd be late. As I got closer to the cottage, I could see Brian's truck was already parked in front of his house. Jenna and Jack were bouncing a ball in front of the garage door, and I saw Brian talking to someone in my front yard.

I pulled into the driveway and saw an unfamiliar car parked on the side. I looked over again at Brian and the person he was talking to. The air went out of my lungs when I realized that the man Brian was speaking to was my ex-husband.

I got out of the car and walked toward the two of them, but Brian didn't make eye contact with me. I was caught off-guard, trying to make sense of what was unfolding.

"Our first day at daycare was awesome!" Jenna said as she ran over to me.

"My teacher said blue is her favorite color, and she'd never had a cupcake with that color of frosting before!" Jack added, coming up to me behind his sister.

They both started telling me about the friends they'd met and how cool the playground was, oblivious to what was happening. I hugged them but didn't hear most of the details about their day. There was something wrong with the scene in front of me, but I couldn't figure out what it was.

"What are you doing here?" I directed my question to Jason with Brian and the kids looking on.

"I need to talk to you. Apparently, your neighbor thinks he's in charge of your visitors," Jason quipped.

"How did you know where I was staying?"

"You put your address in the guest book at Dad's funeral. Remember, my mother asked you to list it for the thank you note?"

"Well, I'll leave the two of you to talk," Brian said coldly. He began to corral the kids and get them back to his house.

"*Brian*—don't go," I said. He'd already turned his back on me and was walking toward his front door. He was angry, but I couldn't figure out why he'd be mad at me because Jason had shown up unexpectedly.

"Go in the house, and I'll be right back," I directed to Jason, giving him my keys as I tried to catch up with Brian.

"Brian—wait!" I called after him again. Brian hesitated by the door, and the kids went inside. "What's going on?" I begged for an answer. It scared me to feel so separated from him with no explanation.

"You tell *me*," he retorted.

"What do you mean? I come home, and my ex-husband is talking to you in the front yard. Obviously, something has happened between you to make you so upset, but I have no idea what it is," I said.

"The problem is that something happened between the two of *you*, and you forgot to tell *me* about it. I should've known this was too good to be true. I wish you'd just been honest with me. I would've understood."

I was dumbfounded and unable to comprehend what Brian was saying. His coldness left me shaking. He was already speaking of us in the past tense.

"Told you what?" I wondered what Jason had said to him.

195

"That the two of you spent the night together when you were in Michigan."

I swallowed hard and fought back tears. "It's not what you think," I whispered, trying to process the situation in my head.

"So, it's true?" he asked, looking at me for the first time since I'd arrived home. The blue eyes that always shared love with me were replaced with sadness and doubt.

"Please hear me out. Let me get rid of him, and I'll explain everything. We didn't sleep together . . . well, we slept together in the same room—but we didn't have sex. I know this looks terrible, but I can explain everything. Okay? Please?" I heard myself pleading with him in a way I'd never done with a man.

I saw the expression on his face change. He wanted to believe me. "Wait until nine before you come over. I want the kids to be in bed before we get into this."

Brian went inside and pulled the door shut. I stood suspended between my two lives and turned back to The Pink Shell to deal with my ex-husband.

***

"What do you think you're doing?" I yelled, plowing through the front door. Jason was sitting on my couch with his feet on the coffee table as if he belonged there.

"I'm here to finish the conversation we started when you came home," he said confidently.

"Muskegon isn't my home anymore. I'm trying to put my life back together, and you've shown up to make sure you can put a wrench in those plans too."

"You're seeing that guy, aren't you?" The shocked look on his face let me know he didn't think I had it in me.

196

"What does it matter to you? We're not married anymore. You have no right to turn up here and make a mess of the life I'm trying to create!" I was crying and not comfortable feeling so out of control. "Why did you tell him we slept together?"

I flopped beside Jason on the couch and buried my head in my hands. I couldn't stop thinking about what I'd say later to Brian to convince him he should trust me.

"We did sleep together. And after I had you close to me all night; I knew we were meant to be together. We can undo this mistake and go home and start over again. We're not the only couple to hit a rough patch in our marriage. We can get through this and be better than we were before."

"Jason, we're divorced. There's no marriage to salvage. I've moved on with my life. Or should I say, I'm *trying* to move on with it. The trip to Muskegon gave me the closure I needed. Please don't take that away from me."

"What about *my* closure? When I woke up that morning and realized you were gone, I was heartbroken. There was so much more I wanted to say to you. I saw my shoes sitting by the bed and the blanket covering me . . . and when I went into the bathroom and saw you'd left a bottle of Tylenol by the sink for my hangover—I knew you still loved me."

I wondered what had happened to my bottle of headache medicine.

"If I left anything in the bathroom, it was because I was in a hurry to get out of there without waking you. It wasn't a cryptic message of love left to encourage you to visit me in Florida."

"You always took such good care of me," he said softly, reaching for my hand.

"I wish I could say the same about you." I pushed his hand away and moved to the chair.

"Let's not do this," he said as if his declaration would clear the air and allow us to move in whatever direction *he* decided was right for us. "I'm sorry about coming to your hotel that night, but I don't regret what I said. I *was* drunk, but it only helped me get rid of my inhibitions. I'm sorry about everything. We grew apart, and I'm willing to take most of the blame for it. There's nothing I can do about it now—except beg you to come back to me."

"I've moved on, Jason. You need to do the same."

"Do you honestly think you're going to have a future with a guy you met on vacation? That's called a summer fling, not a relationship."

"His name is Brian. And I've never been treated better in my life. I love him, and we're going to make a life together if I can explain to him why you and I spent the night together in Muskegon. Was it necessary for you to mess this up for me by mentioning that little detail without further explanation?"

"I didn't realize you two were dating when I said it. He was questioning me about why I was here, and I blurted out that you'd left the hotel room before I woke up, and I needed to see you to clear a few things up."

"Have we cleared everything up?" I asked sarcastically.

"No, we haven't cleared anything up. I can't believe you're seeing someone already. I wish I'd never made that dating profile. It was stupid and cost me our marriage. I haven't even been out on a date since we split."

"It wasn't *just* the profile, Jason."

"Will you even consider trying to put our lives back together? I want you to find happiness, but I want to be the one to give it to you."

"I'm afraid you missed your opportunity," I said quietly.

We sat silently for a few minutes—neither knowing how to proceed. There was nothing left for us, and the finality of that realization was apparent to me, even if Jason was still trying to figure it out.

"You should've called. I could have saved you the flight out here . . . There was a time when this kind of grand gesture was all I wanted from you. But that time has passed."

"I'm sorry. It's all I have to offer," he said.

"It isn't enough," I said firmly. "I think you should go."

We walked toward the door, knowing it was time to say goodbye. I was surprised to feel such sadness that I'd probably never see him again. We may not have been able to make our marriage work, but we'd spent many years together trying.

"I'm staying at the Hard Rock. If you change your mind, I'm here until tomorrow. I'm not going to book my flight until the morning—just in case."

"Jason, I'm not going to call you."

With tears filling our eyes, he pulled me close and held me.

"I'm always going to love you," he whispered, and then he walked out of my life for good.

I went upstairs and flopped on the bed, weighed down by the heavy burdens of my heart. I replayed everything that had happened with Brian *and* Jason and remembered a time in my life when drama and uncertainty were reserved for other people.

I took a ragged breath, knowing I had two hours to figure out what to say to Brian, explaining why I'd chosen to omit important details about my trip to Michigan. If I hadn't blown it completely, my future was waiting next door.

Chapter Twenty-One
August

I arrived at Brian's at precisely 9 p.m.—not wanting to be late and have Brian think I was avoiding our conversation. When he opened the door, he seemed more approachable than he'd been earlier.

"Hi," I said quietly.

"Hi."

At least we had our greetings out of the way.

We walked into the kitchen, and Brian asked me if I wanted something to drink.

"No. I don't know if you'll want me to stay that long," I replied as tears began to flow.

Brian pulled me to him, and I cried into his shoulder until his T-shirt was wet with tears. When I pulled away, I needed to excuse myself to go to the bathroom and freshen up. When I returned, Brian had moved to the great room and had placed a box of tissues from the kitchen on the coffee table. He smiled and motioned for me to sit next to him.

"Tell me everything. I want to hear what you have to say."

"I'm so sorry. I didn't mean to hurt you by not telling you what happened with Jason. And I feel terrible for shifting the attention from Jenna and Jack when they had such an important day today," I said.

"They had no idea anything was wrong. I told them you had an unexpected guest and left it at that. We ordered take-out and played games until bedtime, and everything was fine," he said.

I was grateful they'd had a good day and was happy our misunderstanding hadn't ruined their evening.

I told Brian every detail of Jason's surprise visit to my hotel room at the Baymont Inn. I explained that I'd slipped out early the following morning, arriving at the airport hours before necessary to avoid spending more time with him. I told him about the discussion I'd had with my ex at the cottage and how Jason had begged me to reconsider and take him back.

"Do you want to be with him?" Brian asked. "Because if you do, I will understand. The two of you have a lot of history, and I'll support you in whatever you need to do to be happy."

"And that's exactly why I love you so much. I could never be happy with Jason, especially since I've met you. I want *you*, Brian. I'm so sorry this situation has made you doubt me. It's the last thing I intended. He was too drunk to drive home, and I didn't know what else to do but let him sleep it off in the extra bed. I could have gone to the front desk and booked another room, but I was leaving in a few hours, and at the time, it didn't seem like a big deal."

"I believe you when you say nothing sexual happened between you. He's laid his cards on the table and told you he wants you back. I see you're here and don't want to be with him. I'm not worried about if you want to have a life with him or not."

"What is it then?" I asked.

"The problem is that you didn't tell me in the first place," he continued. "I feel like we've grown close enough that you should've told me about this when you returned. The fact you left it out makes me question how you feel about *me* and how much you trust me."

"This was about Jason and our relationship—the *end* of our relationship, and I didn't feel it was something you needed to know. I'm sure there are many things about you and Jayne you'll never share with me."

"You're right," he interrupted, "but the difference is that your night with Jason happened while we were together. I want someone in my life who doesn't have any secrets from me. If you don't feel the same way, we need to move on and realize we're not meant for each other."

I'd lived many years in a marriage where I kept things hidden inside to keep the peace and salvage some of my dreams. I hadn't shared my online searches for graduate school or my interest in taking a pottery class. I'd spent a few evenings planning a European vacation as a surprise anniversary gift, but the following day when Jason said something hurtful, I'd trashed the file on my desktop and forgotten about the trip. Deception by omission was something I'd become accustomed to in a stagnant marriage. It was a survival technique, and I'd become used to sharing only what I felt was necessary to avoid conflict.

"You're right, Brian. I'm so sorry. I didn't mean to hurt you. I *do* want a relationship based on trust and honesty, and I was wrong to keep this from you."

"Daddy?" I heard Jack's voice from upstairs.

"I should go." I hoped Brian would beg me to stay, but he didn't.

"It would probably be best. We can talk tomorrow," he said.

He hugged me quickly and asked me to see myself out so he could go to Jack. I slipped out the front door and back to the cottage anticipating a long, sleepless night.

***

The beach house was dim, with only the stove light illuminating the first floor. The conversations of the evening rattled in my head, and I didn't turn on any other lights and allow myself such luxury when I felt so dark inside.

I opened the glass door to the porch and slipped into the night air. The waves were pounding on the shore, and my head felt the same way. I needed aspirin and a good night's sleep— but I didn't feel like getting either.

I should have told Brian *everything* about my trip when I got back. The exclusion of that part of my time away had been a mistake. The damage was done, but it hadn't been a calculated move on my part to deceive him. I'd give him the space he needed to think about things and pray it would all work out.

I sat in a wicker chair, feeling empty and scared. Looking out at the ocean, replaying the day's events, I knew there was nothing left for me to do but try to get some rest. Maybe a new day would shed needed light on the subject.

I climbed the stairs to the loft and got ready for bed. Glancing at my phone before pulling the covers up, I saw a text from Brian.

I love you.

Would those three words be enough to solve the problem between us?

I texted back the only thing I had to offer.

You're everything to me. I'm sorry.

***

I saw Brian's truck pull out of the driveway when he took the kids to school. I felt completely separated from them, and I couldn't allow myself to consider a life without the three of them in it.

Morning brought fresh perspective and insight from my point of view about what else could be going on. If Brian loved me as much as he said, he should be able to understand and give me another chance. Maybe it was *him* who was getting cold feet and looking for a way out.

A hot shower made me feel better. My hair was still wet when I came downstairs and poured a cup of coffee. I heard a knock at the door and could see the top of Brian's head in the window. My stomach turned over in anticipation of what was going to happen. The open door revealed a handsome Brian holding a bag from a local bakery.

"The boss told me I could come in late. I was hoping we could have breakfast together unless you're expecting someone else from your past to stop by unannounced."

He was smiling, so I knew he was trying to be funny.

"I think my high school boyfriend is dropping by later, but I could fit you in for a little while," I replied, falling back into a pattern of familiarity with him.

We walked into the kitchen, and Brian put the bag of sweets

on the table. As I reached for another mug, he pulled me toward him and kissed me.

"I'm sorry I was so tough on you," he said, giving me a tight hug. "We can get through this. I know you weren't trying to hurt me. I was so shocked—I couldn't think straight last night."

"I'll never keep anything from you again," I promised.

"Let's try to put this behind us. I love you so much. Let's not spend another hour apart."

It didn't take long to return to the place we'd been before my ex-husband tried to hijack our happiness.

Being the boss had its perks, and Brian took the entire morning off. We spent it together in the bedroom loft of The Pink Shell. The time spent reconnecting was almost worth the misery of the previous twenty-four hours, but I hoped I'd never have to spend another night imagining a life without Brian and the kids.

Chapter Twenty-Two
August

Those first few weeks together flew by. Jack became more comfortable with Brian being in charge and didn't need to call and talk to his Aunt Betsy as much. Jenna was a sweet little girl, and we spent hours together painting our nails and cooking in the kitchen of one of our houses. She loved to help with dinner at night and liked to go grocery shopping with me when possible.

Brian and I adjusted to our new life together, and the situation with Jason was never brought up again. By the time school started at the end of August, we were on our way to becoming a family. The kids were thriving in Brian's care, and he gained more confidence with each passing day.

I talked with Sophie each week, assuring her the eclectic house she called home was being taken care of. I checked it daily and was prepared to move in before Labor Day weekend, so my parents could stay at The Pink Shell when they visited. It would give us the separation we needed to survive the long weekend together. The only downside was that I wouldn't get to spend those last few nights at the summer cottage I adored.

Sophie continued to be vague on the scope of Audrey's illness, citing superstitious reasons for keeping me in the dark. But she was always happy to hear about the details of my love life.

During one conversation, there was music and talking in the background as if Sophie was at a party. I asked where she was, and Sophie assured me the two of them were at home.

I thought I heard someone say, *"Can you make me another drink?"* I asked Sophie if Audrey was well enough to have cocktails, and she said, "No, no—I have to go now. The poor thing said she can't make it to the *sink*. It must be time for her medication. Toodles, darling!"

Sophie always encouraged me to follow my heart at the end of our phone calls. With her support and the love of someone like Brian, I was beginning to think all my dreams could come true. I continued to worry about Audrey but felt deeply grateful for the time her illness allowed me to spend with Brian and the kids.

***

A note came home with Jenna and Jack announcing a family celebration to kick off the school year. It was scheduled for lunchtime, and Brian couldn't get away from work on the day it was to take place, and he asked me if I would be willing to go.

Jack was ecstatic about the prospect of having me at his school and asked if Gus could come along too. I promised to bring him—but added he'd have to stay in the car.

Jenna was quiet, and I sensed she didn't want me to go to

the picnic. I was sure her grandparents would make the trip from St. Augustine to represent the family if that was the case. When Brian and Jack went upstairs to get ready for bed, I took the opportunity to ask her how she felt.

"Hey, Jenna? I couldn't help but notice you were quiet when we talked about the picnic. Is everything okay?"

"Sure," she said. She didn't look up from the puzzle she was working on.

"If you would rather I didn't come with you—I would understand."

"It's not that. I want you to come. It's just that . . ."

"What is it, honey? You can tell me."

"I don't want you to tell the other kids you're not my mom," she said.

I hadn't expected that answer.

"I want to be like everyone else," she continued. "At home, they all know my mom died, so they always feel sorry for me. I don't want the kids to know that about me here."

"Well, how do you think we can keep it from everyone?"

"Could we pretend you're my mom?"

"I'm not sure we should fib about something so important. But what if we do everything we can to keep the attention away from the fact I'm not your mom? I can just tell them 'Hi, I'm Meg.'"

"Do you think it would work?" Jenna asked.

"I think it might."

***

Families were waiting for their kids to be dismissed from

209

classes, and it didn't take long for me to find Jenna and Jack in the school cafeteria.

We got in line and waited to be served. The smell reminded me of my childhood. So many things had changed in the more modern school setting, but they hadn't discovered a way to make the aroma of hot lunch any more appealing in thirty years.

We stood in line next to one of Jenna's new friends and her family. The little girl's mother introduced herself.

"Hi, I'm Adrian—Henley's mom," she said, extending her hand to me.

"I'm Meg," I said, catching a slight grin on Jenna's face. "I'm so happy Jenna and Henley have become friends."

"Yes, it would be great to get the girls together sometime," Adrian added.

No one needed official identification or questioned the biology between the three of us. It was a pleasant outing and made me feel like all of us, given some time, could figure out ways to get around our insecurities about who we were to each other.

The children sang a song before we said goodbye, and I promised both kids we'd have a cookout and spend the evening on the beach. They went back to class feeling like normal kids, and I left believing I could be a pretty good stepmom if I had the chance.

I called Brian on the way home and planned to leave a message, letting him know it had gone well. I was surprised when he answered instead of letting it go to voicemail.

"I figured you would be busy at the job site and unable to pick up. I'm calling to tell you how well the picnic went."

"That's why I have my phone with me. I couldn't wait until

tonight to hear about it," he said.

I filled Brian in on the details, including my promise for a cookout and beach time. He was thrilled things had gone well and said he'd stop by the grocery store on his way home and get something for the kids and the biggest steaks he could find for us. It sounded like a wonderful night to me.

***

It had been a good day, and Brian seasoned the meat while the kids helped me make a salad. I sipped a glass of wine and felt grateful for another day at the beach with such special people. There was laughter and fun, and it felt like we belonged together.

Brian went outside to start the grill. The kids were sitting at the kitchen island when Jack asked, "Jenna, is Meg the mommy who's going to take us to the park?"

"Jack, don't say that. You're not supposed to say that," Jenna said. I could tell she was embarrassed by his question.

Her scolding brought Jack to tears. "Am I in trouble?"

Brian returned to the kitchen just in time to be confused at what had transpired since he'd gone outside. Jack was crying, and Jenna ran off to her room. I was as puzzled about what had occurred as Brian was.

"What happened?" he asked.

"Jenna got upset over something Jack said."

"Jack, what did you say?" Brian questioned.

"I asked Jenna if Meg was the mommy who would take us to the park. I just *wondered* . . ."

"Why don't you run upstairs and play in your room for a little while. I'll call you when dinner is ready. Do you want one or two hot dogs?" Brian asked.

"I want two!" Jack said, grabbing Gus by the ears as he ran upstairs.

Brian started some busy work in the kitchen, not making eye contact with me. When he finally came over, he reached for me and pulled me toward him.

"What is it?" I asked.

"Things are going so well, but we need to remember that this is hard for the kids."

"Of course," I agreed. "What did Jack mean, and why did Jenna get so upset? You need to tell me what's going on."

"This is a good thing. Jack sees you as the important person you are in my life. Even at his age, he knows there's something serious between us."

"What are you talking about?"

"When Jayne died, I wanted to make sure the kids knew she would want us to move on with our lives eventually. I talked with them about what that might look like in the future and tried to help them understand we wouldn't be so sad forever."

"That must have been hard."

"It was," he continued. "I think tonight is my cue to talk with both of them about us and let them know how I feel about you."

"What did Jack mean about the park?" I asked.

"Over the months, I've answered the kids' questions about what might happen. And they've asked about me finding a wife, and I've assured them, if it ever happened, she would love them like their mommy did. It might seem strange to think of me talking to them about a subject like that, but I wanted to keep the lines of communication open about it—hoping someday it would be a reality for us. I told them the new mommy would love and care for them as Jayne did."

We both had tears in our eyes.

"Jack had asked me, *"Will she take us to the park like Mommy did?"* and I assured him she would."

"I'd love to take them to the park," I said, holding Brian close again.

Neither of us said anything else as we let quiet contemplation fill the space too significant for words.

Chapter Twenty-Three
September

My parents rented a car at the airport in Sanford and drove the short distance to Daytona Beach. I was excited to see them, even though I was apprehensive about what the weekend would bring.

Brian's family wouldn't arrive until Saturday, so we had Friday evening alone with my parents. Brian hired one of the teachers from daycare to watch the kids, and we planned to go out for an adult-only dinner.

"Mom and Dad—I'd like you to meet Brian and his children, Jenna and Jack," I said.

"Nice to meet you," Dad said, shaking Brian's hand and moving on to the kids.

"And you must be Virginia," Brian said as he moved toward my mom and gave her a hug she wasn't expecting.

"Please call me Ginny. It's nice to meet you, Brian," she said as she began to let her guard down. My mother was a former pageant queen and runner-up for Miss Iowa from back in the seventies. She was poised and polite no matter what her true feelings were on any subject. An outsider would never have imagined, from the way she greeted him, she was on a fact-finding mission and very leery of Brian Barts.

Mom brought small gifts for both children, and they tore at the tissue-filled bags holding pool toys and orange and purple swim goggles.

"Thank you, Mrs. Royce," Jenna said, followed by the same response from Jack.

"Megan told us you have a swimming pool at your house, and I thought you could always use toys for the water," Mom added. It was a nice gesture, and I was grateful she'd thought of it.

Once the introductions were made and we visited for a little while, Brian and the kids went back next door. We promised to be ready to go by 5:00 p.m., knowing that beach restaurants fill up quickly on a Friday night.

Having already moved most of my things next door to Sophie's, I helped my parents get settled at the cottage. Once they were unpacked and I'd shown them everything they might need for the weekend, we sat down to talk. I missed them more than I'd realized and was happy to have them with me for a few days.

"Tell us more about Brian and the kids," my dad inquired, sipping a gin and tonic.

I told them that Brian was working at the beach, and his job was taking longer than anticipated. His job would keep him and the kids in Daytona for a few more months. I told them how well Brian treated me, and that I was happy to have the opportunity to spend more time with all of them.

"Meg, Brian is a lovely man. But you've only been divorced a short time. Don't you feel like you should date around a little? I don't want you to settle for the first man who comes along . . . just because you're *lonely*."

"I know I need to find a job and figure out what to do with my life. But right now, I'm trying to find out if I might be able to do that here in Florida." I wasn't going to let her make me feel bad about my choices.

"What are Sophie's plans for returning?" Dad asked. I could feel him moving into the role of peacemaker. This had been his task since I was a teenager. Mom always said what she felt, which often contradicted my viewpoint. He was used to running interference and trying to make everything right between us. There was tension in the air, and he was going to try to eliminate it.

"I'm not sure. Her sister is receiving some sort of treatments in Atlanta, and I think she'll be gone until at least the first of the year. She's asked me to stay on until then, and I've agreed."

"Well, that should give you plenty of time to decide if you have a future with this man," my dad added, trying to get Mom on the same page. "He seems nice, and he's obviously successful."

"Meg, don't get me wrong. I want you to find love again. But it's just as easy to find someone in the Midwest as hundreds of miles away. So why put yourself in this position? Don't you want to be closer to home? We've spent years seeing you twice a year, and I was hoping after things didn't work out with Jason—we'd be able to have you close by again."

"I can understand the way you feel. But I need to be happy. I've found a great guy who loves me, and I want to be with him if it's at all possible. I need you to support us and give this a chance. *Please* . . ." Mom's opinion of my relationship with Brian had a lot to do with location, and she didn't seem hesitant to admit it.

"Of course, we'll support you. We're here to have a fun weekend and get to know Brian and his family. I only want the best for you and don't want to see you hurt again," she said.

"I know, Mom." I moved in to give her a hug. Brian would have to work his charm and win the two of them over if this was going to work. I had a feeling he'd be able to rise to the occasion.

***

"I hope the music isn't too loud for your parents," Brian whispered as we took our seats.

We were ushered to a high-top table outside one of our favorite beachside restaurants. The view of the ocean and the live bands were always fantastic. It was hot, but the ocean breeze blew across the deck, making it comfortable.

There was a trio playing hits from James Taylor and Elton John in the corner, and the vibe was mellow. It was already getting crowded, and I was glad we'd come early.

We ordered drinks and appetizers, and Brian and my dad were hitting it off as they bantered back and forth about baseball and fishing. Mom was more reserved, and I hoped she was just taking it all in. If she wanted what was best for me—she would accept Brian and hold true to her word to support us.

"I'm sure Meg has told you I'm working on a condominium project here in Daytona but will eventually be returning to St. Augustine. That's my home and where I'm raising my kids," he offered as the conversation moved to include all of us. "As you probably know, I'm a widower, and the kids and I have been through a lot over the past months. Meeting Meg has been a wonderful surprise, and I want you to know how much she means to me."

I could see my parents were impressed with his sincerity. As he talked, Brian was always connected to me. He either had his hand on my leg, or his arm was brushing against mine. I hoped my parents could see the natural way we fit together. I couldn't remember a time in my marriage to Jason when he'd shown physical affection for me in front of my family.

As the evening progressed, we ate oysters and fried fish. Mom had a couple strawberry daiquiris, which made her more relaxed. I hoped a tipsy Mom wasn't a confrontational Mom and prayed Brian would be able to handle the grilling I feared he would get.

"So, what's your end game in this thing, Brian," Mom asked.

Confrontational Mom made her entrance.

"Do you mean where do I hope things go with Meg?" Brian was calm, and I could tell he wasn't going to let her put him on the defensive. "I'd like to make a life with your daughter—if she'll have me," he said, declaring his intentions without flinching.

"Ginny, let's not put the poor boy on the spot," Dad pleaded.

"We only have the weekend, and I'm not leaving here without knowing what's going on," Mom stated.

"If we were talking about Jenna, I'd be asking the same questions," Brian said. "I want you to know how much I love your daughter. If she decides she wants to stay in Florida with me, you'll never have to worry about her happiness again."

The look on my parents' faces told me they were captivated

by Brian and how he spoke of his feelings for me. His confidence in the life he could give me put me at ease too.

At the end of our meal, Brian picked up the tab, explaining that he wanted to treat all of us. He told my parents that they'd made the trip out to visit at tremendous expense, and he wanted to return the favor by paying for dinner. They allowed him to do it, and their body language told me the gesture was appreciated.

We were home by 8:30 p.m., and my parents said they were tired and wanted to go to bed. After our goodbyes, Brian and I returned to Sophie's place for a debriefing session.

"I'm so glad that's over," I sighed.

"It wasn't that bad. They had questions that needed to be answered. Although it felt like we were discussing an arranged marriage because you hardly said a word. You need to let them know this is something *you* want too. You have all the power here."

I'd talked with my parents privately about my feelings for Brian, but I *had* let him take the brunt of their interrogation without chiming in. Why did I always let my mother get the best of me?

"You know," Brian started, "the kids are in bed, and we've hired the sitter until 11:00 p.m. I don't think we should waste our time alone."

Since Jenna and Jack moved to the beach, time alone had been scarce. We'd managed to sneak around a little—even spending an afternoon together while the kids were at school. We were so preoccupied that we'd almost missed their pick-up time and giggled all the way to the school. I was happy to put the kids' needs first, but time to ourselves hadn't been easy or frequent enough.

Listening to Brian declare his love for me to my parents was a sweet aphrodisiac, and we found each other again in the jungle motif of Sophie's wildly decorated bedroom. It was the first time I'd ever made love to someone with a giraffe head staring at me from above the headboard.

Chapter Twenty-Four
September

My parents and I were already enjoying the beach when Brian's parents arrived. Introductions were made, and both families spent time together soaking up the sun. We all enjoyed drinking ice-cold beer and sodas from a cooler Brian and I had put together earlier.

Our parents hit it off right away. Bob and Linda were as amiable as Brian. The fact he came from good stock wouldn't be overlooked by my parents and would help to make them more accepting of my decision to stay in Florida.

The kids loved playing in the water at the beach, but they always worked on building a sandcastle first. It wasn't long before my mom joined them, giving instructions for making a moat around the perimeter of their creation. I loved watching her talk with Jenna and Jack as they walked along the beach looking for seaweed and small shells to add to their design.

Could she accept two more grandchildren into her life? I wanted to think she would love them but worried that distance and disapproval of our relationship might get in the way of opening her heart wide enough to include them.

We all went out on the town again Saturday night. The kids

wanted to go to the pier and ride the roller coaster, so we chose a restaurant close to the boardwalk. I was happy for the opportunity to enjoy the more commercialized Daytona Beach area again and thought my parents would like it too.

There was something fun about being with tourists from all over the world, and it wasn't a place we'd frequented on our many family trips to Florida over the years. We were more likely to stay off the beaten path and avoid the crowds. I liked that I could give my parents a new experience to take as a memory from their trip south.

On Sunday night, we had a cookout to celebrate Jenna's ninth birthday. There was chocolate cake, Neapolitan ice cream, and lots of presents to open.

The final gift for Jenna was the one I was most excited for her to open. Brian knew Jenna wanted to be an astronaut, so he purchased four tickets for us to go to Kennedy Space Center. He'd wrapped a *Future Astronaut* T-shirt around the four tickets, and we planned to drive to Merritt Island to take in the attraction the following weekend.

Jenna tore open the box and pulled out the purple shirt with black lettering.

"I love it," she exclaimed, reading the front aloud. "When do we get to go, Daddy?"

"Next weekend, you can wear your shirt to the park so everyone knows you'll be working there as an astronaut someday. I even purchased an add-on with your ticket, so you can meet and talk with a real astronaut."

"Can Meg and her parents come too?" she asked.

"We'll be gone by then, but I think you'll be the cutest little astronaut they've ever seen," Mom answered. She looked enamored with Jenna, and that was encouraging.

"I've always wanted to go to the space center," I said. "If you'll have me, I'd love to go!"

"Can Gus come too?" Jack never wanted to leave his little friend behind.

"He can come, but he's going to have to behave himself this time," Brian joked.

After Jenna and Jack went to bed, we all sat on the outside deck and shared stories and drank wine. By 9:00 p.m., my mom was tired and went to bed, but Dad stayed on until later. He and Brian's parents talked and laughed as if they were old friends. I was happy with how the weekend had gone—but was ready to get back to our routine.

I could see Brian yawning as he started to clean up the glasses and bottles and take them inside. I cleared some of them myself and joined him.

"You look tired," I said. We needed to get going, but Dad didn't seem ready to go.

"I am—but I'm so glad they're having a good time together!" Brian said.

"Want me to get Dad out of here so you can all go to bed?" I asked.

"No, let's not intrude. Let them stay awake and enjoy the evening if they're having fun. However, I may have to turn in for the night. I'm beat."

"Me too. I'll just put these dishes away and get out of here," I said, opening the front of the dishwasher.

Brian took two glasses from my hands and set them on the counter. Then, he pulled me close as he said, "You know what I wish?"

"What?" I asked.

"I wish we had one more night alone at your cottage, with

223

no kids or parents in the mix. Just us—celebrating the end of our first summer together."

"That would be heaven," I responded.

"You'd like it?" he asked.

"Yes, but I'm also thrilled to have it end like this. Our families seem to be hitting it off, and that's a good thing. I need my parents to understand why I'm staying. I want their support, and this is an important step in getting it. Plus, I'll only be a few feet further from you at Sophie's."

"Sophie's is nothing like The Pink Shell. That beach house has been a part of us. It's like an old friend I don't want to lose."

"What if I'd chosen another place to rent and wasn't your summer neighbor?" I asked.

"You'd probably be hooked up with some guy at the other end of the beach, and I'd still be lost and lonely," he lamented.

"We were meant to be, so I'd have jogged down here and looked for you every day until I found you."

"Luckily, we found *each other*, and we don't have to worry about how fate might have cheated us out of another chance at love."

We said our goodbyes, and I returned to the deck to retrieve my sweater and inform Dad I was going back to Sophie's.

"I'm calling it a night. Sleep well, everyone. I'll see you tomorrow."

"Honey, wait—I'll come with you. I didn't realize it was so late," Dad said.

He thanked everyone for their hospitality and followed me next door, where I hugged him goodnight in front of the flower boxes. By this time in the summer, they were overflowing with pink and purple blooms. The protective shade of the beach house had given the colorful flowers the perfect spot to flourish—just like me.

"Goodnight, Dad. I'm so glad you're here," I said.

"Me too, sweetheart. You get to bed, and I'll see you in the morning."

I was starting toward Sophie's house when I heard my dad's voice behind me. "Hey," he called out in a loud whisper. "Brian and his family are good people. You chose well, Peanut!"

"Thanks, that means so much to me!" I said with tears filling my eyes.

Labor Day weekend put an end to the summer that changed my life. I'd unpacked my car in late May, anticipating a time of solitude and reflection. I was ending my stay at The Pink Shell with a different outlook and love filling my heart.

***

Monday morning came too soon. I knew it was time for my parents to leave, but I wished they could stay for a few more days. Things had gone well, and I knew it was better to leave each other wanting more instead of the other way around. They pulled out of the driveway before noon, and I headed out for a walk.

When I returned, Brian was sitting in a beach chair on the sand between our houses. As I approached him, I could see he had a big smile and was up to something.

"Hi there," he said.

"Hi. What's going on?" I asked. "Where are the kids?"

"Well, you know how I like to make you happy—right?"

"It's one of the things I love the most about you," I teased.

"I've got a surprise for you."

The entire summer had been a surprise.

"A surprise? What is it?" I asked.

"Mom and Dad have taken the kids home for the rest of the day and night. So, we can spend your last night at The Pink Shell together."

"How did you pull that off?"

"The kids were missing home, and Mom and Dad volunteered to take them for the night and meet me halfway tomorrow to get them back here. It won't hurt for them to miss one day of school. And they're fantastic parents who want this to work out between the two of us. They're sick of taking care of me," he said.

"I'm happy to take care of you."

"I'm happy to *have* you take care of me," he said, pulling me into his lap. "Now we need to figure out what to do with our day."

"I've already moved my things next door to Sophie's, but technically, I have possession of the place until noon tomorrow when the cleaners show up," I said.

We spent the rest of the day alone in my beachfront cottage, only venturing out to get Chinese food and take a moonlit walk on the beach.

I couldn't have asked for any better ending to my time at The Pink Shell.

Chapter Twenty-Five
September

We got on the road early the day we left for Kennedy Space Center. We stopped to eat breakfast on our way out of town, choosing a restaurant off Dunlawton Avenue advertising the best waffles in Volusia County. After our orders were taken, we settled in with coffees and chocolate milks while we waited for our award-winning meal.

Brian and I discussed the plan for the day while Jenna and Jack played games on the restaurant placemats. They colored pictures with crayons given to them by the server and talked about how excited they were to get to the space center.

"How many rockets do you think we'll see?" Jack asked.

"I can't wait to meet a real astronaut. I'm going to ask him what his favorite freeze-dried food is. I wonder if they get to eat ice cream in space?" Jenna asked.

"I've heard they have some of the same food for sale in the gift shop if you want to try it. We can see for ourselves if they have space ice cream," Brian answered.

"I've got to go to the bathroom," Jenna said, squirming.

"Okay, I'll go with you," I offered, leading Jenna toward the restroom sign I'd seen earlier.

We walked through a tiny gift shop and toward the back of the restaurant. We found the bathrooms behind the cash register, and I told Jenna I'd browse while she used the facilities.

I noticed an older woman in the back corner looking at candles and thought she looked familiar. I moved closer, trying to get a better view, and realized it was Sophie's friend, Barbara.

"Well, hello there," I said. Barbara turned to face me as recognition began to register on her face. It had been several weeks since I'd been with Sophie's friends, but she greeted me with a warm smile.

"Meg, how are you?" She hugged me and asked about Brian and the children. I wasn't surprised she knew of the changes taking place in my life since Sophie's group of friends were close.

"Everyone's fine. In fact, we're off to Kennedy Space Center today. We're enjoying our time together, and I'm taking good care of Sophie's place while she's gone."

Jenna came out of the bathroom at about the same time a gentleman left the men's bathroom. I was surprised to see it was Sam and noted Barbara and Sam must have been together. Maybe I wasn't the only one with a budding summer romance.

"Hi, Sam. It's nice to see you again," I said, leaning in to give him a hug.

"Fancy seeing you here, Meg. We were hoping you could have joined us more this summer, but from my understanding, you have been quite busy," he said with a smile.

I knew we should be getting back to the table before our breakfast arrived and began to move the conversation to a conclusion.

"It was so nice to see the two of you. I hope Audrey feels better soon so Sophie can return to Florida and begin hosting parties again!"

"What's wrong with Audrey?" Sam asked. I was surprised he didn't know the reason for Sophie's extended absence.

"Audrey's sick, and Sophie's been staying in Atlanta with her," I said. "I'm house-sitting for her until she gets back. I figured you would know what was going on."

"Audrey's sick?" Sam looked bewildered. "But I thought Sophie . . ."

"Sam," Barbara interrupted, "we've talked about this a hundred times. Here—get the car started, and I'll be out in a minute," she said, bossing him out the door. I'd never seen Barbara be so forceful.

Sam took the car keys and said goodbye. Barbara watched until he got outside before she said anything else.

"I'm sorry to tell you that Sam hasn't been himself lately. I'm worried about him. His memory is beginning to fail. Sometimes he's completely off his rocker," she added, rolling her eyes.

Jenna and I returned to the table where heaping plates of breakfast entrees were arriving. The food smelled delicious, and we all dug in, knowing it would be a while before we ate again.

We were back on the road before 8:30 a.m. The kids kept asking how much longer it would be before we got there, and Brian assured them if they would put their headphones on and watch the movie he'd downloaded for them—we'd be there before they knew it. They followed his instructions, and they were both asleep the next time I looked back at them.

I smiled when I saw Jack had Gus tucked under his arm.

229

Brian had agreed to let the little dog come along if he stayed in the backpack among the snacks and water bottles needed for the day.

After the short drive, we entered Kennedy Space Center, and I was overwhelmed by the size of the place. It wasn't as big as the Disney theme parks I'd visited, but we'd need a game plan to make sure we had time to see everything.

We grabbed a map and started to plan our day. Brian opened the backpack and began to apply sunscreen to both kids. I double-checked to make sure we had everything needed from the car, and we got ready to embark on our day of fun.

"Daddy, can I carry Gus so he can see all the rockets?"

"No, Jack. We'll leave him right here in the backpack, so we don't lose him again. You remember what happened at The Pizza Pit—right?"

"But he can't see anything inside there," Jack pointed out.

"Jack, Gus isn't alive. He's a stuffed dog. He doesn't care about space," Jenna pointed out.

"Gus is too alive. You don't know what you're talking about. Daddy, make her stop saying that," he argued back.

"We're not going to start the day with a fight. Gus will remain in the backpack, and both of you will stay with Meg and me, and we're going to have a fun day." Brian was almost shouting when he told them how much fun we were going to have.

We started by exploring the Rocket Garden. We stood next to actual spaceships and then made our way to the first of several exhibits telling the story of space exploration. We took part in a launch experience, which gave us the sensation of blasting off aboard the space shuttle. It was thrilling for me as an adult, and I could only imagine how much the kids enjoyed it.

After stopping for ice cream, we rode a bus to the operational facilities for future American space flights and, after seeing several more exhibits, made our way to the main staging area for Jenna's meeting with an astronaut.

While Brian and Jenna attended her VIP activity, I took Jack to Planet Play. While he climbed on space-themed recreation equipment, I relaxed on a bench and drank an expensive Diet Coke in the air-conditioning. It was exhausting having so much fun.

***

"Meg, the astronaut I met was a *girl*!" Jenna said as she and Brian made their way toward us after the presentation.

"How exciting," I said. "Did you tell her you want to be an astronaut too?"

"Yes, and she said I needed to study math and science in school and apply for space camp when I'm old enough!" Jenna was riding high after her exciting visit.

"How much do you suppose space camp is?" I asked Brian as the kids walked ahead of us.

"Who knows, but she made it sound so cool, I might want to go myself," he joked.

We'd seen almost everything offered, and we were hungry and tired by evening. We went to one of the restaurants near the park entrance to eat dinner and then made our way out of the attraction to head home. It took about ten minutes to get back to the van, and I was already looking forward to being off my feet for the duration of the car ride.

"Can I hold Gus on the way home?" Jack asked as Brian

got him into his booster seat.

I unzipped the backpack, grabbed my sweater, and looked for Gus so I could give him to Jack. I didn't see him at the top of the bag, so I dug deeper, feeling for his fluffy ears.

"Jack, did you put Gus in another part of the backpack?" I asked, hoping he'd been zipped in a different pocket by mistake.

"No," Jack said. "Isn't he in there?" I could hear fear start to creep into his little voice.

I looked at Brian helplessly, and he joined me in the search for Gus in the backpack—now stuffed with souvenirs and a half-eaten box of candy.

"Did you already take him out?" Brian asked, hoping Jack had forgotten that his little friend was already sitting beside him in the van.

"No," the frightened child replied.

I looked at Jack's face and then at Brian. I opened the bag's main section and poured everything out on the floor of the van as I willed the little dog to appear.

"I lost him again," Jack said quietly.

"What do you mean?" Brian asked.

"I took him out when we were riding out to the launch pad. I didn't think it would hurt if he sat with me in the seat, and I was going to put him back before we got off the bus—but I think I forgot and left him on the seat."

"Was it on our way out or on our way back? I might be able to figure out which bus we were on." I could see Brian formulating a plan to backtrack and try to find Gus.

"I don't know," Jack said as he began to cry.

It was useless to have a five-year-old retrace his steps at a place as big as Kennedy Space Center, but it was closing time,

232

and we were in panic mode.

"I think it was on the way there," he said through tears.

"I'm going to see if there's time for me to run back to the bus entrance. Maybe someone turned him in, or I can hop on the buses and see if I can find him."

Only a few transports were making a continuous loop out to the launch pad and back, so it wasn't out of the question to be able to find the ones we were on.

"I'll stay with the kids, and you go back. Hurry!" I said as Brian turned toward the entrance. I didn't have much hope for finding Jack's little friend and wondered if I could buy another one at the grocery store. It had been weeks, and finding a replacement Gus was a long shot.

Brian began dodging in and out of the crowd as he hurried through the families ending their day. His head looked like a fishing bobber bouncing up and down in a choppy current as he made his way back into Kennedy Space Center.

"Do you think he'll find him?" Jenna asked me.

"I know he's going to try. That's all he can do."

I felt such deep love for this man who tried to do the best he could for his family. Like Jayne's death, I feared Gus's mishap would be another thing this caring father would have to explain to his young son. Despite what Sophie always said, some things couldn't be wished away because a different outcome was desired.

As the attraction cleared out and cars began to stream out of the parking lot, it became evident that we'd be going home without Gus. It wasn't long before I saw Brian walking toward the car. I knew by the way he was carrying himself that Jack's little dog was lost forever.

"Did you find him?" Jack asked as Brian opened his door

and got in.

"No, Buddy. He's gone." Brian was out of breath, and sweat was dripping down the side of his face.

"It's okay. I shouldn't have taken him out of the backpack. It's my fault Gus is lost." Jack hung his head in despair.

"Let's go home," Brian said quietly.

I made one final attempt to ease the pain of the situation by promising to call the Kennedy Space Center lost and found the next day, but we all knew the chances of Gus being found were slim. I didn't have to be Jack's mother to know this would be another difficult loss for such a sensitive little boy.

We were one of the last vehicles out of the parking lot. Our fun day had ended abruptly, and we were all drained and overwhelmed with emotion.

"What do you think will happen to Gus, Daddy?" Jack asked as we drove home.

"I'm sure someone will find him and take good care of him. He'll miss you so much, but he'll be okay."

"Kind of like Meg found *us*?" Jack asked.

"Yes, Jack. Exactly like that."

We drove toward home in silence, each lost in our own thoughts.

Chapter Twenty-Six
November

It was late fall, and I looked out Sophie's window and saw a young man and woman unloading their suitcases and sacks of groceries into The Pink Shell. It looked like another couple on their honeymoon, and I hoped the magic Brian and I had experienced during our time at the beach house would ignite a memorable week for them too.

I was finishing a batch of potato salad to take to Brian's for dinner. He was grilling brats, and I'd bring the salad and some potato chips to fill out the dinner menu. We didn't spend much time at Sophie's house. The setup wasn't ideal for the kids, and the crazy décor was less than relaxing. I was lucky to have Brian's place as a refuge, but I couldn't help but feel jealous when a new renter was starting their week at the cottage.

I loaded my arms with food and walked the short distance to Brian's house.

"Hi, Meg," Jenna said as she opened the door.

"Hi, honey. How was your day? What did you get on your spelling test?" I asked, handing her part of the food I'd carried over.

"I got them all right!" she exclaimed.

We'd been working on her spelling lists each week since she moved to the beach. After I'd told her I was a spelling bee champion in my hometown, she thought my help would give her some supernatural ability at acing her tests, and so far it had.

"Hi, babe," Brian said, leaning in to kiss me.

"It sounds like Jenna had a good day," I replied. "How was yours?"

"Well, I knew as soon as I finished work I could spend the evening with you, so it was pretty awesome."

Brian was always in a good mood. When I was married to Jason, I found myself dreading our evenings at home after a stressful day at work. We could never separate the two parts of our lives, and it was hard to relax and enjoy ourselves as a couple. Never getting a break from your partner was a sure way to annoy each other, and I enjoyed having a romantic relationship that didn't include business decisions.

After dinner and a rousing game of Sorry, it was time for baths and bed. I finished my wine and washed the dishes while Brian took care of the kids.

"Jack wants you to go upstairs and tuck him in," Brian said when he returned to the kitchen.

"Really? That's so sweet. I'll run up and tell him goodnight."

Jenna and Jack had become such a big part of my life, and they accepted the relationship between Brian and me better than I could have imagined. I'd fallen in love with the entire Barts family and never wanted to be without them.

I entered Jack's room and sat on the edge of his bed. He was a light sleeper and had a sound machine playing beside him to soothe him into sleep and keep him there. The soft music lulled me too, and I felt drowsy and relaxed.

"Goodnight, Jack," I said, holding in a yawn.

"I miss Gus. It's so hard to fall asleep without him," Jack lamented.

Being without Brian every night, I could relate to Jack's heartache. "I know . . . do you want me to get one of your other stuffed animals?"

"No, they're not as good," he said as he rolled over in bed. "Goodnight. I love you, Meg,"

"I love you too, buddy. You get to sleep, and I'll see you tomorrow."

"I'm glad we moved to the beach," he said.

"I'm glad too," I answered.

As I left his room and pulled the door shut, I walked across the hall to Jenna's room.

"Goodnight, Jen," I said, sticking my head through the opening in the door.

"Night, Meg. Hey, will you take me shopping for a swimsuit this weekend? Mine has a rip in it, and Dad is terrible at shopping," she added.

"Of course. I'd love that."

I went downstairs, where Brian was building a fire outside and had pulled two chairs near the orange glow of the flames. A beautiful moon illuminated the ocean, and the night sky was clear and bright. The flickering fire added a romantic touch to the already beautiful setting. The fall air was the right temperature to enjoy Brian's deck after the kids went to bed each night, and I'd come to look forward to our evening chats. They always brought us closer and made me fall more in love with a man I adored.

"I found out today my contract will be up at the end of

January," Brian said out of nowhere. He'd been preoccupied, and I'd wondered what was on his mind.

"I figured it was getting close to being done," I said. Brian was anxious to move on to other projects and get the kids back home.

"I want you to move to St. Augustine with us and look for a job there."

This was a conversation we needed to have. My decision to stay in Florida for a few extra months had been complicated enough, but it was time to move forward with more permanent plans.

"What would that look like for the two of us?" I asked.

"That's up to you. I don't want to pressure you, but I can't lose you. Things will be changing, and I want us to have a plan in place for what we need to do. The time will move quickly, and if you start looking for a job now—there's a decent chance you'd have one by then."

"I want to move with all of you, but I'm apprehensive about it. Would we live together, or would I find my own place? How will the people in our lives react to this when we've only known each other for a few months?"

"I don't care what anyone else thinks. This is about us. You've changed my life. I couldn't see a future for myself for such a long time. I don't want to lose all of it by putting thousands of miles between us. It isn't that I don't think we could sustain a long-distance relationship if you went back to Iowa. I just don't want to be without you. If it made sense for me to move the kids and my business—I'd do it in a heartbeat. But we both know that isn't very logical."

"No, the kids need to be in their home, and your business is already thriving." I thought about my weekend in St. Augustine and how challenging that option might be for me.

There was no reason I couldn't move to St. Augustine. It would be a difficult transition, but I had to make a fresh start somewhere—it might as well be there.

Even though I was a grown woman, I dreaded the thought of disappointing my parents. I was hesitant to trust my heart and ignore my mother's voice inside my head telling me to move home.

"You get to make this decision, but I'm asking you to give us the chance we deserve. And if something unforeseen happens, you can always go back to Iowa," he said.

My heart couldn't even consider that possibility.

"I don't know why it's so hard for me to commit to staying in Florida. I'm scared, I guess."

"You know how I feel about you, and I'm never going to do anything to hurt you. It will be your choice if you decide you don't want to be here. I will do whatever it takes to have you in my life."

I believed him, but something was holding me back.

***

With each passing day, Brian and the kids became more comfortable in their new life, blossoming into a family they'd never been before. We continued to spend our evenings together, but I made sure some nights were reserved for only the three of them. Homework and family time didn't always need another person involved, and I tried to give them the space they needed.

Jack still talked about Gus. We always tried to ease his pain by telling him we were sure Gus was happy wherever he ended up. Sometimes we'd make a game out of it by saying, *"I think Gus lives in Greece and gets to eat olives whenever he wants."* Jack would respond with something like, *"I think Gus ended up at the Grand Canyon and gets to ride on a donkey every day."* The conversations always ended in laughter when someone came up with the most outlandish place Gus might have landed. It seemed like a healthy way to handle another loss in Jack's young life.

***

Being in Florida during the fall was different for me. I missed the vibrant colors of Iowa and the traditions of making pumpkin bread and chili as the weeks turned cooler. Days at the beach were still warm, but my favorite season of the year was slipping away like dried leaves skimming across the lawn on an autumn day.

The holidays were coming quickly, and Brian invited me to join the Barts clan in St. Augustine for Thanksgiving. I wanted to be with them but couldn't disappoint my own family and miss the time at home. I wanted to see my siblings and nieces and knew a trip home would allow me to share my plans about moving to St. Augustine in person.

Brian and the kids drove me to the airport, and as they stood and told me goodbye, I knew I would be missed. I was anxious to see my family for the holiday but wasn't sure where home was anymore. I knew it wasn't Michigan. I didn't think it was Iowa, but I wasn't sure it was Florida either.

Jack made a turkey out of construction paper and gave it to me as a goodbye gift. He insisted I fold it and put it in my purse to look at while I was gone. He wanted to make sure I wouldn't forget him during my absence. As we said goodbye, I could feel they needed and loved me as much as I did them.

Brian asked Jenna for something as I pulled away from the hug he was giving me. She had a bag with her and pulled out a wrapped gift about the size of a tissue box. Brian gave it to me and made me promise I wouldn't open it until Thanksgiving morning.

"What's this?" I asked, wondering if I could get a wrapped gift through security.

"It's a Thanksgiving present. I couldn't let Jack outdo me with the handmade turkey, could I?"

Jack beamed, not understanding Brian's sweet sarcasm.

"Thank you, that was so thoughtful of you. I won't peek until tomorrow."

I gave Jenna and Jack each a final hug and planted a kiss on Brian's lips.

"I'll see you all on Sunday. I'm going to miss you so much!" I said, wishing I could take them with me.

I stood in line with the fifty or so passengers who had already made their way to security. After showing my ID and boarding pass, I put my personal belongings on the conveyer belt and hoped the gift would make it through.

"What's in here?" The stern-looking TSA officer didn't look moved by Brian's gesture.

"I'm not sure. My boyfriend gave it to me and asked me not to open it until Thanksgiving."

"That's sweet," he mocked. "However, safety trumps romance on this airline. It'll have to pass through the x-ray machine, or you won't be allowed to take it on the plane."

"Well, of course," I replied, forcing a smile as I tried to cooperate with a guy who didn't seem to have a soft spot for love.

The gift passed inspection and was waiting for me at the end of the security line, piled up against the belongings of several other people. I plucked it out of the pile like a beautiful flower and was on my way.

***

Dad picked me up in Cedar Rapids, and we drove toward my hometown of Washington. We talked about the muted fall colors I'd seen over the countryside as the airplane came in for a landing and discussed my mother's Thanksgiving "to-do" list. I was happy to have time alone with him before getting home.

Iowa didn't have mountains or the ocean, but its beauty was visible in the rolling hills and colorful barn quilts hung on red outbuildings, which dotted the landscape in every direction. Before long, we pulled into the familiar driveway of my childhood home. Mom greeted me in the entryway of our two-story colonial as if I'd been away at war.

"You're finally here!" she exclaimed. "Are you hungry? Would you like something to drink?" Even though she was busy in the kitchen, preparing food, she was dressed to the nines and had her hair coiffed and nails perfectly polished.

"No, Mom—I'm fine."

Dad carried my suitcase in along with the wrapped box I'd put in the car's back seat.

"What's this, Meg?" he asked as he started up the stairs with my belongings like a bellhop at a fancy hotel.

"That's a Thanksgiving gift from Brian," I responded. "I'm not supposed to open it until tomorrow."

"Well, how nice," he said, winking at me as he carried my things upstairs, and I joined my mother in the kitchen.

The house was beginning to smell like a holiday. Pies were cooling on the top of the stove, and Mom was in the middle of making cranberry stuffing. The kitchen island had a variety of ingredients already sliced, and spices were lined up—ready to add flavor to the traditional recipes. I loved this part of the festivities and was looking forward to helping her finish what needed to be done.

We ordered a pizza, and Dad opened a bottle of wine for us to share. I liked having my parents to myself. Thanksgiving Day would be busy, but my first evening in Iowa was all about being with the two of them. After we ate, I relaxed in a leather chair in front of the fireplace where we spent the evening watching television together.

I didn't like their choices in programming, but it didn't matter. I'd hoped to be able to talk with them about my decision to move south permanently, but I couldn't find the right moment to broach the subject.

I drifted off to sleep more than once during the evening as I enjoyed the familiarity of where I'd grown up. It was good to be home.

Chapter Twenty-Seven
November

The smell of turkey began to seep into every nook of our family home, reminding me there was a day of feasting ahead, and I'd better get up and prepare for it. I knew Mom had been working since before dawn, preparing the dinner our family would share at 12:00 p.m. sharp. Thanksgiving had always been at noon at our house. The meal at another time of day would not have been an option in the Royce household.

I smiled and looked over at the wrapped box on top of the desk I'd used throughout high school. It was strange to be sleeping as an adult in a bedroom that still had a tub of stuffed animals in the corner and soccer trophies lining the bookshelves.

The black and white checked comforter on the bed had been part of a set I'd received as a birthday gift my senior year in high school. It still had a pink fingernail polish stain in the corner from the night of my senior prom when I'd quickly painted my toenails and knocked the bottle over.

Time had stood still in my adolescent bedroom, and I couldn't help but feel my parents were hoping they'd have that younger and more naive Meg Parsons at home again soon. They weren't equipped to deal with the grown-up woman I'd become, along with the choices and opinions of an adult who didn't always agree with what *they* felt was best.

Brian's last text of the evening reminded me not to spoil the surprise by opening my gift early, and I'd kept my word. Brian was so thoughtful. When I'd told him I collected Christmas ornaments, the next week, he'd presented me with a beautifully wrapped shell decoration with the words *"The Sea Is Calling You Home."* He told me he wanted me to think of our first summer together each year when I decorated my tree, so I was excited to see what was in the box he'd sent with me.

I slid out of bed and made my way to the desk. The hardwood floor was cold on the bottom of my feet, so I quickly grabbed the box and jumped back under the covers. I slid the gray and white ribbon off and tore at the wrapping paper. Inside, there was a card and a smaller box underneath. The Thanksgiving card contained a handwritten letter.

Meg,

By the time you read this, we'll be hundreds of miles apart. I'm counting every second until you get back to Florida, and we can be together again. Thanksgiving seems like the perfect time to tell you how grateful I am for you and how blessed I feel to know you. I can't believe taking a job in Daytona put me right in the spot to meet someone as wonderful as you.

There was a time when I couldn't think about love again. I couldn't imagine having anyone beside me to share our lives. You've changed all of that for me.

Now I wake up wanting to see you, longing to smell your perfume and feel your touch. I dream about sharing every part of my life with you. I'm so thankful for that precious gift. It was something I wasn't sure I would ever have again.

I know you're scared we might be rushing things, and our feelings for each other might be infatuation. There are no guarantees in life, but if I had to take a bet—I'd bet on us. I know I won't let anything keep me from you if you want the same thing. I promise to love you and be good to you. If it's possible, I'll make all of your dreams come true.

I've learned over the past few years that life is short. Sometimes you have to take a leap of faith and have the courage to ask for and receive exactly what you want in life.

You may wonder why I've chosen to give you this special gift when I'm not with you. I wanted you to be in familiar surroundings when you open this, not lured by the romance and excitement of our life at the beach. This is real life from here on out, and I want you to do what your heart tells you is right, even if it isn't what I want to hear.

I'm hoping this gift proves to you and everyone else where my heart is. The rest will fall into place if it's meant to be. I love you.

Brian

Tears were running down my cheeks as I opened the smaller package inside. A velvet jewelry box revealed a gorgeous princess-cut diamond. The band had smaller diamonds, which encircled the circumference of the exquisite piece of jewelry.

I'd been divorced for less than a year, and someone was asking me to marry them. And I was going to say yes.

Until I realized Brian was proposing to me, I hadn't been

sure he genuinely loved and wanted me in his life. Sophie had been right. The failure of my marriage to Jason had made me doubt myself and my ability to be loved by another man. My own fears could have cheated us out of the life we deserved. Brian's confidence allowed us to get to where we needed to be. He trusted our relationship enough for both of us, but it was time I stopped holding back and allowed him to love me in the way only he could.

I picked up my cell phone and called Brian. I was expecting to hear his voice on the other end, but instead, Jack said, "Hi, Meg!"

"Hi, Jack. I sure miss you."

"I miss you too! When are you coming home? I've been sad this morning because you're not here."

"What if I spend Thanksgiving with you next year?" I asked, knowing I would never miss another holiday with them.

"Okay . . . Here's Daddy!"

"Hello?" Brian answered.

"Hi. Happy Thanksgiving."

"Well, the same to you. How's your day going so far?" he asked.

"It's been fairly uneventful," I lied. "Unless you count the most romantic proposal I could have ever hoped for."

"You liked it?"

"I loved it. I love *you*."

"Enough to marry me?" he asked.

"Enough to marry you, move to St. Augustine, and be the best wife and stepmother you could ever imagine."

"No reservations? You *really* want this as much as I do?"

"Yes. More than you will ever know. I didn't realize until I saw this beautiful ring and realized you were asking me to marry you just how *much* I wanted this! Maybe I wasn't sure you loved me as much as I loved you until I saw the ring and understood what it meant. But I believe you now, and I'm never looking back."

"Meg, you're not going to regret this. Now get back here so we can make some plans!"

"That's the only downside to your romantic proposal. We aren't together. I wish you were here with me so we could share this moment with my family and be together to celebrate."

"I'm sorry about that. I wanted you to have the space you needed to make a decision that was right for you. And Iowa seemed like the only place for that to occur."

We finished our conversation and vowed to celebrate when I got back to Florida. I couldn't wait to be Brian's wife.

***

I gave Dad a big hug as I came into the kitchen. "Happy Thanksgiving!" I said cheerfully, kissing him on the cheek.

"Same to you, sweetie. Did you sleep well?"

"Always. There's nothing like sleeping in your old bed." Despite the childish décor, it was still *my* bedroom.

"Would you like coffee?" Mom asked.

"Yes," I said as she handed me a mug. I chose a piece of pumpkin bread from a silver tray and placed it on a colorful napkin adorned with fall leaves. My mom had a way of making everything perfect. There were always holiday napkins and cornucopias filled with gourds and pumpkins to make Thanksgiving festive.

Today was no different, and I appreciated her efforts. I was excited to think I'd have my own family to fuss over and hoped I'd be as good at it as she was. I was grinning from ear to ear, thinking of the sparkly diamond ring tucked away in the box on top of my dresser upstairs, but no one seemed to notice.

"Can you help me set the table, honey?" Mom asked.

"Sure, I'd love to," I said. I started helping with the morning duties and wondered when my siblings and their families would arrive.

"Well, you're in a good mood today. See what being at home has done for you?" Mom said as we finished the table arrangements.

My mom and dad usually got to the point, and today was no different.

"When are you coming home, Meg?" she asked.

"You mean home to Iowa?" I asked.

"Yes. Where else would I be talking about? I know you like this young man, and so do we. But Sophie will return soon, and you'll need to get on with your life. It's time to think about those things," Mom said with intent.

"Honey, we understand wanting to take a few months to yourself. But, if you're meant to be with Brian—your relationship will withstand the distance," Dad added.

"I've already decided what I'm going to do," I said, preparing to take a stand for myself.

At that very moment, the front door opened, and the house was filled with the holiday entrance of my brother and his family. They lived in Ottumwa and didn't see my parents as often as my sister's family, who lived just a few blocks away in Washington. First, my nieces ran to their grandma, and then they landed in my arms with hugs and kisses all around.

"Hi, Aunt Meg!" they screamed in unison. The celebratory scene was repeated several minutes later when my sister's family bolted through the door too.

The next couple of hours were full of last-minute details to put the perfect Thanksgiving dinner on for our family of ten. There was laughter, talking, and plenty of holiday favorites cooking in the oven and on top of every burner. There were even several crock pots full of other side dishes to be enjoyed. The smell of ham and turkey and all the trimmings melded into one another, making the house smell like home. My senses were overloaded with Thanksgiving memories, and I was happy to be with so many people I loved.

***

We sat at the dining room table as Dad carved the turkey. We bowed our heads, thanking God for the many blessings we'd been given. I said a silent thank you for the gift of the man who'd come into my life. As soon as the prayer was finished, the room erupted again in energetic chatter. The clanging of silverware was almost as loud as we passed serving dishes from person to person and heaped our plates with food.

Feeling the closeness of my family at the table, I realized I felt the same way with Brian and the kids. They felt right to me, just like my own family did. Now *they* were my family too.

"Aunt Meg, did Mom tell you I tried out for the basketball team?" my niece asked.

"No—really? Is Coach Davis still there?" I asked, enjoying the chance to catch up on the lives of my family members.

"Does anyone want to donate to our trip for Spanish class?"

my other niece asked, not wanting to be outdone by her sister.

There were several side conversations going on as my brother discussed the latest at his workplace with my brother-in-law, and my mom mentioned how much she loved my sister's new haircut. It was familiar and comfortable, and I was thankful for my life, old and new. If I'd known I would be in such a good place only months after my divorce, I wouldn't have had such a difficult time coping with the loss of my marriage.

"Meg, when are you coming home? You can see there is so much you're missing while you're in Florida. Wouldn't you love to see a few of your niece's basketball games?" Mom wasn't going to let it go.

"Actually, I have some news to share," I said confidently.

"Oh? What news is that?" Dad asked with the others looking on. Even though we were still in the middle of Thanksgiving dinner, everyone's attention fell on me, and a hush came over the table.

"I've decided to move to St. Augustine. Brian and I are getting married."

All eyes were on me, and the boisterous mood from earlier was replaced by stunned silence.

"When did this happen?" my mother asked.

"When I got up this morning," I replied, leaving out the details of the gift I'd opened.

This brought the banter to a rolling boil of excitement, tension, inquisition, and disbelief as everyone asked me questions at once.

"This morning, Brian asked me to marry him, and I said yes. So, I will be moving to St. Augustine with my new family soon, and my life will be in Florida."

"Oh, my goodness," Mom said. "We'll talk about this later. It doesn't seem like the right time or place to discuss something so serious." Her curt response put me on edge and told me everything I needed to know about her opinion on the subject.

The rest of the meal was tense, and I was sorry I'd chosen that moment to share the news of my engagement.

***

The male members of the family all gathered to watch football as the women began to clean up the mess. I always wondered why this was the natural order of the world. Maybe it came from when the men had done their Thanksgiving chores by hunting for the turkey and growing the food. However, it seemed outdated when most women were purchasing everything for the celebration at their local grocery store and slaving over a hot stove for hours—even days—before the meal was served.

I didn't think my dad's contribution of carving the turkey at the table should get him off the hook. But, since I'd already made a powerful personal statement at the Thanksgiving meal, I thought it best if I quietly resumed my gender-assigned duties without a fight.

My sister and sister-in-law joined me in clearing the plates from the dining room. We scraped the uneaten food into the trash and washed the good dishes by hand. My mother was noticeably absent.

"Congratulations, Meg," my sister, Tracy, said quietly as she gave me a quick hug and looked over her shoulder to make sure Mom wasn't coming into the room. "She'll get over it.

She just wants you in Iowa. This will pass, don't worry about it."

"That's right," my sister-in-law, Kathy, piped in. "This is *your* life, and from the photos I saw from their trip to see you in September—this guy is hot!"

"He's so much more than *hot*, Kathy. If Mom knew how great he was and the life I was walking into—she wouldn't be giving me such a hard time."

"You *are* talking about our mother, aren't you? You're a grown woman," Tracy reminded me. "You don't need their permission."

"I know," I replied, keeping my voice quiet. "But I want their support. It would be easier for me if they could be happy for us."

Mom appeared in the kitchen doorway and began taking stock of what needed to be done. The conversation quickly turned to the meal plan for the rest of the weekend and sleeping arrangements for everyone. I wasn't the only out-of-town guest. Although my sister and her family lived in town, I was sure my niece would join her cousins on the floor in the family room while my brother and his wife would take another room.

***

As with most Thanksgiving gatherings, everyone fell asleep in the late afternoon. When I opened my eyes, my dad was the only other person who was awake. He was looking at me from across the room. I wondered if his stare had roused me from a nap brought on by too much food and a chenille throw.

He smiled at me and cocked his head to the side, indicating he wanted me to join him outside. We both quietly found our way to the sun porch and sat on the comfortable rattan furniture.

"I'm sorry about how things went down at dinner," he started.

"Me too," I added.

"Do you love this man, and do you think he can make you happy?"

"Yes, Dad," I said as tears filled my eyes.

"Okay then, you leave your mother to me," he said. "She loves you so much. We both do. It would kill us if you were hurt again. If Brian and those two beautiful kids make you happy—you'll have our support. You need to follow your heart."

I got up from my chair, bent down next to my dad, and hugged him. "Thank you, Dad! I know this is the right decision for me. I'll come back and visit, and you and Mom can come to Florida whenever you want."

"That'll be a welcome offer once the snow starts to fly!" he said.

My dad always knew the right thing to say. Hopefully, he'd be able to find the words to convince my mom too.

Chapter Twenty-Eight
November

It was early on the Friday morning after Thanksgiving. I heard a commotion downstairs but chose to turn over and try to continue sleeping. A house full of relatives was never a quiet place unless it was the middle of the night, or someone was announcing life-changing news that didn't go over well.

I figured the kids were up early, and Mom was starting breakfast for the entire crew. It wouldn't be long until the aroma of another big meal made its way to every bedroom in the house, beckoning the family to join together again.

I was drifting back to sleep when there was a soft knock on my bedroom door. Before I could answer, I heard someone slip into the room and close the door again. I assumed it was one of my nieces. First, I would let them feel like they surprised me, and then I would scare them by opening my eyes and exclaiming, "Gotcha!"

As I anticipated the next move of my unknown visitor, I felt a heavy weight on the bed and a soft brush of lips on my cheek. My heart skipped a beat when I opened my eyes and saw Brian lying beside me.

"Good morning, beautiful!" he said.

"Brian," I gasped. "What are you doing here? Are the kids

with you?" I sat up in bed and threw my arms around his neck.

We hugged and kissed, and I was overjoyed to have him with me.

"I promised if you committed yourself to me, I would do whatever I could to make your dreams come true. You told me you wished I was here with you and your family. After thinking about it, I realized I could easily make that happen for a few days. Once I told my family what I wanted to do, they were more than willing to keep the kids. I thought I'd fly back with you on Sunday. I hope you don't mind," he said.

"Mind? I'm thrilled! Now you can meet my brother and sister and my nieces—and spend more time with my parents. But I need to tell you something. I don't know how your family took the news, but my mom is a little apprehensive. It doesn't change anything for us, but I wanted you to know you might be walking in on more than you bargained for."

"What about your dad and the rest of the family?" Brian asked. "Are they more receptive to this stranger coming into your life and stealing you away to Florida?"

"Yes. Everyone is happy except for my mom. She'll come around. She needs to see us together more to get used to the idea. Maybe this couple of days will help."

"Do you think she'll give me the cold shoulder?" he asked.

"My mother would never make you feel unwelcome. She'll be the ideal host—no matter how she really feels. You'll see when we go downstairs for breakfast in a few minutes."

"A few minutes? I was hoping we might have a little time alone up here," Brian said, slipping his hand under the covers playfully.

"I wish," I replied coyly. "There will be plenty of time for fooling around when we get back to Florida. But, right now, you've got some work to do with my mom, and taking advantage of her daughter under her roof is not a good way to start!"

I was only half-joking with my comment.

***

The mood at breakfast was a lot better than the day before. My family welcomed Brian and had many questions for him about a number of topics. My sister was gushing over my beautiful engagement ring, and my nieces insisted on trying it on.

Brian conducted himself in his truly "Brian" way and had the family eating out of his hand before the end of the morning. Tracy gave me a knowing look more than once, letting me know I had her full support. My mother was pleasant but didn't have much to add to the conversation.

The women of the family were going Black Friday shopping, but I hesitated to leave Brian at home. He assured me he was a grown man, and there was no reason to babysit him. He convinced me he could do a little behind-the-scenes work with the guys, which might prove valuable with my mom. I agreed, not wanting to miss the outing with the girls.

We hit some sales at a few major department stores, but many deals were already gone since we didn't arrive at the first store until after noon. However, I did find gifts to take back to Jenna and Jack, to which my mother replied, "I guess I'll have three more names to add to my Christmas list this year."

It was a start.

***

When we pulled into the driveway, the guys were playing football in the front yard, and my dad was planted in a lawn chair acting as referee.

"You all look like you're having a good time—but it's time to get cleaned up for the evening. I'll have appetizers and drinks ready for everyone in a little while. And my famous chili will be done in a couple of hours," Mom said.

It made me smile to think about cocktails, and I wondered how Sophie was doing at her sister's house. I also thought about her beach friends. I was sure she was the Thanksgiving host for her group, and I hoped no one had to spend the holiday alone due to her absence.

Mom offered Brian the last bedroom in the house, but I was happy when he declined her invitation opting for a hotel not far away. I was glad he wouldn't assume there'd be room for him in a house where he was an unexpected guest. I knew this wouldn't go unnoticed by my mother, who was conservative in how she felt certain situations should be handled and wouldn't have approved of us sharing a bedroom.

I walked Brian to his rental car, kissed him, and told him to hurry and return to the house. We had a fun evening ahead of us, and I wanted him with me.

"I can't wait," he replied. "You have an awesome family. Even your mom," he added with a sly smile.

Brian left for the hotel, giving me an hour to myself to shower and face any inquisitions the family had planned for me.

My parents were sitting in the living room perusing the newspaper when I came back through the front door. "I'm heading up for a shower," I said quickly.

"Meg," my mom started.

"Yes?" I hesitated at the steps.

"I really like Brian."

"Thanks." I caught my dad's smile behind the front page. We were making progress.

***

We all gathered around the island in the kitchen. My dad opened two bottles of wine as my brother, Michael, handed out beers to those who wanted them. Mom laid out a spread of food, including cold shrimp, cheese and crackers, and a hot mushroom dip.

My nieces played in the family room as the adults laughed and joked. Brian was one of those people whose magnetic personality and friendly smile made you like him immediately, and he fit in well with my siblings and their spouses.

The evening was spent eating chili and playing games— including a ping pong tournament, which Brian won handily. There was laughter and love everywhere, and it reminded me of the weekend we spent with Brian's family at the beach house.

When we said goodnight and Brian drove away toward his hotel, I felt like everything would be okay.

***

Saturday gave me the chance to show Brian my hometown. He'd never been to Iowa before, and I hated to have him leave without experiencing where I came from. Dad had announced he was taking the entire family to our favorite restaurant on Saturday night, but everyone had the day to themselves.

The late November morning was chilly, a precursor for what was coming. The fountain in the middle of town was already shut down for the winter, but tiny white lights twinkled in bare branches of trees in the downtown square giving it the beauty I'd always remembered. There was something charming about a holiday weekend in a small town, where people returned to their roots as if their souls were pulled home, even though their lives took them elsewhere.

"This place is so Norman Rockwell," Brian said as we walked hand in hand.

It was the kickoff to the Christmas season in Washington, and all the storefronts were beautifully decorated. As we meandered in and out of the shops, we were offered hot cider and cookies and greeted with the friendliness of Midwestern hospitality.

"I want you to try something," I said, leading Brian into a candy store. "We'll take the salted caramel apple," I said to the young girl behind the counter. She put the gooey apple in a box, and we sat at a table near the front window.

"I've had a caramel apple before, but it never looked like this one," Brian said as I pulled it out and offered him the first bite. The brown caramel was speckled with chunks of sea salt, and the apple was drizzled with dark chocolate.

"Oh. My. God. This is to die for," he said.

"I know," I agreed, taking a bite from the other side. The juicy apple dripped down my chin, and the sticky caramel stuck to my teeth. "They have them all year long, but I only get them in the fall. It's a Washington tradition," I said, smiling.

"Well, it's a good one. Do they ship to Florida? I'll take a hundred of them!" Brian said, reaching for the apple and another bite.

I drove Brian past my old high school and took him to the lake where I used to hang out with my friends. We spent the day traveling down *my* memory lane, and by mid-afternoon, we'd been to every corner of town.

"Have we seen all your favorite haunts?" Brian asked.

"It's funny you would say *"haunts"* because there's just one more place I want to take you. If you think you're brave enough," I teased.

"Oh, I'm up for anything you can dish out," he volleyed back.

"How do you feel about heights?" I asked.

"That depends. How high are we talking about?"

"You'll see," I said as I drove out of town toward Lover's Leap Bridge. I'd been scared of it as a kid but had grown to love the spot over the years. It would take us less than a half hour to get to Columbus Junction where the bridge was located.

After the short drive, we parked the car, and I led Brian to a marker telling the story of the popular site. Legend said that a native American woman threw herself off the cliff after learning that her true love had been killed in battle. She was rumored to be buried at the bottom of the ravine, and if you visited at night—you could hear her crying in the forest.

"Wow, this is . . . *high*," he said, looking over the side. "Tell me this thing doesn't swing back and forth."

"Do you want me to lie to you?" I asked.

"Oh, Lord."

I took his hand, and we started across the bridge.

"If you walk in a straight line behind me, it won't swing too much," I said as I let go of him. "Just go slow, and we'll make

261

it to the other side in no time. You haven't been to Southeast Iowa unless you've crossed this bridge, and I can't let you leave without experiencing it."

I made it to the other side but didn't feel Brian behind me. I looked back, and he was still in the middle holding onto the railing and looking out over the trees below. He was standing very still so the bridge wouldn't move and was smiling with his hand extended to me.

"This bridge reminds me that we can do anything together," he said. "I didn't tell you the truth about my fear of heights. They are my worst nightmare, and when you brought me to this spot, I didn't think I'd be able to cross."

"You haven't crossed yet—you're still in the middle," I pointed out. "Come on over to this side."

"Come back to the center with me," he said.

I sauntered toward Brian, and as I got close to him, he dropped to one knee.

"Meg Parsons, I know you're already wearing my ring, but I need to ask you an important question. Will you trust me as much as I trust you—to take every day of our lives and make them the best they can be for each other? Will you help me overcome my fears and let me help you overcome yours? Will you marry me?"

I helped an unsteady Brian to his feet, and we hugged each other tightly.

"Yes, to all of those things. I love you, and I never want to be without you," I said.

"Okay, let's get to the other side before I lose my courage." He took my hand, and we finished crossing.

We stood on solid ground, kissing each other, knowing that getting back to our car would be easier because we'd already done it once together.

"This reminds me of the night I took you to the top of my construction project. Remember when we looked out and saw the shore, the houses, and the red lighthouse?"

"Yes, it was beautiful. I couldn't believe you'd set the entire thing up and had a backpack waiting with a bottle of wine and everything."

"Are we having wine?" Brian joked as he looked around, hopefully. "Because I could really use a drink right about now."

"No, but it is like that night. Only this time, I'm showing you *my* world. This is where I grew up, and I can't believe I've had a chance to share it with you."

"You grew up on this bridge?" he said, continuing to poke fun at me.

"You know what I mean."

"I'm sorry for giving you a hard time," Brian said, pulling me close. "I love this, and I can't wait for us to start our life together. Do you know how many wonderful things we have ahead of us?"

"I can't wait," I said. "But first, I have to get you back across this bridge."

Chapter Twenty-Nine
November

My parents reserved the small private dining room at DiBonito's. We'd celebrated so many birthdays and special occasions there that just entering through the doors made me giddy.

The restaurant was dark, with red upholstered booths lining each wall. There were tables of varying sizes in the middle of the room covered with white linens. A single red rose was at the center of each one. The DiBonitos had lived a few blocks from us for years, and they always greeted our family with hugs and kisses on both cheeks.

"Hello, my dear friends," Mr. DiBonito said as he welcomed us. "What are we celebrating tonight?"

"We're celebrating family," Dad offered. "I want you to bring us several bottles of your best Cabernet!" He was in a good mood, and I knew we'd have a fun evening.

"And what shall I bring for the little girls?" he asked as he turned his attention to my nieces. I have a nice kiddie cocktail I would love to serve you—on the house!" Mr. DiBonito offered.

"With extra cherries!" my father requested to the appreciation of his granddaughters who were excited to get to drink out of fancy glasses.

We were seated at a long table covered in white with votive candles scattered across the entire length. A large rose bowl was stationed in the middle of the table with several floating roses inside. The deep red petals were beginning to open, and the rich color made them look like they were made of crushed velvet.

There was fragrance in the air from the fresh flowers, and the room was bathed in light from sconces along each wall. Beautiful Italian scenes from photos taken by the owners during their travels to their homeland were hanging throughout the room. The ambiance was warm and happy, and I felt the same way after a glass of wine.

Things were going well, and everyone seemed at ease. Even my mother was enjoying herself. We all ordered dinner and continued our lively conversation and laughter.

Brian joined in with the stories of my brother and brother-in-law, but he always had his hand on my leg or around my shoulders. Like the night we had dinner with my parents in Florida, he was always close enough to me to let me know he was there without being overly clingy. Brian was smooth without being obnoxious. Everything about him was attractive, and I could see each member of my family falling for his irresistible charm.

It took three waiters to deliver the food that the eleven of us had ordered. I was amazed at how they could get so many different dishes prepared and ready to come out simultaneously. We all waited for the last plate to be served so we could dig into the mounds of pasta and Italian meatballs set before us. As we were about to begin eating, Brian stood at his chair as the rest of us looked on, and I wondered what he was going to do.

"I know we're all hungry, but if you will indulge me for a second," he started. "If you would all raise your glass with me, I would like to propose a toast." My stomach churned with nerves about what he was going to say.

"First, thank you for accepting a virtual stranger into your home on a holiday weekend. I was taking a chance by showing up, but it's what I needed to do," he said as he looked toward me. "I know from experience that there are things we have no control over. Sometimes life's challenges aren't part of the plans we've made for ourselves. I also believe we have a certain responsibility in forging our own destiny, even if it doesn't always fit with what others would hope for us. So, I decided to make this trip to be with the woman I love—the woman I have asked to marry me. I love her more than anything, and I've pledged to do whatever it takes to make sure she's taken care of. I know we *all* love Meg, and I promise to do what is needed to make this woman happy if you'll do the same by supporting us."

"Here, here!" Dad added as everyone raised their glasses toward us.

"You two are going to have to up your game," Kathy said as she wiped a tear away and pointed toward my brother and brother-in-law in mock disgust.

"We're lucky this guy came along after we were already married," my brother joked as everyone clinked their glasses and dove into the food.

Brian leaned in and gave me a tender kiss after my nieces banged their spoons against their glasses, insisting on a smooch.

"Well," my mother said with a sincere smile, "It looks like we have a wedding to plan!"

***

"I hope you don't mind. I left the kids in Daytona. They were so excited about the two of you coming home that I didn't want to have them in the car!" Betsy said when she picked us up at the airport.

Betsy and her parents had driven out to the beach house with the children after Brian had flown to Iowa so they could have the rest of the weekend there. She warned us that there was a celebration planned, and the kids had been working all day on a party to welcome us back to Florida.

It was nice to have time alone with Betsy. She told us about her job in St. Augustine and hinted at a romance brewing with someone who worked in the office building next to hers.

"We met in a downtown parking garage when he took the space I'd been waiting for. I was so mad that I hung out by the elevator so I could give him a piece of my mind. But, when I saw how cute he was, I decided to tone it down a little. I acted like I was joking when I told him he'd stolen my spot—and he claimed he hadn't seen me waiting and would make it up to me by taking me to dinner. We've had two dates since then, and I really like him," she said.

"Don't tell your big brother a story like this. You're lucky you're not on a missing person poster," Brian joked.

"I'm not stupid. I checked him out before I agreed to go on our first date. He happens to be the brother of a gal I work with, so it's all good," she answered. I was happy to see Betsy moving on with her life, and the smile on her face told me everything I needed to know about the guy.

We spent the rest of the ride back to the beach telling her about our weekend with my family. We also shared our plans

267

for a small wedding sometime in the early summer. She immediately said she'd watch the kids while we took a honeymoon, and we accepted her offer. Before we knew it, we were pulling into Brian's beach house.

The front door flew open, evidence the kids had been watching out the window for us. As soon as we got out of the car, we could hear salsa music playing from the house. Jenna and Jack rushed toward us, each wearing a colorful sombrero.

"We're having a party to welcome you home!" Jenna exclaimed, grinning from ear to ear. Jack followed behind, trying to keep the sizeable hat from covering his entire face.

"We ordered food from Fiesta del Mar!" he added.

Bob and Linda appeared in the doorway, relieved to be free of kid duty. Brian's parents embraced us and shared how happy they were we were getting married.

Linda whispered, "You've given us our Brian again. He's so happy, and we have you to thank."

I hugged her tightly and felt the sincerity in the words she shared privately with me. She was going to be a wonderful mother-in-law. I was looking forward to having that unique relationship in my life again.

The house smelled delicious, and the spicy food was already laid out for us to devour. There were various things to eat—including our favorites from the authentic family-owned restaurant, which had become one of our preferred spots of the summer. After traveling most of the day, I was famished, and the homemade tortilla chips and fresh guacamole hit the spot.

Bob had made his secret-recipe margaritas, and I sipped on one as I looked at all the bright-colored decorations Jenna and Jack had hung in the dining area. They'd taken the welcome sign I'd made for them when they arrived earlier in the summer and turned it into an engagement greeting for us. They'd both drawn pictures on the poster board, and Jenna had printed the words:

Congratulations Daddy and Meg
We Love You!

They loved me. It was more than I could have hoped for when I'd opened the front door to The Pink Shell in May and had the entire summer ahead of me.

***

It was mid-morning when I dialed Sophie's cell phone number.

"There isn't a hurricane brewing, is there?" Sophie asked without a greeting.

"No," I answered. "Why would you think that?"

"Well, even though it isn't hurricane season anymore, one could still pop up. Those weather people don't know everything. What's going on, darling?"

"First of all, how's Audrey doing?" I asked, feeling it was proper to ask about important health issues before sharing my news.

"Oh, you know . . . these things take time."

I didn't know. Sophie was always vague when discussing Audrey's *situation*.

"How are things at my beautiful beach house? I miss it so much," Sophie lamented.

"Things are fine. I'm taking good care of the place. But I do have something I wanted to tell you."

"What's that, sweetheart?" she asked.

"Over the weekend, Brian asked me to marry him, and I said yes!"

There was silence on the other end of the phone.

"Sophie—did you hear me?"

"I heard you! I had to put the phone down and dance right here in the middle of my bedroom! Oh, my sweet Lord—it's about time! I'll be home tomorrow!" she yelled into the phone.

"Home tomorrow? What do you mean—what about Audrey? Doesn't she need you?" I asked.

"Honey, that woman is driving me crazy. I can't wait to pack my car and skedaddle back to Daytona. Audrey is a terrible cook, she cheats at cards, and she snores. I've about had it being with her for the past three months."

"But . . . who will take care of her if you come back?"

"Audrey is fully capable of taking care of herself."

"She isn't sick anymore?" I asked, trying to figure out this puzzle of a conversation I was having with Sophie.

"Darling, Audrey was never sick—although I did want to kill her a couple of times!"

"What?" I was confused.

"Meg, I decided to get out of Daytona and let you stay at my house so you and Brian would have the time to fall in love deep enough to keep you in Florida. I knew you were leaning toward going back to Iowa because you couldn't figure out a way that you could stay. So—I provided the opportunity, and you did the rest!"

"Sophie . . . you did that for us?" I was crying.

"I knew you had a chance at the kind of love I had with my sweet Charlie. So, I chose to do something drastic to make it happen. I don't mean to put a damper on this celebratory phone call, but do you know why I swim out into the ocean every day and turn around and come back?"

"No, I figured you like to get a little exercise."

"After Charlie died, I was so lost. I didn't know what to do with myself and couldn't figure out how to go on without him. On one particularly depressing night, I decided to take my own life. I went out on the beach in the moonlight, shed my clothes, and swam into the dark ocean. I'd planned to go out so far that I couldn't get back in, and I'd drown."

"Oh, Sophie . . ."

"Well, it obviously didn't work, so stop your blubbering and let me finish my story. Anyway, when I got out about as far as I go each day, I stopped myself and thought, *"what are you doing?"* and I started back to safety. Only, there was a riptide, and I had difficulty getting back to where I'd started. I swam, and fought, and prayed for the strength to return to the shore. I eventually did it, but it was nearly impossible in the dark night, and I was afraid I'd lose my life in the process. I decided the moment I landed on the beach that I'd spend the rest of my life taking care of other people. I'd found my purpose in that fateful swim, which forever changed my life. Now, I swim out there each morning and make a conscious decision to come back and live another day."

Sophie had revealed her innermost secret to me, but before I could let it sink in or respond, she changed the subject again.

"We're having a wedding! I simply must host the reception. No one throws a party like me, and this calls for a celebration!"

"I can't believe you'd go to such lengths for us," I said quietly, overwhelmed by what she'd done. "So, you're saying that Audrey is just fine?"

"No, she's *nuts*, and I can't wait to get home!"

I'd heard Sophie talk about Audrey in this way before. They had the kind of relationship where they loved each other deeply but knew how to push each other's buttons. Knowing Audrey's health wasn't in jeopardy, I could laugh at the thought of Sophie and her sister living together in a small apartment while Brian and I had the run of three beachfront properties in which to fall in love. The sacrifices made in the name of love were incredible.

"How will I ever thank you, Sophie?" I asked, still trying to process the information.

"Use your life mulligan wisely, sweetheart. That's all I ask. Simply allow yourself to be happy."

It was the best advice I'd ever been given.

Epilogue
Eighteen Months Later

It was a typical day at the beach, and it was already hot for an early summer morning. Jenna sat at the kitchen island eating cereal and drawing a picture of a boat on her sketch pad. Jack was on my lap, and I snuggled him as he purred like a kitten. He was getting so big. His legs hung down at least five inches more than when I'd first met him. He was almost seven and a little old to be cuddling like a baby, but I knew he was still making up for the time he didn't have his mother's affection.

I could hear the shower turn off in the bathroom upstairs. Brian would be coming down in a few minutes, and we would start our first full day of vacation. We'd spent our honeymoon at The Pink Shell, but Brian had arranged for the four of us to stay in the gray house next door to celebrate our first wedding anniversary. It was a special treat for our family before our lives underwent another significant life change.

It was hard to believe it had been a year since our families joined us on the sand in front of the three beach houses to celebrate our wedding. The only other person in attendance was Sophie. We hadn't allowed her to host our reception as she'd requested, but when she insisted on going online to become an officiant for our ceremony—we didn't deny her the honor. After all the sacrifices she'd made to make sure we got together, we decided it was the least we could do.

She'd shared a heartfelt message about the two of us being a sign of hope. She talked about how you never knew what was around the next corner of your life, but that happiness was always waiting after heartache if you were willing to hold out for it. She said second chances were like wishes and shouldn't be wasted.

Brian and I listened intently and vowed to love each other forever as the sun hung low in the sky, and a warm breeze blew through my hair adorned with baby's breath.

Sophie ended the simple service by asking everyone to join hands and form a circle around us. We all bowed our heads as she offered a beautiful prayer asking God and our loved ones to bless us as we established our new family. It felt fitting to have so much love surrounding us as we committed our lives to each other.

That was the same week we found out Barbara and Sam from Sophie's party crew were getting married too. I was happy to know Sam *wasn't* suffering from dementia after all. The ladies had forgotten to fill him in on the made-up story of Audrey's illness, so he was at a loss about what was going on when we'd seen them at the restaurant earlier that first summer.

As a wedding gift, I designed Sam and Barbara's wedding invitations at the graphic arts studio I'd opened once I moved to St. Augustine. Brian had converted the guest room into my office, which allowed me to work during the day and be a full-time mom to Jenna and Jack when they got home from school. I created custom event materials and business newsletters and had seen enough success in the first year to feel like I was contributing to the household income. I was able to take the creative side of what I'd done in Michigan and turn it into a home-based business with a workload I could control. It made me happy to have my personal and professional lives balanced for the first time in my life.

Sophie performed Barbara and Sam's wedding on Labor Day weekend at the end of the same summer we were married, and she hosted a small party for them at her home afterward. We'd driven down for the day and laughed when Sophie worked into their ceremony that she was happy she'd been able to perform two weddings for the price of one online ordination fee.

Later, Sophie cornered me and asked if I'd design business cards for her as she loved her role of helping people as a certified minister. I held back laughter when she asked me if I would add pet funerals, house sagings, and séance coordination to her growing list of services offered.

I had the project done for her in less than a week.

"Do you think we can come back here for vacation every year?" Jenna asked, without looking away from her drawing.

Our golden retriever puppy, aptly named "Goldie," slept curled up near her on the floor. He'd been a Christmas present for the kids, but everyone knew he was *my* dog—including Goldie himself.

"I think that's a great idea," I said as Jack shifted in my arms and I tried to get comfortable. "Are you ready for breakfast, Jack?"

He nodded in the affirmative as he kept his head on my shoulder. He had a new little stuffed animal named Rascal on his lap—a gift we'd given him for being the ring bearer at our wedding. He kept a closer eye on Rascal than he had on Gus.

"Can I have cinnamon toast with the crust cut off?" he asked.

"Of course. Do you want me to make it now or wait until your daddy comes downstairs?"

"I want to wait for Daddy so he can hold me while you make the toast."

I cuddled him closer and kissed him on the head, content at having this beautiful child so close to me for a few more minutes.

After breakfast, we all headed to the beach. I took the kids out first, and Brian followed with coffee for both of us. Mine was decaf. It wasn't as good as what I usually drank, but Brian did his best to mix the creamer and sweetener precisely as I liked it. The kids played in the sand, and Brian gave directions from his chair for building the best sandcastle possible.

I looked back at The Pink Shell standing modestly beside the gray contemporary. I remembered seeing Betsy and Brian at the beach with the kids that first weekend two years earlier. Another couple was in the cottage now, and if they looked out and saw us enjoying our day, they'd see a typical family—a mom and dad with two kids and one on the way. They would have no idea of the journey we'd traveled to find each other.

"Are you feeling all right?" Brian asked.

"I'm feeling pregnant!" I replied, looking down at my swollen ankles made worse by the Florida heat.

"Oh babe, I'm so sorry. If I could do anything for you, I would," he said.

"I think you've done enough!" I said, patting my bulging belly.

"Okay, let's look at the names again," he said, taking out the sheet of paper with the list of possibilities.

We had a month before our baby girl was due, and we wanted to settle on a name soon.

"I think I've already decided," I said.

"I don't get a say in this thing?" he said with a smile, knowing I would never be so selfish.

"I'm pretty sure you'll like this one," I said. "I think we should name her Sophia Jayne Barts."

It was a few seconds before Brian could answer, and even then, his voice broke with emotion.

"It's perfect," he said.

Acknowledgments

The First Summer has been years in the making. Although it's my second published book, the story was the first full-length novel I wrote and holds a special place in my heart. The working title of that manuscript was, *The Pink Shell*. Many family and friends were gracious enough to read those first versions and encourage my growing aspiration of becoming an author. You know who you are, and I'm grateful to each of you.

As this book evolved into *The First Summer*, several people went above and beyond to help me prepare for publication by reading an early copy and helping with edits or promotion. Thank you to Valerie Austyn, Kathy Bailey, Lainey Cameron, Charlotte Dune, Laurie Garrison, Lori Johnson, Kendra Richman, Suzzanne Shelton, and Teri Sporer for your contributions.

I also have immense gratitude for Emily Rollins and Lauren Nelson, who continue to help me with edits, technology, and questions about social media. I trust your instincts, and I appreciate your opinions on things like cover design and whether my author photo is good enough to put on the back of a book.

I'm lucky to be the wife, mom, and grandma to the best blended family I could have hoped for. You are all so good at urging me to keep moving forward. To know you are proud of me is the biggest reward I could ask for. All my love goes to Emily, Nick, Olivia, and Mia Rollins; Lauren Nelson and Riley Rue; Rob Nelson and Morgan Potts; Holly, Jeff, Jake, and Morgan Bradley. And, of course, I have to send love to my sweet pup, Murphy Olds, who spends hours by my side as I write and edit.

Finally, I want to express my deep appreciation for my husband, Doug. I'm fortunate to have a partner in life who believes I can do anything, and his faith in my abilities makes me feel like I can.

Thank You

Thanks for reading my book—I hope you enjoyed it and will consider sharing it with friends and family and leaving a review on Amazon and Goodreads. I'm an independent author and consider myself a small business owner through publishing. Your support and feedback allow me to continue writing books and sharing them with readers, and I'm grateful to each of you.

Check out the latest news on books by

Christina Edgar Olds:

christinaedgarolds.com

Facebook: Christina Edgar Olds, Author

Instagram: @christinaedgarolds

E-mail: info@christinaedgarolds.com

Want to read more from this author? Here's a sneak peek of her debut novel, *Giving Up Grace*. Use the QR code below to order today!

Giving Up Grace

A Novel

By

Christina Edgar Olds

Chapter One
December 2014

It was almost Christmas, and the cloudless sky covered Southern California in robin's egg blue. I sat in the window seat at the back of the house looking out over the large yard and pool area. A soft breeze that turned the ceiling fan above the outdoor kitchen reminded me of better times, but empty chairs arranged among brightly colored flowerpots only underscored my loneliness.

The morning air was cool as it leaked in from the small opening of the bay window. My skin prickled from the cold, and tiny goosebumps appeared on my forearms. I shivered and took another sip of herbal tea before leaning in to crank the window closed. I'd become a Californian; chilly now when the temperature outside reached anything below seventy degrees. How could I have forgotten the Iowa winters of my childhood when it dipped to twenty below zero on some January nights?

I removed the tie from my small ponytail and tousled my new shorter and darker hair. Mom would be happy to see me looking more like my old self again. Graham was the one who thought I looked good with shoulder-length blond hair that never seemed to fit my personality, but his opinion didn't matter anymore.

His voice echoed in my head, *"This isn't what you think…"* and the familiar feeling of betrayal washed over me.

I should've said, *"Oh really, Graham? What is it then?"* and hung around to hear his response as he attempted to explain. Instead, I closed the door to our walk-in closet and went back to the guests at his surprise birthday party, hoping another glass of wine would make it all go away.

I remember the first time I questioned whether Graham was the one for me. It was about a month before our wedding, and we were standing in front of our favorite Thai restaurant waiting for the valet driver to bring the car around.

"I don't want to take an unfulfilling job," I'd said. "The position at the hospital would pay more, but private practice is where I can make the greatest difference in my patients' lives," I'd argued, hoping he would recognize my need to do something meaningful with my new medical degree.

"If you already know what you're going to do, why ask my opinion? We've got more than two-hundred thousand in school loans to pay off so it seems pretty obvious to me which job you should take."

"I want to know you'll support my decision on this, no matter which one I choose," I'd answered, searching his eyes for common ground.

"It's not my job to make you feel secure. That's on you." His voice was flat and uncaring.

Those few words had taken my breath away and made me feel small. Through that simple exchange, I realized we had different expectations of a relationship.

I believed marriage was about taking care of each other. Not in a way diminishing either's ability to be an independent person but in a mutual way making that bond different than all the others in your life. I guess it wasn't a value we shared.

At that moment, I felt alone in our relationship for the first time. I should have trusted my gut, calling my mom to tell her she'd been right. We *didn't* know each other well enough to make a lifetime commitment.

I pushed the feelings aside, not allowing myself to comprehend he'd just told me he'd never love me in the way I needed to be loved. I married him anyway, giving myself to a man who didn't begin to deserve me.

Our marriage had been a difficult one—two people joined in matrimony and not much else, and the birthday party incident had hammered the final nail into our marital coffin.

Ever since I'd opened the door to the master bedroom closet and discovered Graham and Becca together, I'd been on a downward spiral. The sting of rejection was humiliating, even if the outcome was a blessing.

Suddenly, I could see everything that was wrong with our relationship. We didn't have the same political views or taste in music. I'd never taken his last name or joined our checking accounts and wasn't completely sure of his favorite color. Maybe we'd been doomed from the beginning, as if we'd settled for a roommate instead of putting in the work to find a soulmate.

After I filed for divorce, I couldn't eat or sleep and felt like I'd lost control of everything. Eight years of a bad marriage had sucked the life out of me, and it took every ounce of strength I had to hold it all together.

Preoccupied and short with my colleagues, I'd even had an outburst with a patient. I'd let my personal life affect my medical practice, and a formal grievance had been filed against me. Apparently, my emotional eruption hadn't been the only thing reported to my boss. Staff members had complained of my moodiness and neglect of duties like forgetting to give prescriptions and lab orders to the nurses.

Even a stellar record wasn't going to keep me from answering for my actions. Dr. Peele didn't hold back, giving me a six-week suspension. I'd always felt like one of his favorites, but there was no doubt he'd never look at me in the same way again.

I thought my time off work would drag on, but it had flown by faster than expected. I'd spent a month trying to get my focus in place again with yoga and days at the beach giving me the respite I needed, but now it was almost time to get back to work and begin the difficult job of reclaiming my career.

I'd worked up the courage to make a trip back to Iowa for the last two weeks of my employment hiatus. I wanted to eat some home cooked food and sleep in a bed that didn't remind me of Graham. Although hesitant about my return, I was excited to see my mom and get one of her big hugs that made everything better.

Our mother-daughter relationship had taken a beating when I left without much of an explanation the summer after my senior year of high school. Although we'd slowly made our way to being close again, I'd only been back home a handful of times since graduation.

I preferred living the life I'd created for myself on the West Coast, and Mom enjoyed trips out to see me a couple of times per year to take in the sights and enjoy the California weather. There were too many memories in Elmwood, and shame always accompanied me home like an invisible companion I couldn't shake.

Mom knew I'd be alone for Christmas, and she insisted I fly back for a few days. I'd tried to convince her to visit me instead, bribing her with a first-class ticket, but she wouldn't hear of leaving home during the holidays. She was thrilled when I agreed to come and never imagined my time away from work wasn't exactly voluntary.

***

The cab dropped me off with less than two hours to spare. At LAX you needed as much time as possible to make a flight, and I'd be cutting it close.

"Excuse me," I repeated, racing through the throngs of people, always the well-mannered Midwesterner at heart. A part of me hoped a missed departure would give me an excuse to cancel the entire trip, but delaying the inevitable wasn't going to change anything.

Security was a nightmare, and I had to wait in line for nearly a half-hour while people fought with TSA agents about everything from taking a jacket off to why they couldn't bring a large pocketknife on the flight. I finally made my way to the gate where they were already beginning to board the plane.

I found my seat next to an elderly woman and silently thanked God she seemed normal. I struggled to get past her in the aisle seat taking my place next to the window, hoping to put my earbuds in and take a nap during the long flight. After learning she was on her way home from visiting her grandchildren in Pasadena, the brief chat eventually turned to my profession.

"I'm a doctor," I shared, feeling apprehensive about my current status.

How would I reclaim my reputation after doing something so unprofessional?

"That must be rewarding . . . I'm sure you're able to help many people with your expertise," she remarked, clueless to how her words hurt considering my recent suspension.

"Yes, I feel privileged to have the opportunity to serve so many in the community," I replied. I was optimistic I'd have many more years to treat patients and families, but going home seemed like an even bigger challenge to overcome.

***

"We've begun our descent into Des Moines, please place your belongings in the overhead bins or under your seat and prepare for landing," the flight attendant said cheerfully. I began to feel pressure in my ears and the anxiety of returning home in the rest of my body.

I looked out the small airplane window to see farmland below highlighted by red barns and fields of dark fertile soil partially covered in snow. Country roads and meandering streams looked like a beautiful piece of artwork from the sky and reminded me I wasn't in California anymore.

I'd been sleeping for a couple of hours, so I pulled my purse out from under the seat in front of me and retrieved my cosmetic bag to freshen up. I reached for a navy jacket tied around the strap to put on after I took my seatbelt off.

It had been eighty degrees when I'd left Los Angeles, but I'd be lucky if the temperature topped thirty once we landed. A shudder went through my body, and it was more than the weather outside giving me a chill.

I closed my eyes and breathed deeply as the aircraft picked up speed, propelling me toward the secrets of my past.